ISBN: 9781068608841

Contents

Prologue

Harry looked up at the ceiling fan, shaking his head as it clicked loudly on every rotation, evidence that his hotel was at the economical level of accommodation. He wiped a bead of sweat from his brow and frowned.

Frickin' overseas assignment. I'm a Pulitzer Prize-winning journalist, and I still have to come to Belize in June.

Despite his mood, he placed the lanyard over his head and saw the badge with the word 'Press' next to his photograph, staring back at him in the mirror.

Every agency will be present—every damn agency, and where am I? I'm kilometres from this century's most important global event, waiting to hear some allegedly important secret.

Harry tried to forget why he'd fallen from grace, but the image of him vomiting on President Kafelnikov's shoes had instantly gone viral. Even after five years, lowly reporters sniggered when they heard his name.

Bloody seafood in Moscow. Never again.

He checked his smartphone for the umpteenth time despite having memorised the time and location where he was to meet a whistleblower. Harry tapped his UV level monitor and grunted in satisfaction when it showed the dimly lit number zero before heading out the door.

Out on the street, he watched a taxi pass him, undoubtedly going to one of the pricier hotels. With his editor's words, 'Don't spend a damn cent more than you have to,' still ringing in his ears, he didn't raise an arm to flag it down. The bar was only a twenty-minute walk away, and the day's heat was decreasing quicker outside than inside.

***

Harry stared at the man's image on his smartphone and had to look twice at the guy who walked into the bar. The photograph on the phone showed a twenty-something bespectacled professional. The man who'd just arrived was far from it. He wore a sweat-stained T-shirt and shorts that were torn and bloodied. With messed-up hair, dirt smeared across his face, and a haunted look on his face, Harry couldn't distinguish between the whistleblower and the street bum he'd avoided on his walk to the bar.

'Fred?'

'Harry?'

Harry nodded and couldn't help but return Fred's smile.

'So, what story is so important that I have to miss the unveiling of the first space tower?' he asked, sarcasm dripping from every syllable.

Harry felt Fred's piercing stare and was disconcerted by the enigmatic smile that crossed Fred's face.

'I've just come back from Planet 27.'

Harry's eyes widened. 'And you have a story to tell?'

Fred nodded.

'So, why me?'

'You're a journalist with a Pulitzer.'

'But...' Harry reddened. 'Even after...'

Fred smiled. 'I saw the—' He coughed. 'I saw the event.'

'Yeah.' Harry couldn't stop indignation from creeping into his voice. 'So why me?'

'Everyone deserves a second chance; after all, you still have that Pulitzer.' Fred's eyes kept returning to the doorway.

'Are you expecting someone?'

'I haven't got much time.' Fred glanced at the doorway before sitting in the booth opposite Harry. 'The construction is flawed.'

'What?'

Fred nodded at the TV, which was showing Tower 1.

'Is that your story? You think something's wrong with the space tower?'

Fred fixed Harry with his intense stare. 'They haven't allowed for the stress of the cumulative weight on the lower framework.'

'What?'

'They haven't used strong enough materials. The design is flawed. It isn't strong enough to support itself.'

'And you know this how?'

Fred looked at the doorway again. 'The ore I brought back from Planet 27 wasn't used when constructing the tower.'

'Why not?'

'I dunno. Cost, or maybe they don't want the tower to work.'

The bartender turned the volume up on the TV. Harry's eyes flicked across to take in the image of the event he was missing out on. Thousands of reporters and camera operators were jostling against a single rope line. Before them stood the massive structure known as Space Tower 1; it was so large that the news camera struggled to capture a proper perspective.

As the camera zoomed out, the screen showed the horde of protesters surrounding the gigantic edifice.

'Sorry, I have to go.' Fred frowned.

Harry turned back to him. 'Is that all you have? It's hardly a story. What evidence do you have?'

Both men glanced at the screen, not understanding the local news anchor's Spanish dialect. They could sense the excitement in the female reporter's tone, though. Harry, Fred, and the bartender stared at the TV.

Something wasn't right with the image of the tower.

Fred frowned.

Harry put a hand up to his mouth as the reporter's words became more strident.

Suddenly, a loud crashing sound sliced through all conversation. The reporters at the base of the tower turned to flee. The female reporter on the TV was speechless.

Tower 1 was collapsing. Sounds of furious, contorting metal filled the air.

The three men stared as the TV showed chunks of the tower falling on top of the fleeing journalists and protesters. Even after the image turned to a grainy, grey screen, the men in the bar struggled to comprehend the disaster that had just occurred.

The ground shook under them, and the shock wave swept air into the bar, buffeting them for a few seconds.

'Oh, my God.' Harry turned to Fred. 'Oh, my God.'

Fred nodded. His face had lost all colour. The bartender looked at his only two customers, tears streaming down his face.

'How did you know?' Harry whispered in disbelief.

'My name isn't Fred. It's Benjamin Dawson. My father runs Coben Engineering.'

'Coben Engineering?' Harry struggled to process any information after watching the disaster live on TV. 'Didn't they bid for the contract to build all the space towers?'

'Yeah, they did. Our bid was never selected.' Benjamin stood up. 'I gotta go.'

'What? Why?'

'My father wants me back. He shouldn't have told me about...' They both looked at the TV screen as images of carnage showed the disaster unfiltered.

When Harry turned away from the TV, Benjamin Dawson had gone.

Chapter One

When Joe opened his eyes, he saw a young man staring at him through the clear Perspex. The face disappeared, and there was a hiss as the lid of his suspension pod rose and swung open.

'Not again.'

'Captain, the stowaway survived, and he's now waking up.' The young crewman clicked off the intercom and turned back to stare at Joe. 'Do you know who you are?'

'Yes. Where am I?'

'We're orbiting Earth.'

Joe closed his eyes and swore under his breath. 'How long have I been asleep?'

'You've been in the pod since I fished you out of the ore.'

'How long ago was that?'

'Almost four months now, I guess.'

'Don't you know for definite?'

The crew member shook his head.

The captain walked into the room and smiled. 'Our John Doe has survived.'

Joe put his hand to his stomach and then looked down at his midriff. The captain grabbed Joe's hand and pulled it away. The young crew member peered over the captain's shoulder as they both looked at the smooth, unbroken skin of Joe's belly.

'There isn't even a scar,' the young man whispered.

'Yeah,' the captain agreed. 'Earl, there isn't even a scratch. Are you a hundred percent certain that the blood was his?'

'I was positive it was his.' Earl stared into the distance, clearly attempting to recall when he put Joe into the suspension pod four months ago.

'Did you check?'

Earl looked at the floor. 'I don't think I did, Captain.'

'Remember for next time, Earl.'

'Aye, sir. But hopefully, we won't have another stowaway.'

'Humph.'

'Captain, where am I?'

'You are aboard *La Pinta*. But I should be the one asking the questions. What is your name?'

'I'm Lieutenant Joe Wolfe, Acting Head of Security for New Trinidad. Well, I was when I left. I suppose I'm back to being a security specialist.'

Captain Richard Ackerly nodded slowly. 'Can you remember how you ended up aboard my ship?' he asked with a raised eyebrow.

Joe raised a hand and massaged his temples. 'Melanie Young... I can remember Melanie Young.'

'Ah, I thought it would be about a woman.' The captain grinned and winked at Earl. 'Well, I'm sure the port authorities will have some questions for you.'

'What?'

'Well, you aren't gonna stay aboard my ship any longer.'

The ship shook, and the three men looked out the window.

'You won't be able to see the shuttle. It's underneath us,' Earl told him with a grin. 'Here, grab my arm.'

'But...'

'You gotta go, Lieutenant. You're not getting any of our rations. We're hoping for steak.'

'Aww, Captain. I was dreaming that it would be fish.'

Joe raised his eyebrows. He allowed himself to be pulled upright and managed to grab hold of a control console to stop himself from collapsing onto the floor in a heap.

'We always get a treat whenever we return to port with a full load of ore. Earl, tell...' The captain scratched his head. 'Is it Arty? Did you say he was covering Christmas this year?'

'Aye, Captain. Artemii Vasily. He got the short straw.'

'Well, tell Arty we have an unexpected passenger needing safe passage back to Earth.'

'Aye, Captain.'

Captain Richard Ackerly turned to Joe. 'The crew of *La Pinta* wish you a very merry Christmas when it comes.'

Joe started. 'Christmas?'

'Ho, ho, ho. It's now December. I think it is anyway.' The captain scratched his scalp. 'Time for us doesn't matter much. We go to Planet 27, return, and then go back once more. So, merry Christmas when it comes.' He turned back to the console, leaving Joe to head to the shuttle bay.

***

Joe twisted his neck to see if he could see anything of their return to Earth out of his visor, but only the orange glow of re-entry was visible.

The shuttle vibrated with the turbulence, and Joe saw a cloud scoot past the circular window.

When the shuttle bounced on touchdown, Joe didn't even raise an eyebrow; such was his relief at returning safely. He would have forgiven the pilot anything but crashing.

He unlatched the safety harness, peeled himself out of his spacesuit, and, for some reason, randomly thought that the suit smelled fresh. He popped the helmet back into the overhead locker and folded the suit as neatly as possible before placing it on the bench.

When the side passenger door hissed angrily at him before opening, Joe popped his head out into the unfiltered air of Earth. At the far end of the runway, he could see a gigantic structure reaching into the clouds. When he took his first step out of the shuttle, he saw two military-looking guards staring coldly at him.

'Lieutenant Wolfe?' the first guard asked.

'Yes, Sergeant?' Joe noticed the three chevrons on the man's nearest shoulder.

'You are under arrest. Anything you say will be recorded and may be used in any court case against you.'

'What? What's happening?'

'That is what Coben Engineering is wondering too.'

A brief smile flashed across the other guard's face.

'Come on. There is a hearing awaiting your arrival.'

***

Joe was shoved into a dimly lit room and bumped into a table. As his eyes adjusted to the lighting, he saw a series of monitors facing him.

They flashed on, and Joe found himself surrounded by the images of staring faces.

'Lieutenant Wolfe?'

Joe nodded to the image of the person who had asked the first question.

'Yes, sir.'

'Why are you back on Earth so soon?'

Joe scratched his scalp.

'I don't exactly know, sir.' He looked around at the frowning faces. 'I remember arriving on Planet 27, then...' He shook his head.

'Then what?' another disembodied head asked.

'There was a nurse. There was the commander.'

'Commander Trent?'

'Yes, that's him.' Joe looked downwards. 'Something went wrong...' He shook his head.

Images flashed through his mind. He remembered falling. A wolf ran at him. His father was talking to him.

'My father?' Joe whispered.

'What?'

'I'm remembering things.' Joe massaged his temples with his palms.

A grey veil hung over a chunk of memories. A knife flashed in front of Joe. The memory of being stabbed in the stomach shocked him, and he staggered.

'Lieutenant Wolfe? Are you unwell?' a clipped voice with a hint of a Russian accent asked.

In his mind's eye, he saw the inside of a shuttle, and he must have been climbing up a set of ladders. Then there was the sensation of drowning. He couldn't move. Joe was sinking.

'Lieutenant Wolfe!' a heavily accented voice yelled.

Joe opened his eyes wide.

'Someone tried to kill me.'

'What? Who?' an American voice asked.

'I dunno. It's all blurry. I remember falling into what must have been ore. I should have suffocated.' Joe looked up only to see most of the faces of his inquisitors showing surprise. One person just nodded.

He put a hand to his belly.

'Are you injured, Lieutenant?'

He ran a hand under his shirt and felt smooth skin. 'I thought I was. I must have been imagining things.'

'You must be experiencing amnesia,' the American voice guessed.

Joe looked at the screen and shrugged.

'What can you remember?' a Russian-accented female voice demanded. 'What more can you remember?' she corrected herself.

Joe saw the Russian's eyes glance to her side and, after a brief pause, nod.

'What do you know about Doctor Dawson?' she pressed.

'Which one?' he shot back automatically.

'Doctor Benjamin Dawson.'

Joe scratched his head. 'Doctor Benjamin Dawson,' he mused. 'I think he was my friend, but he always seemed to be hiding something from me. He always had an agenda.'

'What did he tell you about the ore?' an Asian-accented voice called out.

'The ore? He didn't tell me anything about the ore.'

'Didn't he?' the American voice queried.

'The ore... he... told me it was stronger than steel.'

'What else?' Another question was fired at him.

'Nothing... but something is at the back of my mind.'

'What?' the American asked.

'I can't think... I can't remember exactly. The ore seemed special... different.' Joe suddenly remembered a woman falling to her death and yet returning without a scratch back at New Trinidad. 'Does it have magical healing properties?' he whispered.

'What did you say?' the Asian voice barked.

Joe looked up and saw the shocked faces on the screens.

'I don't know. There are things that I can't remember for sure. My mind is playing tricks on me.'

***

'Lieutenant Wolfe, it has been decided that you will keep your rank.'

Joe looked from face to face. 'I didn't realise that was what was being reviewed.'

'You left Planet 27 without good reason.'

'But I cannot remember what happened.'

'Ignorance is no excuse.'

'But...'

'You will travel to Russia and take up the post of Deputy Commander of Tower 3's security force with immediate effect.'

'Tower 3?'

'That is all.'

The screens all went blank, with the inscrutable American face being the last one Joe noticed staring at him. He turned at the sound of the doors behind him opening. He was hauled out into a brightly lit corridor.

'Transport awaits,' a gruff voice told him.

'But what about my possessions? My clothes?'

'You will be issued a uniform when you get there.'

Chapter Two

Joe eased back his chair and put on his headphones to hear the last of the news headlines.

'With the anniversary of the tower disaster coming up, what is the mood on the streets, Ritchie?'

'Thanks, Gloria. I've been speaking to several people, all of whom did not want to be on camera. Some were scared, and some were angry.'

'What were they angry about?'

'As you know, in recent months, there have been gatherings and speeches about the science behind the need for mass evacuation of Earth being fake news. The anniversary here in Mexico polarises the people. Many are concerned about the future of those who aren't selected or cannot afford a ticket, and many are protesting the launches from the towers, wanting to see unequivocal proof. Those are the ones angry at the money spent in building the towers and the cost of every launch.'

'They want to see the science?'

'Yes, Gloria.'

Joe changed the channel and settled on the first channel showing a movie. He snorted as *The Poseidon Adventure* started. He tapped the screen and raised his eyebrows.

'Released in 1972.'

A flight attendant paused at his shoulder.

'What was that, sir?'

Joe moved the headphones from one ear to the other. 'I said this movie was released in 1972.'

'I'm told it's a classic, sir. A group of people faced challenges time and time again.' The flight attendant had a faint accent which hinted at her Slavic genes.

Joe nodded, noticing the pencil-thin eyebrows and piercing, cerulean-coloured eyes before the flight attendant carried on up the aisle, automatically adjusting to every jerk of the aircraft responding to a patch of mild turbulence.

'Do you think she's Russian?' a bespectacled young man with the whitest of faces asked from the window seat.

'Mmm,' Joe answered noncommittally.

'I'm Marvin. What's your name?'

'Joe.'

'Are you a scientist too?' Marvin pushed his spectacles back up his nose.

Joe shook his head and saw a bead of perspiration running down the side of Marvin's face.

'Oh? I thought only scientists and engineers could afford flights these days?'

'Security.'

'Ahh, okay. I should have guessed. I think I'm usually a good judge of character,' Marvin said, wiping another bead of sweat from his temple.

'You feeling okay, Marvin?'

'Just nerves, Joe.'

Joe nodded and let the unending one-sided conversation lull him to the edge of sleep. When there was a pause, he looked over at Marvin, who appeared to be waiting for his response.

'What was that?'

'You here on promotion?'

Joe breathed deeply. 'A sideways promotion, you could say.'

Marvin frowned. 'I never heard of a sideways promotion to Russia before. Where did you say you were last based?'

'I didn't.' Joe felt Marvin's interest quicken. 'Off-planet security.' He said it as deadpan as possible, trying to make it sound as uninteresting as he could.

'Wow. Off-planet. I've never met anyone who has been off-planet before. What was Mars like?'

'I wouldn't know. I've never been to Mars,' Joe said, already knowing that Marvin's interest was getting more and more piqued. 'Planet 27.'

'Never heard of Planet 27. What is it like?'

'Just like Earth.'

'Does it have any aliens... or... I suppose you would call them natives.'

Joe stared at Marvin, who looked unflinchingly back, then shook his head.

'So, what goes on at Planet 27?'

'Just mining.'

'Precious metals?'

Joe nodded, remembering the weight of a bag of gold in his hands. 'And diamonds.'

'What metals?'

Joe looked at Marvin again. 'No idea. I was only security.'

Marvin nodded, then continued with his one-way conversation as if he'd only stopped for breath. 'So, why did you leave?'

Joe stared at him for a moment that was long enough to make the conversation awkward. 'Because I did,' he replied, shutting down any further questions.

Marvin opened his mouth, and Joe's mouth tightened into a slit. Marvin decided against saying anything more and wiped his brow with the back of his hand.

Joe felt something lingering at the back of his mind, like a sticking plaster that had one little edge ruffled and sticking up, ready for ripping off. He scratched the top of his head and didn't see Marvin glance over at him, registering the subconscious movement.

***

'We are approaching Kafelnikov airport. Please fasten your seat belts as we prepare to land. Cabin crew to stations.'

Joe felt the vibration through the floor as the landing gear locked into place. He tried not to look at Marvin, as he dreaded it would prompt the chatterbox back into another diatribe.

Marvin breathed out heavily as the aircraft touched down and the wheels shrieked as they hit the runway.

Joe looked down the aisle, seeing row upon row of empty seats, and frowned.

There were so many empty seats, and I got stuck sitting beside motor-mouth Marvin.

The lights came on, and the few passengers unbuckled their seat belts and grabbed their belongings. Joe grabbed his rucksack and grunted when Marvin said goodbye.

'I may see you about. Maybe we could catch a beer...'

Joe raised a hand in the air as he walked to the exit.

The flight attendant gave him a wide smile. 'Hope to see you again soon, Captain Wolfe.'

'Only Lieutenant. Thanks.'

The flight attendant shook her head. 'According to our flight manifest, you're a captain.'

'Oh, well. These mistakes happen.' Joe smiled and walked down the gangplank towards customs. The walkway was situated down the centre of a tubular skybridge, and the end opened out into a large, bright, white concourse. He walked in the direction of the arrows, hoping that Marvin was far behind.

On the other side of Customs was a soldier in fatigues that were as black as coal. A beret with the International Space Federation badge topped the stony-faced head. The soldier lifted a sign: **Captain Wolfe**.

Another mistake?

Another man held a sign for **M Franklin**. That man looked nothing like a scientist. The thousand-yard stare and the crew cut of the man wearing loose but formal clothes were incongruous.

Is someone waiting for Marvin? Not a suit? Not a soldier? Maybe paramilitary? Joe rubbed his chin, and his eyebrows rose. *A spy*

Chapter Three

Joe knew they'd arrived before the driver confirmed it. The barbed wire perimeter fence, visible for the past 200 metres, gave it away. Nobody was outside jogging or doing their daily PT.

'Nobody is doing PT.'

'Yeah. I guess there ain't anyone who thinks they need to be fit here.'

Joe nodded, then reached for his face mask. He'd been advised to wear one anywhere without air conditioning after returning to Earth.

'No need for a mask here, Captain,' the driver informed him before pressing the button to open the door.

Being the only passenger, Joe took his time retrieving his rucksack. 'What do you mean, no face mask?'

'Air is fine here, that's all,' the driver said before returning his gaze forwards.

Joe raised an eyebrow but hopped off the last step and landed lightly on the pavement. The door closed with a pneumatic hiss behind him, and the bus pulled away from the gate at the front of the site.

'Captain Wolfe?' The guard in black fatigues looked at him expectantly.

'Corporal,' he said, nodding, no longer correcting anyone on his rank.

'Major Wentworth is expecting you.'

'Where?'

'His office.' The guard pointed at the nearest drab grey building.

'No need to salute,' Joe advised before heading off.

The guard nodded in agreement.

***

'Captain Wolfe?'

Joe snapped to attention and fired off a salute.

Major Wentworth's mouth tightened. 'No saluting here,' he said before leaning back in his chair, exposing a bulging belly that was attempting to pop a shirt button or two.

Joe saw what must have been a dinner plate from the major's last meal. An empty glass tumbler was in his superior officer's hand, and a half-full bottle of clear spirit sat open on the office desk.

'Yes, sir.'

The major stared at him with glazed eyes. 'Your priority is to ensure security is adequate and we have sufficient staffing levels. Manage the rota and keep the guys focused.'

'Yes, sir. Do we have full staff levels, sir?'

The major shrugged and peered out the window at the grey Russian weather. 'I trust you will find out. That is all, Captain.'

Joe thought to ask about his promotion to the rank of captain, then had second thoughts after seeing dust on the major's dress uniform jacket hanging up in the corner. He turned on his heels and quietly left the major's office. When he exited the building and stepped out into the compound, he saw it—the tower. To be exact, he saw a glimpse of the lower section as the grey clouds parted for a brief moment of awesomeness.

'It's enormous, ain't it, Captain?

Joe glanced at the person who spoke and recognised the bus driver from earlier.

'How tall is it?'

'You asking me? God knows how tall.' The soldier scratched his head. 'I guess around eight kilometres, but that's me just plucking a number out of the air.'

Joe nodded, then returned his gaze to ground level when the grey clouds consumed the base of the tower once more.

'So, where does everyone hang out when they're not on shift?'

'That would be the Woddy Bar over there.'

'Woddy Bar?'

'Yeah, you know how the Russians call their drink Wodka? Wodka—woddy.'

'Thanks. Hey, can I buy you a drink?'

'Nah, too much of the clear stuff will make me go blind. You never know who brewed the stuff and where. It can be worse than moonshine. Thanks, though. I've never had an officer offer to buy a round before.'

The driver walked away, leaving Joe to himself. He rearranged the rucksack on his shoulder and headed to the Woddy Bar.

***

As Joe opened the door and stepped inside, the bar went quiet. Several men sat around a coffee table at one end of the room. At the other end was a bar—a counter where a completely bald bartender was drying a glass with a cloth. A small flat-screen TV was positioned to face the bartender.

'You can always tell when it's the news, even here in the good ol' motherland.' The bartender turned and smiled. 'What can I get you, Captain?'

'How do you know I'm the captain?'

'It's not a holiday destination, sir.' The bartender grinned. 'Plus, all the guys were expecting you.'

Joe looked at *the guys*, who didn't seem in the slightest interested that he'd arrived. 'You don't say.'

'Yeah, well, it's an easy gig here. Nobody gives a shit.'

'What's your name?'

'Sergeant Edison.'

'Sarge, as my priorities seem to be looking after the rota, making sure we have sufficient staffing levels, and keeping everyone focused, maybe you can tell me all about this gig?'

'You're doing the rota? Great, that makes my life easier...'

Both men's attention flicked to the TV, attracted by the flashlights and shouting showing on the screen.

'That'll be the princess released.' Edison returned his attention to polishing glasses.

'Princess?'

'Didn't you hear? Ex-President Kafelnikov's daughter was detained for protesting. We all call her the princess.'

Joe saw a twenty-something-looking blonde woman turn to face the camera and give a practised pose.

'What did she protest about? Must have been serious if her father couldn't keep her out of jail.'

'S'pose. She wasn't the only one. 'Bout a dozen all rounded up at the front gate. They caused no end of problems for us.'

Joe raised his eyebrows.

'Especially since we're low on numbers. Skeleton staffing. Day shifts are fine, but a pain in the butt when doing the rota for the night shift.'

'Recruitment?'

Edison sniggered. 'We get the occasional greenhorn. But nobody volunteers to come to Russia when there are much more appealing towers to go to.'

'Like?'

'The US, Canada, Mexico, Argentina, Nigeria, Nepal, and loads more. I think there is even one in Australia.'

'Don't forget Bali!' someone shouted from the group across the other side of the room.

'Oh yeah, and Bali.'

'And you all volunteered for here?' Joe asked with a smile.

'We all volunteered to be here, didn't we guys?' Edison shouted at the other end of the room.

'First in the queue, I was,' a well-spoken Brit returned.

'After me, you were,' a French accent added.

'And I was the very first,' a Russian joked.

'That is only because you didn't have to travel far, Vlad!' Edison shouted back. He turned to Joe. 'And you, Captain? Why did you volunteer?'

Joe had a wan smile. 'I couldn't remember the reason I came back to Earth.'

'What?'

'That is the real reason.' He smiled.

'Hey, guys. The captain here couldn't remember why he came to Earth.'

'Is he an alien?'

'Yeah, he's one of those Martians that can take on the same shape of who they look at.'

'You're thinking of that classic movie.'

'Yeah, *The Terminator*.'

Edison held a glass up to the light and polished it whilst looking at Captain Joe Wolfe. 'Have you seen it yet?'

'What? The movie *The Terminator*?'

Edison stopped polishing the glass. 'The tower. Have you seen it yet?'

Joe looked steadily at Edison. 'The tower? Yeah. Some size, ain't it?'

'Same as all the others.' Edison stared at Joe, watching his reaction.

Joe nodded, then dropped his shoulders. 'I guess I'll have the local brew.'

'Hear that, guys? The captain is having the local drink.'

Joe saw someone wave a hand dismissively before getting back into an argument about which *Terminator* movie was the best.

Edison took a large, unbranded bottle of spirits down from the shelf and poured a shot. He paused, saw Joe's unimpressed face, and poured another slug into the crystal-clear glass.

Joe slowly twirled the glass in his fingers as he would if looking for flaws in a diamond. He downed the contents in one swig.

Edison grunted and replaced the bottle on the shelf.

Joe swallowed, stifled a cough, and refrained from wiping the tears that had appeared at the corners of his eyes. He breathed out through his mouth.

'Warms you from the inside out, doesn't it?' Edison asked, not expecting an answer.

Joe coughed. 'It sure does.'

Chapter Four

Joe rubbed his temples and opened his eyes. The dull ache of unforgiving alcohol pounded the inside of his skull. He sat in front of a holographic screen, and his eyes lost focus. A feeling of seasickness washed over him, and he breathed in deeply to quell his riotous stomach. After several deep breaths, his senses returned to normal.

'Aleksander—why do you want to come to Russia?'

The cursor blinked at him imperiously.

Aleksander Kovalenko.

I should be thankful for a volunteer, but I'm not sure.

Aleksander's file showed everything was in order. Every box was ticked, and everything seemed above board.

So why do I feel discomfort about this?

The cursor blinked between Accepted and Declined.

'Captain, the cloud has lifted!' Sergeant Edison shouted through his doorway.

Joe got up and stretched. Pain shot through his skull.

'Damn woddy!' he whispered and moved away from the digital record of a Ukrainian applying to be part of the security detail for the Russian tower.

***

This must be like Jack and the Beanstalk.

Joe looked at the thick base and couldn't determine its shape as it was so vast. Straining his eyes upwards, he could see the tower stretching into the heavens in a never-ending double helix.

Just like DNA.

A pair of engineers opened the door of the lift. Joe watched as the men checked each other's breathing apparatus. The doors closed, and the lift shot up the inside of the tower.

'What are they going to...?'

'Probably some routine maintenance before the launch next week,' Sergeant Edison answered before Joe completed his question. 'That is, if nobody decides that now is a good time to start a protest again.'

Joe pursed his lips and watched the lift shoot up the inside of the tower and disappear from view disconcertingly quickly.

He breathed in deeply and remembered his face mask was back in his room. 'How come we can breathe without masks here?' He glanced at Edison.

Sergeant Edison shrugged. 'Our sensors always confirm that there is absolutely no problem breathing freely.'

'And how often...?'

'Do they get checked? Monthly. So far, there have been no issues with any equipment. It's one thing that never causes concern. They never go wrong.'

Joe frowned.

'In Moscow, the UV values continue to exceed expectations. Every person, resident or visitor, is required to wear an oxygen-generating mask due to the quality of air.'

'So why not here? Why is this area different?'

This time, it was Denison who shrugged.

Joe looked up into the sky until his neck ached, and a different sort of ache reached his consciousness.

'Hi, Charlie.' Denison broke Joe's reverie.

'Hi, Dennis.'

Joe turned and saw a woman in black fatigues. She had short, dark hair under her beret, and her brown eyes watched him steadily. He turned back to Denison. 'Dennis Denison?'

'Yeah. I don't know if my parents were having a laugh at my expense or they lacked imagination.' Denison pointed at the woman. 'Captain, meet Sergeant Charlie Fowler.'

'Sarge,' Joe said, nodding.

'Sir.' She nodded back.

'Where are you from?'

'Carlisle, England. And you, sir?'

'The US.' Joe turned to Denison and raised his eyebrows.

'Me? I'm from Ontario, Canada.'

'UK, Canada, and the US, and that's just the three of us.'

'Yeah, the team is a motley crew that covers the world.'

'So, Sarge, what made you come here?' Joe looked again at Fowler.

'I volunteered, sir. There isn't a tower in the UK yet.'

'Yet?'

'I hear one is planned, but our sodding government are so slow to make a decision where it will be.'

'How long have they been thinking about it?'

'Since the Tower 1 accident.'

'Wow. That must be almost thirty years.'

Fowler nodded. 'We had some politicians who didn't believe the science behind the story of the worsening air quality and the increasing UV levels.'

Joe's eyebrows raised.

'They only really came on board when Coben Engineering was chosen to supply the off-planet ore to build the towers. And even then, they couldn't decide where the best launch site would be.'

'Coben Engineering, again,' Joe muttered.

'What, sir?' Fowler asked first.

'Nothing. I was thinking of a friend I once knew.'

Both sergeants looked at Joe and waited for more. Nothing came.

'So, do you want to show me it?' He nodded at the monstrous construction attempting to hide behind an ethereal veil of cloud.

'Okay, but don't blame us if your first meeting with Tower 3 is an anticlimax,' Denison said before heading off to the tower's base.

Joe looked at Fowler and was about to suggest that she go first.

'After you, sir.'

***

The tower's three gargantuan legs stood on a concrete base and, as they neared the base, Joe couldn't see more than one at a time.

'So, this is made of ore from Planet 27?'

'Yep,' Fowler answered, nodding.

Joe held a hand to his stomach.

'Last night's vodka affecting you, sir?' Denison asked with a grin.

'No, just a flashback to another time.'

'Oh?'

Joe thought of the panel of international representatives who had quizzed him over his early return from his last tour of duty and closed his mouth firmly. 'A story for another time, Denison.' He looked up and saw lights on what must have been the base of the lift that the engineers used to board. 'How high does it go?'

The attention of the three of them swivelled to the sound of someone smacking the fence line.

'Friggin' protesters,' Fowler muttered before grabbing a communicator and pressing the On button. 'Chatelan, *où es-tu*?'

Joe's eyebrows shot up.

'Sergeant Fowler, I am here,' a heavily French-accented voice replied clearly through the device.

'Où es-tu? Vite. Il y a des manifestants à la clôture.'

'D'accord, j'y vais.'

'Rapidement! Le capitaine est ici avec moi.'

'Et quoi, alors?'

'Vas-y ou je te fouetterai le cul, paresseux.'

Joe looked at Fowler, who gave a brief smile. 'You don't want to know, sir.'

Some of the protestors were shaking the chain of the fence, whilst a few of them were hitting the chain links with metal bars. Three guards sauntered over in front of the protestors and must have calmed them down. Some walked away, and most of them sat down. A guard passed something through the fence.

'Some of the local vodka works a treat,' Denison said before giving Fowler a long look.

Joe glanced at Fowler and saw her coquettish smile before a quick frown as she remembered her new captain was standing right there.

So, that's how it is between them. Joe looked away and smiled.

'So, is this all of the protestors?' Joe nodded at the dozen or so sprawled about on a grass verge on the other side of the fence.

'You expect more, *mon capitaine*?' asked Corporal Jacques Chatelan, every word loaded with disdain.

Joe frowned and looked at Chatelan, who had other ideas. The handsome corporal was closing in on Fowler, right in front of Edison.

'So, what happens if there are more, Corporal?' Joe asked, over-emphasising the Frenchman's rank.

'Ach.' Chatelan turned and let his arm drop from around Fowler's hip.

Joe sensed Edison was fizzing. 'Corporal, I asked you a question.'

'*Oui, bien sûr*. Of course you did, *Capitaine*.'

'Have you been drinking, Chatelan?'

'No more and no less than yesterday.' Chatelan yawned.

'Is this acceptable here?' Joe whispered in Edison's ear.

'As long as it doesn't affect the security of the site,' Edison said between gritted teeth.

'I suggest you take a break, Chatelan,' Joe said sharply and realised that the Frenchman wasn't responding. 'Now, Corporal. That is an order.'

Chatelan looked longingly at Fowler, turned, and bowed at Joe. '*Bien sûr, mon capitaine.*' The French corporal sauntered off.

'Sergeant Edison, go and get someone who is more sober to replace him.'

'But what about—'

'Sergeant Fowler and I will continue patrolling the fence line.'

Chapter Five

'Captain Wolfe?'

Joe looked up from the holographic screen and saw the major in the office doorway. 'Sir?'

'I hear we have a new staff member. Some young Ukrainian.'

'Not quite, sir. I haven't yet approved the application.'

'What? Why not?'

'I just don't—'

'Don't give me any excuse. Don't let your laziness get in the way of doing your duties, Captain.'

Joe raised his eyebrows.

'You have to ask yourself, are we needing more staff?' The major stared at him angrily through glassy eyes. 'Well?'

'Yes, sir.'

'So, get the man started,' the major instructed before huffing angrily and walking back down the corridor to his comfortable own office.

Joe shrugged and tapped the green accepted button. 'Be it on your head, Major,' he whispered to himself.

***

Aleksander Kovalenko was of average height, with a slim build, and had a set of grey eyes that looked straight through Joe with a thousand-metre stare.

'So, Kovalenko, why did you apply for the Russia Tower security team?'

'I don't like the warmth.' Kovalenko smirked.

Joe looked at his screen and then back at the Ukrainian. 'Go and see Sergeant Edison. He'll sort you out.'

'Yes, sir.'

Joe glanced at the now empty doorway and pursed his lips, then shook his head. He tapped the cursor on the word ARRIVED, and the page closed. The rota showed up in one empty slot, and he pressed it with his forefinger. Up came the one name still to be placed: A. Kovalenko. With another tap, his admin work was complete.

He stared out of his window and saw the tower's majesty in a break in the murky clouds. The weather forecast had predicted the wind would bring the dirty Moscow air into their clean zone, and Joe felt disquiet in his silent office. It wasn't just the Moscow air that was dirty; pretty much every city on Earth suffered from the crappy conditions.

Joe scratched his head. *I returned from Planet 27 quicker than I wanted to, only to find that humankind was ramping up their planned evacuation of Earth.* A feeling of malaise filled him.

'Captain Wolfe?' Joe's communicator squawked with the recognisable voice of Sergeant Fowler.

'Yes, Sergeant?'

'I think you need to get down here.'

'What is it?'

'More protestors than before.'

'Nothing that you can't handle.'

'Sir, we have the princess herself heading the group.'

'What's your location?'

'Front gate, northeast quadrant.'

'I'm on my way.'

'As fast as you can, Captain.'

Joe pulled one edge of a painting of the Eiffel Tower away from the wall, revealing a safe with a digital keypad. He entered an eight-digit code and opened the safe, showing a pistol. Just as he slipped the firearm into his side holster, his communicator squawked again.

'Captain? Are you there?'

'I am. Who is asking?'

'Corporal Jenson,' a British voice answered.

'Yes, Jenson?'

'Captain, you need to get here. There is a group of protesters here making a racket.'

'That doesn't sound serious. Give them some vodka.'

'They chucked it back at us. It hit Barnes right in the face.'

'Where are you?'

'Section Two, sir.'

'I'm on my way.' Joe clipped the communicator back onto the holder on his chest. *Crap. Section Two is a couple hundred metres from the front gate. Just what I friggin' feared. Two groups of protestors at the same time.*

***

Joe stood in the doorway to the Woddy Bar.

'Everyone sober enough to handle a weapon, get up off your lazy backsides. We've got work to do.'

Aleksander Kovalenko grinned and jumped up from the stool at the bar.

Joe looked his way. 'Sergeant Denison, you and Kovalenko with me. The rest of you go and sort out the protestors at Section Two.'

'Where are we going, sir?' Edison asked, moving out from behind the bar.

'Main gate. The protestors have mounted a two-pronged attack. Come on, guys. Move your backsides. NOW!'

Joe ran out of the building with Kovalenko at his shoulder and Denison not far behind. He heard the sound of grumbling soldiers getting to their feet, and he grimaced. He thought of contacting the major and remembered his superior's attitude during the only two times he'd spoken with him.

Captain Joe Wolfe raced towards the front gate using the quickest route he knew. Although the three of them would miss Section Two, he had to trust that the rest of the team was sober enough to deal with whatever was happening there.

Joe glanced around. Kovalenko was still keeping up. Denison, on the other hand, was red-faced and breathing loudly.

'Come on, Dennis.' Joe smiled. 'Keep up.'

Kovalenko's teeth showed in a wolfish grin.

***

Joe and Kovalenko pulled away further and further from Denison, and he was no longer to be seen when they reached the front gate. The protestors were swarming around the front entrance. The fence bulged with their cumulative weight.

'Come on!' someone screamed.

The gate burst open, and the first couple of ranks of protesters staggered a few paces, with many of them falling to the ground. The crowd roared with a mixture of excitement and rage.

'Captain! Watch out!' Fowler yelled at him.

Kovalenko flattened the nearest protestor with a punch to the temple.

An empty vodka bottle flew through the air towards Joe, who ducked. The bottle hit Fowler's forehead, and she dropped instantly.

A blonde woman pounced on Joe, who staggered. Before he knew what was happening, she'd grabbed his pistol out of its holster and fired it over their heads. Everyone ducked instinctively except the woman and Joe. Then the screaming started.

In a slow-motion daze, Joe realised it was the princess who had his gun. The ex-president of Russia's daughter had his gun!

She smacked him on the nose with the pistol. Joe staggered, and blood flowed from his nostrils.

'Captain,' Fowler shrieked as she staggered to her knees.

Joe stared at her, seeing Chatelan pulling her to her feet. Fowler was pointing at him. He turned. The princess was levelling his firearm at him. The sounds of multiple shots at once filled the air. Joe was thrown about like a rag doll. Pain shot through his leg and shoulder. The last thing he saw was a look of adrenaline-fuelled excitement mixed with utter horror in the princess's eyes.

'You're okay, miss,' Joe mumbled before darkness took him.

***

Someone gently raised his wrist and took his pulse. Joe saw a nurse with extremely dark eyebrows and hair pulled back so severely that she had no lines on her forehead or around her eyes.

'My mouth... so dry.'

Someone pressed a cup to his lips, and he gulped down water.

He saw Sergeant Fowler with a paler face than usual.

'What is it, Sarge?'

'Two deaths. There were two deaths. The major is blaming you.' She glanced about. 'I shouldn't be here...'

'Who?'

'I gotta go...'

'Who was killed?'

'Jacques Chatelan and Aleksander Kovalenko.'

'What? No! What about the protestors?'

Fowler was hurrying away.

'Nurse? Do you speak English?'

'*Da*.' She smiled at him.

'What happened to the protestors? Were any of them hurt?'

'Only... how do you say it? Cuts and bruises. Yes, cuts and bruises.'

'Thank goodness.'

'No, thank you, Captain. You a hero.'

Joe frowned. 'What?'

'You saved her.'

'Who? Fowler?'

'*Nyet*. Anastasia. You saved Anastasia.' The nurse beamed at him.

Joe felt the darkness come on again. 'I don't understand. Who is Anastasia?' He heard the words 'Anastasia Kafelnikov' before he passed out.

***

The next time Joe awoke, he felt more comfortable, and his face was no longer bandaged. Although shades were blocking the light from the window, he could tell something wasn't quite right.

'Ah, the hero is awake.' The nurse came over to sort the pillows. 'How you feel?'

'What is wrong outside?

The nurse grabbed one of Joe's wrists and looked at a digital timer that she held in her other hand.

'Nurse? What is wrong outside?' Joe saw she didn't understand him. 'The window? The sky?' Joe pointed.

'Ah, outside. Nothing. Just Moscow weather visiting.'

A man's head popped around the doorway, looked around the room, and disappeared. Joe looked up and saw the shapes of three figures through the opaque windows.

'You have visitors. I go now.' The nurse fled the room and escaped in the opposite direction of the three figures.

The man who had surveyed the room moments ago entered first. He wore a long, dark raincoat despite it not having rained recently. Joe sensed this man was huge. A monster. He must have spent much of his life in the weights room of the gym.

The monster popped his head out of the room and said something.

Joe had only seen the person who entered the room once, and that was on TV. Mr Kafelnikov, the former president of Russia, was standing there, looking at Joe. A hulking figure of another bodyguard filled the doorway.

'Mister President?'

'Call me Sergey.' Sergey Kafelnikov smiled. He turned to each of his bodyguards and nodded. They left the room and filled the corridor outside. 'How are you feeling, Major Wolfe?'

'I'm just a captain, Sergey.' Joe touched his shoulder and winced. Then he moved his legs to sit up, and an explosion of pain shot through his whole body.

'For the moment, Joe, for the moment.' Sergey stepped close to the head of the bed and pressed Joe back down to a lying position. 'I was told you had been shot twice. Let me see what they did to your shoulder.' He peeled back the tape which held the bandage to his shoulder. 'I have experience with such matters from a... how do you say it? Ah, yes. From a past life.'

The ex-president of Russia bent over and sniffed Joe's shoulder wound. 'I am guessing that your wound has got infected.'

Joe was overwhelmed and surprised on so many levels. He didn't know what to say. He tilted his head and attempted to sniff his shoulder without bringing back the pain. The faintest hint of a sour smell reached his nostrils.

Sergey reached inside his suit jacket and brought out a leather pouch. 'Major Wolfe, did you know that we have a mutual friend? No, of course not, as I told him to keep it secret. Benjamin has kept his word, I am guessing, as you seem surprised.'

Sergey opened the top of the pouch, peered down inside, and nodded. 'I helped Benjamin when... how do you say it? Yes, when he and his father didn't see eye to eye.' He tipped some of the dust out of the pouch and onto Joe's shoulder wound.

Joe instinctively winced, but no pain came.

'So, Benjamin gave me a present when he could.' Sergey held up the pouch and felt the new weight of the contents before nodding to himself. 'Some magic powder from the planet you so recently returned from.'

'How did you know?'

'After my wife died, I lost all interest in my job, so I resigned. I became a businessman. I became a very busy businessman. I helped fund the trip to Planet 27. And in return, Benjamin gave me this.' Sergey tapped the pouch, now inside his jacket breast pocket. He looked with satisfaction at Joe's shoulder and replaced the bandage and tape.

'Thank you.'

'No, thank you, Major. You see, I came here to apologise and thank you for your recent actions: my daughter, ach. I can't control her. She has become quite wild without her mother's calming influence. So, I am here to apologise that she shot you.' Sergey looked at Joe's shoulder.

Joe was feeling energised. If he didn't know better, he would have guessed that his morphine level had been increased. 'And you said you were here to thank me also?'

'Yes.' Sergey smiled. 'I need to thank you for saving my daughter's life.' He pointed at Joe's leg. 'I understand that a bullet meant for my princess was stopped by your leg.'

Joe raised his eyebrows.

'I truly love my daughter despite her recent activities. I would be heartbroken if someone had killed her. So, thank you, Major. If you ever need my help, contact me.' Sergey placed a card into Joe's hand.

Joe looked down at the card in the palm of his hand and didn't know what to say. As he looked back up, all he saw was the back of ex-president Kafelnikov leaving the room.

***

A young man in black fatigues stood in the doorway when Joe next opened his eyes.

'What day is it?'

'Sunday, sir.'

'What's your name? No, wait. Your British accent... is it Benson?'

'Almost, sir. Jenson.' Jenson smiled.

'How long since the protestors stormed the gate?'

'A week, sir.'

'A week? Wow. I have been so out of it.' Joe put a hand on his shoulder and was surprised to feel no pain. He turned to face Jenson. 'So, what can I do for you, Corporal?'

'Nothing, sir. I was checking to see if you were up for attending the funerals.'

'I think I'll be laid up here for a while. Oh, by the way. Where is Denison? Sergeant Denison?'

'Haven't you heard, sir?'

'What?'

'Sergeant Denison is still in a coma.'

'Oh my God. What? Why? How?'

'We think that new Ukrainian shot him.'

Joe shook his head. 'What? Why?'

'Sergeant Denison's rifle was recovered and was missing one round. He'd fired his rifle. Word is he had a disliking for Sergeant Chatelan.' Jenson looked at the door. 'Of course, that is only what I heard. I wouldn't count on it in a court of law.'

Joe cocked his head. *A court of law. Have things got that serious that fast?*

'Well, I shall inform the major that you haven't recovered enough to attend the funerals. But you are awake. Now you can receive your promotion.'

'What? What are you talking about?'

'Sorry, sir. I didn't think it was a secret. Everybody knows you took a bullet to save the princess. Saving her after she shot you too. Didn't you hear?'

Joe was speechless.

Jenson paused at the door. 'I hope you get better soon, sir. It's been hellish without you.' The young corporal gave an encouraging smile and disappeared down the corridor.

***

'Joe Wolfe.' The major's voice cut through his dreams like a hot knife through butter.

'What?' Joe mumbled, blinking slowly as he returned from a deep sleep.

'I am still your commanding officer. Call me sir.'

Joe was instantly awake. 'Yes, sir.'

The major threw a clear packet with something dark in it onto the bed. Joe looked down and saw it was a major's insignia.

'I don't know who you know, Joe,' the major said, using Joe's first name for the very first time. 'But someone loves the ground you walk on. You've been promoted to major.'

Joe's mouth dropped open.

'Of course, this means good news for me too. I get to see the back of you, and I received a commendation of my own.'

'I don't understand.'

'You tried to keep the glory all to yourself, didn't you?' Major Wentworth rubbed his nose with his sleeve.

Joe saw a faint white smear on the man's wrist.

'I heard everything over the airwaves and came out to the front gate. I saw that peckerhead Ukrainian you insisted on hiring take a pop at Sergeant Denison. So, I took him out.'

'You killed Kovalenko?'

'Course I did. Nasty piece of work you brought into the group.' Wentworth shook his head. 'Course, I didn't get a bullet, so I only got a commendation.'

'Am I leaving?'

'Yeah, as soon as you're up to it, you will be outta here. You got your team to build at Tower 17.' Wentworth smiled.

Joe cringed.

'Remember me, buddy, when you're in Scotland. Won't ya?'

'Why Scotland?'

'That is where Tower 17 is, of course,' Wentworth replied before leaving the room, chuckling.

Chapter Six

Joe looked around the aircraft and saw two other passengers spaced apart and far away from his designated seat.

At least there is no nosy Parker on this flight.

The flight attendant smiled, and Joe saw no emotion in her eyes—just his reflection off her dark brown irises. There were smudges under her eyes barely concealed by makeup, and the dark shade of lipstick advised him of her seriousness. Although her uniform was spotless, Joe noticed that the front of her tunic was faded in comparison to the underarms when she checked his overhead locker.

'Thank you,' he said and noticed she inclined her head but didn't reply.

Joe massaged his right leg before automatically touching his completely healed shoulder. He settled down for a nap but stayed awake until the flight attendant came back to ask whether he wanted anything to eat or drink.

'No thanks,' he said before closing his eyes.

***

Joe didn't know if he was in a dream or not; such was the intensity of the experience. He was being chased, and this time, he knew why. All of the security forces of Planet 27 were on high alert. The mining team had revolted, and he was somehow involved. They didn't understand his logic: if humanity had the technology to cross the galaxies and set up a colony on Planet 27, then why didn't they have the technology to mine without manual labour?

Joe's mouth tightened into a thin line. Coben Engineering had 'recruited' all of the Native Americans who were willing and physically able to travel. In Joe's mind, they were slaves to the mining corporation. It had taken five deaths before someone mentioned it, and when the toll had gone into double figures, a union was hastily established.

The stars were threatening to expose Joe, hiding in the foliage, despite his year-long natural tanned look. Joe moved one large leaf and saw the line of flickering torches moving.

'Joe, you must go.'

'But...' Tears welled at the corners of his eyes.

'They still don't know you helped the tribe leave the mine.'

'But what about you?'

'No, Joe. If I'm caught, they'll put me back down there.'

'Even with your limp?' Joe looked at the old man.

'You have given me hope. That is all I need. I shall tell them that I didn't want to go.'

Joe looked at him and then at the advancing line of lights.

'Go! I shall hold them back from chasing you for as long as I can.'

'Thank you, Adam.'

'Thank you, boss,' the old man, Adam, said with a wink.

Joe smiled, then sprinted off into the darkness, and after a few hundred metres, he heard the commotion. Adam was yelling at the top of his voice, no doubt attracting all of the search party and stopping them in their tracks.

***

Joe awoke to the juddering of the aircraft and the pinging of seat belt notifications.

'This is the captain speaking. Please ensure you fasten your seatbelts. We have made good time, and Mother Nature has been kind to us. If you look out the port side window, you may see the landing lights of Glasgow Airport.'

Joe looked out the window and saw a double line of lights a moment before the aircraft turned to line up with the runway. He breathed deeply and attempted to settle his mind. The dream or memory, whichever it was, was both unsettling and yet positively affirming.

A second after the aircraft's tyres touched the tarmac, the seatbelt lights pinged off, and Joe and the other two passengers clambered out of their seats and grabbed their possessions.

Joe saw a man with patches on the elbows of his jacket and horn-rimmed glasses perched on the end of a beak of a nose. The other passenger was further back, with their back to him. He grabbed his rucksack and wandered up to the exit doors.

The flight attendant put on a face mask and handed another mask to Joe. 'You'll need this, sir,' she said through the muffling mask.

Joe nodded and twanged the elastic of the retaining straps before easing them over his face. He blew out automatically before realising that the exit door had only opened and any bad air had yet to circulate through the aircraft. The two other passengers, wearing their face masks, were ambling up the aisle towards him.

With a nod, the flight attendant pressed the big green release button, and the door opened up with an exasperated hiss.

Joe and the other passengers stepped across the smallest of gaps and onto the mobile gangway. With only one direction to go, Joe went onwards, down the steps, and opened a door at the bottom to find he was in the airport. Someone at the far side of the arrival hall waved the three passengers over and pointed at the solitary bus waiting to whisk them away.

Seeing the driver's blank stare and large face mask gave Joe second thoughts about questioning him about their destination or the expected duration of their drive.

He sat down and deduced by the position of the sun, barely visible through the grey clouds, that they were northbound, at least initially. Joe glanced around and saw that the other passenger from the plane was a woman. Her curled eyelashes were visible through the glass pane on the front of her face mask. She looked straight back at him without flinching. The male passenger, sitting behind her, reached out a hand and tapped her shoulder. She responded by holding up a hand, stopping any communication he'd intended.

So, she's in charge.

Joe nodded deferentially and turned back to look out the front of the bus. The bus they were travelling on was unlike the typical bus in the States that he knew. However, he was familiar with the shade of green in the interior. The military green paint covered all of the metalwork throughout the inside of the vehicle. Black faux leather covered the seats, and not a seatbelt was to be seen. The aisle down the centre of the bus was spotless; whether through lack of use or the driver's pride in keeping everything clean, Joe couldn't guess. Metal coverings on the wheel arches dominated the interior of the vehicle, reducing the usable seating area.

Joe nodded to himself. *It must be some size of tyres. Thick treads? But why?*

Occasional streetlights stood to attention as they passed, and many of them that still had intact bulbs were blinking sleepily at their passing. As the bus hummed along the motorway, decrepit and fading signs adorned with contemporary naive artwork and sometimes rusted bullet holes stood shyly every few kilometres. The quality of the road surface diminished as the murkiness of the clouds lessened with every kilometre they travelled.

Is that blue sky?

Joe peered through the smudged fingerprints on the outside of the glass of his face mask.

And is that green vegetation?

He stared at the shades of green whizzing past them. The brakes squealed, and Joe swayed forward with the sudden deceleration. The driver was picking out a route around a large motorway sign lying peacefully on its side.

Welcome to Perth & Kinross-shire

Joe thought back to the brief computer searches he'd conducted in the few minutes he had available to investigate the country. Perth & Kinross-shire was the fourth-largest county in Scotland and had been the seventh most populated before the exodus from Earth began. The Scots who could afford it had fled the country to England and then across the channel to the nearest space tower. The French were outraged that the British would occupy any of their seats.

The bus leapt forwards with a burst of acceleration that pushed Joe back into the cushion of his seat. He looked skywards and was pleasantly surprised to see pale blue sky peeking through the large, pillowy clouds. The bus jerked sideways, and the driver held up a hand by way of apologising. The quality of the road surface must have been decreasing, as was the speed at which they were travelling. Joe saw through the side windows that potholes and craters pockmarked the motorway.

***

Joe was beginning to feel motion sickness due to all of the jerking and sudden movements the driver had to make to avoid popping a tyre. But when the bus slowed further, he craned his neck to see a fence being put up by a couple of guys wearing the flimsiest-looking masks he'd ever seen. The sign arrested his attention.

Danger: Tower 17 under construction

The bus swung in a wide arc and veered away from the sign. Joe stared into the distance and saw a cluster of buildings. They kept his gaze as the bus plodded along a track which was in far better condition than the roads that had brought them this far.

The bus exhaled loudly, and the double doors opened, allowing Joe to step down onto Scottish soil. He took in the majestic scenery. The site for the tower was on a plinth of solid rock, which had survived the scouring of a glacier's journey many millennia ago. Joe stared in awe at the surrounding hills, putting him just off centre of the U-shaped valley. Where clouds held back from caressing the hilltops, he noticed that the hills had been dusted with snow. A river etched the centre of the U-shape on its southeasterly trajectory, only hiding from view behind the protective line of trees.

Joe saw the smudge of sickly air above a town or city, and he automatically tightened his face mask.

The two other passengers walked past him, with the woman taking the lead at a fast-paced walk towards the nearest building. Joe swung his rucksack onto his shoulder and followed suit. He caught up with them as they reached the door and found he was breathing hard, much harder than he cared to admit, and much louder than the two other passengers ahead of him were.

Joe saw the woman type in 1-3-1-4 onto the keypad at the right-hand side of the door. A strip of red light flashed on around the door as it opened, and the woman stepped inside whilst the man stood stock still. The door closed hermetically, and Joe felt his hair tousled by the puff of air that was forced out of the building. The light around the door frame turned green, and the male passenger went next. Again, a puff of air, and again, the light turned green.

Joe typed in 1-3-1-4 and stepped inside. The door clicked shut behind him and, for a second, all of the air was sucked out of the small, dark room he stood in. A second later, air filled the room, and he breathed it in gratefully. Lights came on, and a door popped open in front of him. Joe unslung his rucksack from his shoulder and opened the door wide.

The male passenger was walking down a corridor leading away from the entrance vestibule he'd just come through. Joe saw him take off his face mask in mid-stride. On the ceiling of the corridor was a dotted line of small bulbs lit in a reassuring green. Joe ripped off his face mask and took a deep breath.

Clean yet slightly stale air filled his lungs.

'Major Wolfe,' a voice called from down the corridor.

Joe saw a white-haired head leaning out from a doorway.

'Hi.' Joe held a hand up, and the head disappeared back into the room. He saw the name on the door which he was guessing the white-haired man had leaned out from: **Doctor Wardle**

'Doctor?' Joe knocked and opened the door.

Dr Wardle spun around on his chair to face him and removed a pair of spectacles before placing them next to an ancient-looking computer keyboard. He looked far younger without his glasses, and had it not been for the shock of white hair, Joe would have guessed the doctor was in his early forties. Fresh-faced with no liver spots or blemishes, the doctor looked the picture of health and vitality. His eyes were a startling sky blue, and he peered at Joe with a disarmingly direct gaze.

'You wanted to see me, Doc?'

'Ahem, yes. I *wanted* to see you. Arrival medical, I'm afraid. Let's get this over with, shall we?' Dr Wardle said. He put his glasses back on, perching them on the end of his nose before swinging around to face a computer screen.

'Is that an actual computer monitor? I can't remember seeing one,' Joe remarked.

'Old school, I'm afraid. Not on the internet. Less chance of... erm... more secure, that is.' The doctor swung around. 'Age?' he asked, then returned to face the monitor.

'I don't know.'

The doctor swung around. 'Come, come now, Major. You must know your own age.'

Joe rubbed his forehead. 'Excluding induced sleep, I would guess twenty-nine.'

Dr Wardle swung around and stood up. 'Excellent.'

Joe stepped back a pace as the doctor moved so close to his face he could feel the man's breath on his cheek.

I'm curious, that is all. I haven't seen a long-liver—a space traveller.' He pressed a fingertip into Joe's cheek. 'Wow. Elasticity is good.' The doctor looked Joe up and down. 'How is your liver?'

'Working well, I think.'

'Digestion?'

'Good.'

'Bowels and bladder?'

'Both good.'

'Eyesight?' The doctor held a magnifying glass up to Joe's face and peered intently into his eyes.

'I'm perfectly healthy. Well, apart from...'

'Yes?'

'I'm still recovering from a bullet wound in the leg,' Joe said, automatically rubbing his thigh.

'Of course. Your records say you were shot twice. Let's see, let's see,' the doctor said eagerly.

Joe opened his shirt at the neck and popped a few buttons until he could show the clean, unmarked skin where the bullet had hit.

The doctor mumbled his agreement. 'And the leg?'

Joe dropped his uniform trousers, and the doctor dropped down onto his knees to take a closer look.

'Doctor Wardle, have you seen Major Wolfe? He was on the flight in today?' A woman asked as she entered the office without knocking.

Both Joe and the doctor looked up.

'Ahh, I see you're getting acquainted,' she said before backing out of the office.

Speechless, Joe looked down at the doctor, who was grinning.

'Occupational hazard,' he said. 'That reminds me. I should have a "do not disturb" sign on the door for such occasions.'

Joe nodded.

'Did you have anything special put on your shoulder wound?'

Joe felt the piercing gaze of the bright blue eyes. 'You could say that.'

'What was it?'

'I don't know exactly.'

'Was it space ore?'

Joe raised his eyebrows in surprise. 'What? How did you know?'

'We have a fair amount of it on site. I find it has remarkable properties.' The doctor tore open a packet of bandages, grabbed a vial of what appeared to be grey sand, and tipped the contents onto the centre of the bandage. 'Now, don't tell anyone. But keep this poultice in place for a couple of days, or until you sense a change.'

'Sense a change?' Joe asked as the doctor taped the poultice over his leg wound.

'You'll know when you know.' Dr Wardle stood up and positioned himself in his chair, facing the monitor, and tapped away at the keyboard. 'Come back when you want. But for now, I think the site director wants to speak to you.'

Joe pulled his trousers back up and sorted himself out as the doctor tapped away at the keyboard, humming to himself. Walking out into the corridor, he could swear that he felt some tingling down his injured leg. He knocked on the door marked **Site Director** and waited.

'Come in.'

Joe opened the door and stepped into the office. At first glance, it appeared to be the same small square office that the doctor had, apart from a hanging mobile display of the solar system. The planets had been naively decorated with patchy colouring and weren't quite spherical.

'Hello, Major Wolfe. I am the site director, Helen Ogilvy.'

Joe nodded. Having undergone such a rapid transition from Russia to Scotland, he hadn't even thought of meeting his new boss, let alone being prepared for it.

'I hope coming in at the ground level won't be too much of a disappointment for you,' Director Ogilvy said, looking deep into his eyes. 'I should imagine it will be a bit of a come down from the excitement of a fully operational tower.'

Joe's attention was on the display hanging from the ceiling in the corner.

'You like my orrery?' Director Ogilvy asked, noticing where Joe's attention was fixed.

'I—yes. I didn't know that was what it's called.'

She nodded and stared at the display, immediately getting lost in thought.

After a few awkward seconds, Joe broke the silence. 'How long has this site been in existence?'

'Tower 17 has yet to be built. They're starting the printing tomorrow.'

'Printing?'

'That's what I call it. They look like enormous 3-D printers to me. But what would an astrophysicist know about tower structure composition and construction?'

Joe cocked his head to one side.

'That comes under Professor Viggenson, who was also on the same flight as you and I.'

Director Ogilvy's dark eyelashes were the ones he'd seen on the face-masked woman on his flight in from Russia. She was wearing thick, black-rimmed spectacles, which she hadn't had on under her mask. With prominent cheekbones and a perfectly proportioned nose on a pale-skinned face all framed by hair the colour of midnight, Joe found himself staring at her for a few seconds too long.

'So, my main tasks?' he asked, recovering himself.

'Same as in Russia, I'm guessing. Your team will be provided by the company, but of course, you can always ask for specific people, should you wish.'

'Umm, no. I'm sure that will be perfect.'

The site director nodded before continuing. 'You saw the last of the fence being erected on our way in today. Until the politicians announce the location of Tower 17, I can't imagine there will be any trouble.' She glanced at his injured leg. 'How are you after your Russian experience?'

Joe nodded. 'I'm okay overall. Got a sore leg, but hopefully what the doctor gave me will sort it out.'

'Good, good. Well, if you need anything, holler, and I'll see what can be done.'

'Thank you, Director.'

'Please call me Helen,' she said, already turning to face her computer monitor.

Joe backed out of her office and turned to see a friendly, smiling face.

'Sergeant Fowler. It's good to see someone I know. How long have you been here?'

'A couple of weeks. Shall I show you around?'

'That would be great.'

Chapter Seven

Sergeant Fowler pointed at the cirrus clouds being blown south-eastwards.

'No need for a face mask, Major.'

Joe turned to Fowler and saw her smiling face as she held out her face mask. It hung down her front, held in place by a canvas necklace. He peeled off his mask and breathed deeply, closing his eyes as he did so.

'Better conditions here,' he remarked.

'Definitely.'

'Okay, so show me around, Sarge.'

'Have you been to the workshop?'

'Not yet.'

Fowler strode around the building, Joe had just exited to the rear. He was amazed when Fowler walked down a flight of stairs, which weren't immediately noticeable. She pressed the intercom button next to the wrought-iron door.

'What?' The question was barked out.

'Professor, it's Sergeant Fowler and Major Wolfe.'

'You have Major Wolfe with you?' The voice instantly warmed.

'Yes, Professor.'

A buzzer sounded, and the door clicked.

'Come on, sir. It seems the professor has a soft spot for you.'

***

On the inside of the door, a spiral staircase took them deeper and stopped at another door, which wasn't locked. It opened to reveal a long corridor with the smell of oil and metal.

Joe felt a puff of air as the door closed behind them. 'Air-conditioned?'

Fowler nodded.

A shaft of light flooded the corridor ahead of them.

'It seems he couldn't wait for you, sir.'

Joe raised an eyebrow but didn't say anything.

'Major Wolfe,' the professor purred. 'It is good to see you.' The man removed his spectacles and cleaned them with the tiniest piece of fabric. He looked up straight at Joe. 'Sergeant Fowler, could you check the security of each of the labs?'

Fowler raised her eyebrows. 'All of them?'

'Yes, please.'

Fowler looked at the professor, then at Joe and back at the professor. 'As you wish.'

As soon as Fowler was out of the office, the professor perched his spectacles on the end of his nose and looked over them at Joe.

'Joe... May I call you Joe?' The professor smiled. 'I understand you have been on Planet 27?'

'Yeah,' Joe answered slowly. 'I went there with a friend...' His voice tailed off, unsure of whether he should divulge anything further.

'What was it like—Planet 27, that is?'

'Quite a challenge. I was lucky to get back to Earth alive.'

'Oh, did your friend not help?'

'Benjamin?' Joe pulled a face. 'I can't tell whether he was a help or a hindrance. If it wasn't for the ore, I don't think I would be alive.'

'Is your friend Benjamin Dawson? Benjamin Dawson of Coben Engineering?'

Joe nodded and noticed that the professor was staring at him, dumbfounded.

Professor Viggenson turned and pointed at a poster on the office wall. 'Have you ever studied the Earth and its atmosphere?'

Joe moved over and looked at the poster closely. 'Can't say I have.'

'It is amazing. There is the troposphere, which extends from ground level to approximately ten kilometres. Then the stratosphere from about ten to thirty kilometres...'

Joe was tracing the lines on the poster of the planet as the professor described the Earth's atmosphere.

'...then the mesosphere from thirty to fifty kilometres, the thermosphere from fifty to four hundred kilometres and finally, the exosphere from four hundred kilometres until it fades between 100,000 and 190,000 kilometres above the surface of Earth.'

'Wow. I didn't know the atmosphere went that high. How tall is the tower gonna be?'

'Anywhere between fifteen and thirty kilometres. Of course, it all depends on my design, and...'

Joe turned to face the professor. 'And?'

'How good a friend are you with Benjamin Dawson?'

Joe was confused. 'Benjamin?' He rubbed the side of his face. 'I saved his life.'

'So, you could say he owes you?'

Joe looked into the distance. 'You could say that.'

'Our tower could be the best in the world, you know. Imagine that. Looking after the biggest and best tower in the world.'

Joe was confused at the change in conversation again.

'Of course, we would benefit if you could ask a favour.'

'A favour? Oh.' Joe gave a small smile in realisation. 'You want me to ask a favour from Benjamin?'

'Would you?'

'Depends.'

'On?'

'What the favour is.'

'Ummm, well. We would like you to ask Benjamin to double our allocation of ore.'

'How much do you want me to ask for?'

'Well, if he could allocate us 100 million tonnes of ore, that would be a start,' the professor said with a straight face, awaiting Joe's response.

'That sounds like a lot.'

'It would certainly get us closer to the Karman line.'

'What's that?' Joe looked back at the poster.

'No use looking at that. It's not on there. Joe, the Karman line is what is termed the edge of space.'

'How high?'

'Approximately one hundred kilometres.'

Joe looked at the poster again and traced his finger up through the layers. 'That is in the thermosphere. Why there?'

'If we get closer to the Karman line, then the shuttles will need to use less fuel. The less fuel needed for each flight means that we can provide more flights, and more flights mean the common man and woman can join the exodus from Earth before it's too late.'

'If I ask the favour, can I ask a favour in return?'

The professor smiled. 'What would that be?'

'Anybody from my tribe who wants to leave gets a free flight.'

'How many are in your tribe?'

Joe looked straight at the professor. 'Could be dozens or could be thousands. It depends if they want to join the exodus.'

'Thousands, eh?'

Joe nodded.

The professor paused, then gave a slow nod. 'I will tell you what. If Benjamin agrees and we get all the ore that we need, then yes. Everybody from your tribe who wants to leave Earth will get a free flight.'

'Everyone?'

'Yes. Everyone.'

Joe held out his hand, and the professor shook it.

***

'Did you enjoy your chat with the professor?' Fowler asked as they walked along the corridor.

The pealing of an old-style telephone sounded out from the office they'd just left.

'It just reminds me of the saying—it's not what you know but who you know.' Joe paused and attempted to listen to the professor on the telephone.

'Uh-huh. Yes. As much as possible. Yes, but one proviso. Yes. The whole tribe. But... Well, I couldn't say no. Anyway, it's only if he can deliver. Yes. I know. I couldn't force him. If you think you could have done better, then you should have been on site here and talked to him yourself.'

Fowler stared at Joe, who frowned. He set off again down the corridor to get back to the entrance to the underground building.

'Was that about you, sir?'

'Mmm. As I said, it's not what you know. It's who you know.'

'You must know some people in high places.'

'Why do you think that?'

She looked at the rank badge on his shoulder and paused. 'From lieutenant to major and then getting posted in charge of this new site.'

Joe smiled. 'I know a few people. But if you think about it... it has taken me over twenty-seven years to get from lieutenant to major.'

Fowler opened the outer door, and they went up the sunken stairway into the daylight. Joe glanced back and saw the age to the door.

Maybe not as new as Fowler thinks.

'So, the site is a thousand acres. Most of it's fenced.'

'Most?'

'We didn't think that the cliff needed fencing.'

'Let's see that then.'

'I'll get a buggy.'

'Make sure the battery is fully charged,' Joe whispered as Fowler disappeared around the corner of the building in front of him.

Joe breathed deeply and struggled to recall the last time he'd been in a buggy. The battery had died, and he almost had too. With Planet 27's summer sun sucking the moisture out of every single one of his pores, Joe remembered that if it hadn't been for Jameson finding him when he had, he doubted that he would have survived. He shuddered.

How did Jameson get on without me?

The image of Tallulah sprang to mind, and he felt his stomach flip. He pulled a face as he regretted leaving Planet 27 unexpectedly, and the pang of missing her receded.

Sergeant Fowler shot around the corner in a three-wheeled buggy and skidded to a stop at his feet. Joe automatically turned as the cloud of dust washed over him and grit peppered his back.

'Sorry, sir. Couldn't help myself.'

Joe turned, smiling.

'Hop on.'

Joe looked at what appeared to be an overgrown tricycle. With a large wheel at the front that had such a thick tread on the tyre, he was confident that they could travel over any terrain.

Fowler sat behind the steering wheel in a safety harness on the right-hand side. She patted the left-hand seat.

'Fully charged?' he asked.

'Yes. I have a bank of batteries on a charging cycle. Wouldn't want to be stranded a thousand acres away.'

Joe nodded.

As soon as Joe had fastened his harness with a click, Fowler floored the accelerator, flinging him against the moulded plastic seat. He held out his face mask, and Fowler shook her head. She was grinning from ear to ear as the air rushed past them in a mixture of wind and the speed they were achieving.

Joe settled in his seat and smiled. They came out of a copse of trees, and the landscape took his breath away. A patchwork quilt of fields edged by dry-stone walls covered the rolling hills into the distance. The buggy swung right and zipped through a gap in an evil-looking, spike-covered hedgerow onto a lane. Joe assumed it was a lane but accepted that as they were travelling along two barren lines through a grass-covered, three-metre-wide line, it could be simply a route that more than one vehicle had traversed in the wet months.

Fowler seemed to be driving to either scare him or get to their destination in the shortest time possible. The sun was past its zenith and yet was still not emitting any real heat. Between that and the wind chill factor, Joe felt like frostbite was knocking at the door of his ears and nose. Just as he was about to tap her on the shoulder and ask to slow, Fowler took her foot off the accelerator, and the buggy slowed as they came close to the top of the escarpment.

She jumped out and carefully took a step closer to the edge of a cliff. Joe followed suit. Below the sharp drop was the dark grey-blue water of a river.

'What is that?'

'A river?'

'No, that over there on the far bank?'

Fowler pulled a pair of binoculars from her rucksack and took a quick peek before handing them to Joe. 'A tent.'

'What is a tent doing down there?"

'Probably trout or salmon fishing, I would hazard a guess.'

'Fishing? Is the weather good enough? Are there any fish in the rivers still?'

Joe kept the binoculars trained on the door to the tent until it burst open, and a man wearing a camouflage jacket, flat cap, dark green trousers, and boots up past his knees dived out to grab hold of a twitching line.

'So, as you can see, sir, we don't have to worry about anyone getting up this cliff.'

Joe looked down and fought off an adrenaline-boosting moment of vertigo. The river below didn't appear to be that deep. The fisherman was wading out towards the centre. One hand held the fishing rod, and the other had a hand-lift net. He looked at the fisherman and the river, and then another glance took in the severity of the climb up the unforgiving cliff before moving back from the precipice.

He looked at Fowler, who was waiting for his approval.

'Good decision, Sarge,' he said for *now.* He glanced over the edge again. He smiled at her.

'Want to see the rest of the grounds?'

'Yeah, sure.' He sat in the buggy and clicked his harness into place.

***

Much of the journey around the site consisted of heather-lined rectangles, the demarcation of generations of farmers' fields where the dry-stone walls gave shelter from the wind, allowing shrubs to thrive. The hardiest of shrubs displayed their gratitude with an eye-catching covering of glorious yellow blossoms. For a brief second, Joe thought he could smell coconut. Fowler saw his surprise and grinned, swinging the buggy over to the nearest hedgerow and following its line until a gap appeared.

As they topped a rise, Fowler cut the engine and allowed the buggy to stop of its own accord. 'Look.' She pointed down the slope.

Joe stared at the view. The land sloped downwards, and in the distance, he could see the river flashing silver with the daylight. The sky was clear until the pall of the fetid breath of civilisation hung in the air on the horizon.

'What is over there?'

'Industry. Dundee City. It's the same with all cities in the UK, some more than most. Much of Scotland has been untouched by the poisoned air.'

Joe raised his eyebrows but didn't say a word.

'This is the reason for the Earth Exodus. Despite all the warnings from the scientists, industry got its way. Commerce couldn't stop killing the planet. The towers are the only thing that humankind could think was the answer.'

Joe saw Fowler wipe a tear away.

'I'm sorry.'

Fowler looked at Joe. 'No need to apologise. It's not your fault.'

'All the same. I *am* sorry.'

Fowler nodded, and her mouth tightened into a thin line. 'Come on. Let's get you back to your office, sir.'

'Yeah. I've got a message to write,' Joe said softly, the words drowned out by the roar of the buggy.

***

Joe sat at his desk in his office. The walls were off-white and bare. The floor was non-offensive wood, and he couldn't decide whether it was actual wood or imitation. There was a small, square window that provided some natural light and offered a glimpse of the horizon. He turned back to the holographic computer screen.

'Computer.'

'Voice activation confirmed. Major Wolfe's voice recognised.'

'Computer. I want to send a message to Benjamin Dawson.'

'Which Benjamin Dawson do you want to message?'

Joe looked blankly at the wall. 'How many Benjamin Dawsons are there alive?'

'Two hundred and nine on Planet Earth.'

'I want to send a message to Benjamin Dawson on Planet 27.'

A message panel displayed on the screen, and Joe scratched his head.

'Umm.' He breathed in and sighed on the outbreath.

Dear Benjamin,

He pressed the back button and erased the text.

Hi Ben,

He looked down and then nodded.

I don't know if you've heard, but I'm alive. I don't recall exactly what happened in my last moments on Planet 27, but I somehow fell into some ore. I think someone stabbed me. Luckily, when I woke up, I'd healed. But I awoke aboard a ship that was orbiting Earth.

How are you?

How is Tallulah?

What news have you got?

'There is nothing else for it,' he whispered to himself.

The reason I'm sending you this message is to ask for a favour. I haven't ever asked you for a favour, so this has been a long time coming. It is a whopper, too. Just thinking about it makes me amazed that I'm asking, but...

Can we at Tower 17 in Scotland get sent double our allocation of Planet 27 ore?

I know it's a big ask. But if you do, it means that anyone from my tribe on Earth can have a free ticket to the Earth's Exodus programme. Yes, I know it's a horrifying time. The atmosphere of Earth is dying. An exodus has been taking place. Those with enough money have bought tickets to travel to Mars so far.

If you can send us more ore, it means that my tribe will have the choice to join the Exodus or, I suppose, die on the dying planet of Earth.

Joe bent his head, and a tear slid down his face and landed between his feet.

You may be interested in how I ended up in Scotland. Well, I was sent to the tower in Russia on promotion to Captain. When I was working at the tower in Russia, a riot broke out, and, well, some people died, and I managed to survive. The powers that be thought I saved a woman's life, so I got promoted to Major and am now in charge of security at Tower 17 in Scotland.

I'm still struggling to grasp it. Everyone here is great so far. You would like the place.

He glanced out the small window.

You would never guess when looking around this site that the Earth is dying. I haven't had to wear a mask since getting here.

They even have fish in the rivers here. The fish are still alive here!

Oh, I forgot to ask. How is Jameson?

Joe blinked, and memories assaulted him.

***

He was saying goodbye to Tallulah and promising his return. Then he was on the buggy. The buggy died.

Joe's mind fast-forwarded to him awakening in a hospital room. The nurse heard him mention Tallulah's name and ran away in a flood of tears.

Again, time jumped, and he physically flinched at the memory of a knife plunging into his belly. The faces of two men swam into his mind.

Zimmer was one. Trent was the other.

The memory of pain expanding out from his wound was palpable even though it was a memory.

Time jumped once more, and he was drowning in the ore on a ship that was taking off from Planet 27. Then there was nothing.

***

Joe opened his eyes and found his cheeks were damp with tears. He looked at the puddle on the floor as his rushing breath slowed and gradually returned to normal.

He rubbed his eyes and looked at the computer screen. The cursor was blinking expectantly at him. Joe clenched his right hand and felt the tension flow up his wrist. He uncurled his fingers and returned his attention to the message.

I remember now. When I left the hospital, I was attacked by Zimmer and Trent. I was stabbed and left to die.

Joe sat up straight, cocked his head to one side, then nodded.

If you can, let Jameson know what happened. Perhaps he can address the issue.

Anyway, I hope this message finds you and your family well. And, if you can see doubling our ore for Tower 17, I promise it will be the only favour I ask of you.

Wishing you health and happiness.

Your friend,

Joe

Chapter Eight

Joe looked out of the open doorway and shuddered. Only essential staff were allowed out in the pouring rain, and only in full hazmat suits, wearing clumsily large boots, oversized helmets, and essential breathing apparatuses.

'Unfortunately, the wind isn't southeasterly.'

Joe glanced back and saw Fowler's cute face.

'Hmmph.' Some rainwater bounced off the cement outside the doorway and landed on the base of the door frame. With mild curiosity, he saw the dark shadow of the raindrop as mild acid burnt into the top layer of wood.

'Major Wolfe?' a voice shouted from the other end of the corridor.

'Oh, I would watch out, sir. Must be serious if the doctor is calling for you.'

Joe was relieved to see the glimmer of a smile on Fowler's face. She winked and turned away.

'What is it, Doc?'

The doctor pointed at his doorway, and Joe set off to an unplanned appointment with the physician.

'So, what can I do for you?' Joe said with a grin.

Dr Wardle smiled. 'How have you been?'

'Okay.'

'And your leg?'

Joe paused. 'Now that you come to mention it, I haven't noticed the wound recently.'

'Major, drop your trousers, please.'

'Only if you close the door this time, Doctor.'

'What? What? Oh, yes, of course.'

Joe unbuckled his belt and allowed his trousers to drop to the floor. The poultice set in place with a taped bandage was spotless.

'It looks like new.'

'Yes, yes. Looks as I had hoped.' Dr Wardle looked up at Joe. 'Grit your teeth, Major.'

'What? Why?'

The doctor ripped the bandage off Joe's leg in one swift movement.

Joe gritted his teeth but didn't utter a sound.

The doctor held the bandage up, showing the underside of the tape. The bandage had a selection of complete leg hairs stuck to the glue.

They looked at the unblemished flesh of his leg. Apart from the sudden inflammation of the skin from the quick removal of the bandage, there was nothing to signify that Joe had been shot in the leg.

Joe's mouth dropped open, and the doctor muttered under his breath.

Dr Wardle bent down and sniffed where the wound had been. Then he stared at the floor around Joe's foot. 'Yes, yes. No sign of dust.'

'What?'

'Nothing, Major. Nothing at all. I'm just talking to myself. Do you feel fine? Or even better than fine?'

Joe nodded. 'Yes.'

Dr Wardle held the used poultice to the light and turned it around in his hands. 'Marvelous. Just as I'd hoped.'

'What is that, Doctor?'

'The ore is a miracle cure. Dare I say it... a miracle cure. But it seems to be spent after healing you. None remains...' The doctor's voice trailed off into a soft muttering.

***

Joe sat on top of the cliff, staring vacantly into the distance. The grass had turned brown. If he'd been back home in the States, he would have assumed the sun had damaged the plants. But not here. Poisoned rain had burnt the foliage. Thankfully, other rain clouds had swept in from a different direction a day or two afterwards and had diluted the poisonous water before washing it away.

He raised his eyebrows and exhaled loudly.

Is the ore a miracle cure?

He thought back to his time on Planet 27, realising that some unasked questions had been answered. When he buried Clare after someone pushed her over to what he thought was her death, he understood he'd probably saved her life. He'd buried her in the loose sand and shingle so the wolves wouldn't eat her body. When she'd staggered back to town with no memory, he'd doubted his own memory and his sanity. How could a woman without a pulse, whom he'd buried on a beach, turn up alive? Simple. The sand on the beach most probably had a high concentration of ore.

How far does the power of the magic ore stretch?

There was the metal of the crashed aircraft he'd seen. It was rust-free despite decades of having all of the weather of Planet 27 sweep over it, and it was so shiny he thought it was new.

Is it just the ore? Could it be the soil? The seawater? Raindrops? Joe glanced down at the river and noticed nobody was camping on its banks today. *There would have been more miracles if anything other than the ore had healing properties... surely?*

'A penny for them.'

'What?' Joe turned and saw Fowler walking towards him.

'A penny for your thoughts, sir.'

'What?'

'It's a saying. I'm curious what you're thinking about, sat above a dangerous drop.' Fowler leaned over the edge of the cliff and glanced down. 'I see no fishing happening today.'

'Yeah, I noticed that too.' Joe smiled. 'I was just thinking about what the doctor told me.'

'You're not ill, are you?'

'No. Quite the opposite.'

She tilted her head to one side, and Joe watched her long hair cascade down her cheek. Her fine locks fanned out, mesmerising him.

'Sir?'

Joe shook his head. 'What's your first name, Fowler? Is it really Charlie?'

'It's short for Charlotte.'

'Call me Joe.'

'Only if you call me Charlie.' She smiled, her whole face lighting up. 'Is that short for Joseph?' There was a strength to her gaze.

'No. Just Joe.'

Her brown eyes had such depths that he had to shake his head again.

'What's wrong... Joe?'

'Nothing. I just caught myself before I became hypnotised by your eyes.'

Charlie flushed beetroot, and Joe saw cute little dimples in her cheeks.

'I didn't mean that as it sounded. It wasn't a come-on.'

'Oh?' Her eyes flashed.

Joe was confused. There was a moment. But it had passed.

'I was thinking of my... of Tallulah, back on Planet 27.'

The sparkle in Charlie's eyes dimmed slightly. 'Tallulah is a beautiful name.'

'Yeah, she's beautiful too.' Joe glanced at her hair again. 'I just realised. When I first met you, your hair was shorter.'

Charlie was the one to stare into the distance. 'I needed a change.'

Joe nodded.

'After Dennis,' Charlie whispered. 'After Dennis told me he didn't know if he meant to kill Chatelan or not.'

Joe nodded again.

'I couldn't stay, not knowing if he was a killer or not.' She passed a hand through her hair. 'So, I transferred here as soon as I heard. And I grew my hair. No need to keep it as short as the guys.' She turned to face him again. 'And you, Joe? What made you come here?'

Joe remembered the major at the Russian tower site. He also remembered the unannounced visit by ex-president Kafelnikov and Major Wentworth. Even if he hadn't been promoted, Joe knew deep down that he wouldn't have been able to stay much longer. He'd been at the right place at the right time. If he'd stood a metre away from where he stood during the riot, the reason for his leaving the Russian tower would have been for entirely different reasons. Wentworth would have ensured that.

'I got promoted,' he said.

Charlie waited for something further, but Joe wasn't giving away any more. Once again, he stared out into the distance.

'Was that a glint?' Joe put a hand above his eyes.

'Where?' Charlie leaned forward, her face very close to his arm in an attempt to look down his line of sight.

Joe felt the warmth of her breath through the sleeve of his shirt and recoiled.

Charlie didn't notice. 'Can't see anything.'

Joe stood up and stretched his arms above his head in an attempt to cover his confusion. The internal battle between the desire to have close contact with Charlie against the faded memories of Tallulah and her zest for life created awkwardness and frustration.

Charlie looked up. 'You going back?'

'Yeah. But don't let me stop you from staying here.'

'But...'

'No, you stay and I'll go.'

Joe stomped away, unaware that Charlie was frowning and equally confused.

***

Hi Joe,

It's incredible to hear that you're not only alive but have landed on your feet like the proverbial cat. How I envy that in you.

News first and your favour later.

After I showed Jameson your message, he assembled a team and tracked down Trent and Zimmer. They didn't want to be taken in for questioning and stupidly decided to fire off a few shots. The shots went past so close to us... yeah, I know I should have left the hunt to Jameson and his team, but I wanted to see them pay for what they did to you. George, who is a new guy, was a bit trigger-happy and returned fire. Within seconds, bullets were going everywhere as everyone joined in. It didn't take long for Jameson to call a ceasefire, but it took longer to realise Trent and Zimmer weren't coming back alive.

The good news is that they have paid for what they did to you. The bad news is that they didn't know that you survived. I would have loved to have been able to tell them that you're alive so I could see the look on their faces.

Oh, before I forget, Tallulah was overjoyed to hear that you're alive. She even hugged me right in front of my wife, who wasn't impressed. Tallulah asked me if and when you were returning, and she mentioned something about you making a promise. As soon as my wife heard her asking about you, the jealousy disappeared. She forgave me quickly and hugged me. I think she was marking her territory and warning off Tallulah. Yes, we have decided to give our marriage another go. It feels right.

Now on to your 'favour.' My answer is yes, I will give you as much ore as you need. I need to figure out a way to do it without upsetting my paying customers. Don't worry about it. I shall find a way. Have you discovered its secret?

Joe sat up and softly tapped his chin.

I will tell you about it one day.

Let me know what to tell Tallulah.

Your friend forever,

Ben

Chapter Nine

Everyone on site heard the juggernaut before it appeared along the track. Professor Viggenson was first at the gate, whooping and hollering at the arrival of the first delivery.

'He's almost American today?' Charlie elbowed him gently.

Joe nodded and then stared at the cab of the vehicle.

'What is it, sir?' Charlie asked, using his rank in conversation that others would hear.

'It can't be!' Joe stepped forwards one pace. 'It is. It's Jameson. Sergeant Jameson.'

Fowler and Joe watched as the gigantic vehicle, which barely fit on the Scottish roads, trundled through the gates and swung around to the drop-off area. The bus slowed and let out an almighty hiss when it stopped. The front passenger door opened first, and Jameson sauntered over, wearing a full head-covering mask with a clear face panel.

'Hi, sir.' He paused. 'You aren't wearing a mask. Nobody is wearing a mask. Is the air here okay?'

Joe nodded and gave him a big grin. 'No wind today, Sarge.'

Sergeant Jameson pulled off his mask, tilted his face skywards, and let out a loud howl.

'What brings you to Scotland, Sergeant Jameson?'

'I'd heard that you survived your stint on Planet 27 and had to see for myself,' Jameson said as he put his hand out.

Joe ignored the hand and gave Jameson a bear hug. He saw the driver clamber down and hold his mask up, then drop it down in front of him so it dangled against his chest. The driver was wearing high-leg boots, military fatigues, and a tight haircut that showed the shape of his head.

'Who's your driver?' Joe let go of a mildly embarrassed Jameson.

'This is George. George Swift. He, too, was on Planet 27.' Jameson and Joe faced George.

George snapped his legs together and fired off a salute. 'Reporting for duty, sir,'

'No need to shout, George. I'm only a couple steps away.' Joe smiled, softening the rebuke. 'Where are you from, George?'

'Planet 27, sir. Completed a six-month tour, sir.'

Joe nodded. 'Where were you born, George?'

'New York, sir.'

Joe saw the tension in George's jawline and how the man's eyes avoided looking directly into his own.

'Army?'

George nodded.

'Are you both here reporting for duty?'

George and Jameson nodded in unison.

'Off you go, then, to get a checkup with Doctor Wardle.' Joe turned to Fowler. 'Sergeant Fowler. Please show Jameson and George the HQ and make sure they see the doc.'

Fowler nodded. 'Come on, guys. Follow me. You're lucky you arrived today. I hear that tomorrow is going to be a windy day.'

***

Joe watched the professor running from the front of the vehicle, where he'd given instructions to the rear to supervise the pouring of the powdered ore.

'Professor!' Joe yelled. 'I'm sure there are plenty of other people who will look after this first shipment.'

'I don't want a single speck of dust to be lost,' he yelled back without turning his head.

'But Professor...'

The professor waved a dismissive hand at him, still not turning to face Joe.

Joe watched as Professor Viggenson instructed the operator of the extended chute to pour the ore from side to side into the open hatch of the gigantic 3-D printer storage unit. The mammoth device vibrated at such a pitch that Joe felt every cell of his body shaking as he stood too close. The printer was one of two devices that were operational 24/7, and it had two others as replacements when essential scheduled maintenance was required. He glanced at the other base and saw it similarly being filled.

He remembered feeling foolish, having asked the professor how they would fill the printers, as everyone called them, when the tower grew higher.

'What is the purpose of the tower?' the professor asked with a smile.

'For the shuttle to launch closer to space.'

'Where will the shuttle have to be for that to happen?'

Joe craned his neck and stared through the clouds. 'Somewhere up there?' He pointed.

The professor nodded. 'Do you see those vertical rails?'

Joe looked at the inside of the nearest tower leg. Numerous vertical lines were visible facing the tower leg opposite.

'Yeah.'

'The shuttle is transported up the tower on those rails.' The professor looked at him again. 'A tank will travel up to the level of the printers, fill them to the brim, and return to ground level for more ore.'

'The engineers have thought of everything.' Joe glanced at the base of the tower and then back into the clouds.

'I never assume that I've thought of everything,' the professor said softly.

'How bad do the storms get in Scotland?' Joe asked thoughtfully as he continued to look skywards.

'We do get bad weather. Why do you ask?'

'Have you thought of lightning?'

The professor smiled. 'That I have.' He pointed at the metal spikes surrounding the nearest base. Where the base finished on a never-ending concrete plinth, the rods dived through holes deep through the cement.

'Is that all? Some pieces of metal in the ground?'

'Copper. And no, that is not all. The maintenance crew will travel in the cage.'

'Maintenance crew? But it's only being built. Why would it need maintenance?'

'It will likely not need any maintenance for several years. But an inspection team will routinely travel the height of the tower.'

'And in a cage?'

'A Faraday cage.'

Joe looked at him, non-plussed.

'It's a structure that protects what is inside from any electrostatic and magnetic charges.'

'What about the weight of the structure? Isn't this tower going to be many times the height of the first tower, the tower that collapsed?'

The professor frowned.

Joe looked straight at him and waited.

'That tower didn't have ore from Planet 27. It should never have been built that way. The weight of the structure far exceeded what the base could support.' The professor looked downwards. 'I learnt much from that... project. And anyway, ours is a double helix.'

'Isn't that the shape of DNA?'

The professor nodded. Both men turned to the sound of another delivery.

'I can't thank you enough for asking your friend for the extra ore.'

This time, it was Joe who nodded silently.

***

'At last, I can speak to you alone,' Joe said, sitting opposite Jameson.

'You want to know what happened?'

'I want to know about everything since I... since I left abruptly.'

'That is one way to describe it,' Jameson said with a laugh. 'Well, everything went haywire for a while. So much so that I can't remember how long you've been away.' He rubbed his face. 'You'd disappeared, and nobody knew where you were. I arranged search parties. We hunted high and low. I took a team out to the cliffs that ran parallel to the coastline. We went all the way to the village. Nobody, absolutely nobody, had seen you.'

Joe nodded.

'Eventually, we had to stop the search.'

'Oh?'

'Yeah. I was facing a mutiny. The team hadn't slept for longer than four hours a night. I kept pushing. I was sure we would find you. They took me back when I collapsed. Perfect timing, really.'

'Why, what happened then?'

'Clare was looking for me. You know, the woman you thought had died. Her memory was slowly returning, and she was frightened.'

'Frightened of what?'

'Frightened that if Zimmer knew she could remember him pushing her off the cliff, then he might have tried again.'

'Of course. Zimmer.'

'We put an order out for his capture.'

'And?'

'Nothing. He went to ground.' Jameson smiled suddenly. 'Then one day, Benjamin Dawson came whooping and hollering. Something about you having survived and you were at work on Earth in Scotland.' He spread his arms out, pointing at their surroundings. 'I couldn't believe it. He showed us your message.' His eyes narrowed. 'All security staff went on a hunt for Trent and Zimmer. Dawson insisted he come along.'

'And George Swift. Was he on your team?'

'You heard about him then? He's a good kid, really. He'd only been on the planet a couple months since you'd disappeared.' Jameson glanced about, making sure nobody was within earshot. 'We all wanted to kill Trent and Zimmer. But I had the order out to capture them. They were to be sent back to Earth for trial.'

Joe raised his eyebrows but said nothing.

'We found them barely surviving off the land. They must have heard us coming and got a decent vantage point. Their first shot just missed Dawson. George Swift must have seen their muzzle flash and was already firing back before I could order him not to. Well, everybody with a gun joined in. Trent and Zimmer didn't stand a chance. By the time everyone stopped firing, the two of them were dead.'

'What did you do with their bodies? You didn't leave them lying on the ground, did you?'

'What? No. We strung their bodies onto the back of a buggy and took them to the morgue.'

Joe nodded.

'I had to bring their bodies back to Earth.'

'Why?'

'They didn't die of natural causes. The company insisted.'

'And George?'

'He volunteered. I don't know if it was remorse or a desire to ensure Trent and Zimmer were truly dead. But he was very insistent.'

'And now you're both here.'

'Yep. Now we're both here. Ready and willing to be told what to do by the famous Joe Howling Wolfe.'

Joe laughed.

Chapter Ten

Jameson sat in front of Joe and shifted in his seat.

'I realised that I have yet to decide on who my deputy should be. You've earned the right to be in the running.'

Jameson blinked.

'But I need you to confirm that you're not reporting to anyone else?' Joe stared into Jameson's eyes.

'I stopped reporting to anyone out of the chain of command on Planet 27 after we first met.'

Joe saw Jameson's steadfast eyes and nodded.

'Who else are you considering?'

Joe paused. 'You don't need to know that.'

Jameson nodded. 'Have you thought about going back?'

'Yeah. But it would take me twenty-seven years to get there, and by then... well, things would be different.'

'Could you not call in a favour and get a trip through the wormhole?'

Joe looked down and sighed heavily. 'I used my favour up already.'

'What? How?'

'I asked that all of the Seminole people who want to join the exodus get a free ticket.'

Jameson stared at him.

'So, yeah. I'm all out of favours.' Joe stood up and straightened. 'But let's not mope about it. We've got a tower to look after.'

'Tower 17.'

'Tower 17,' Joe agreed, and both men stared out of the window, seeing the nearest leg of the tower in its vastness.

***

'So, Major, how are you feeling?'

Joe thought first before answering. 'I'm okay, I guess.'

Dr Wardle frowned. 'You don't sound it.'

'Yeah. I'm having difficulty in accepting that I may not see someone ever again.'

'A woman?'

Joe looked up and nodded.

The doctor opened a drawer of his desk and pulled out a bottle. 'Care to grab those tumblers?' he said, motioning behind Joe.

Joe placed the tumblers on the desk between them.

'So, Joe, have you ever had whisky before?'

'Does bourbon count?'

'I mean the original Scottish whisky. Made with Scottish water that has run through peat. Made with the finest fermented grains. After malting, mashing, fermentation, and distillation, the liquor is aged in barrels to get its distinctive flavouring.' The doctor poured out two large shots and offered one to Joe.

Joe eyed the drink with suspicion, and his mind released a distant memory.

'And how is your leg? Any noticeable differences?'

Joe glanced down at his right leg. 'Nothing different. But I'm planning to go out for a run soon.'

'Great, great, great.' The doctor poured more whisky. 'Do you know that this whisky came from a distillery that started with Russian investment?' He looked at Joe for a reaction.

Joe glanced at the doctor. 'Russians get everywhere, don't they?' He eyed the amber through the opaque plastic.

***

Joe looked at the half-full bottle of bourbon that his friend held out to him.

'Have some, Joe.'

Joe didn't move.'

'Go on. What are you, chicken?' another boy said.

'He's not a brave.'

Joe removed the cap and took a slug. The hit of alcohol brought tears to his eyes, and he barely stopped himself from coughing.

The other three boys seemed impressed and took it in turns to take a swig for themselves. It was only Joe who didn't splutter, and all jokes of being man enough evaporated.

Joe took another mouthful and felt the fire erupt in his belly. Each of them, in turn, followed suit. Joe took another drink and watched mercilessly as the others copied him. It took another two rounds before the smallest of the group vomited. When the boy who joked about Joe being a chicken followed suit, Joe stood up and staggered away home.

***

Joe downed the whisky in one gulp and felt the burn in his belly. The doctor copied him before adding another shot of whisky to each glass. Again, Joe tipped all of the whisky in one go, and again, the doctor followed suit.

Only after the seventh drink did the doctor, with glassy eyes, try to estimate how much of the bottle they'd consumed.

'Joe,' the doctor slurred. 'Who... taught you how to drink? Good god, man. You... are a machine.'

Joe grinned and refilled the tumblers.

'No... no. That's me done. You take the bottle if you want. I shall see if I can walk to my room,' the doctor said, wobbling to the door of his office. 'My last prescription. Have a drink of water before you go to sleep.' And with that, he wobbled out the doorway.

Joe sipped his next drink and stared out the window at the night sky. A wisp of cloud covered whatever stars were in the sky.

***

Joe got up from his umpteenth fall and stumbled into the front door. His mother opened it a moment later.

'What have you done, Joe?' She grabbed his arm and expertly guided his forwards movement.

'Don't tell Pa.'

'I won't tell.'

'You won't tell me what?' Joe's father stood at the entrance to the living room, taking everything in. 'You been out partying, Joe?'

'They said I was chicken.'

'Did they now?' his mother said.

'So, I had to show them.'

'Do you need the bathroom?' his father asked, moving close and supporting his son.

'No, I'm all right.'

'Are you going to be sick?' his mother asked.

Joe stopped and thought about it. A hand shot up to cover his mouth. Joe's father took over. 'Why did you ask that?' he scolded his wife over his shoulder whilst half carrying and half frog-marching Joe straight to the toilet. The lid was lifted just in time as Joe knelt and expelled his stomach contents in an acidic jet.

***

With a stumble, Joe left the headquarters and turned to his accommodation.

'Major, you may need some help.'

Glassy-eyed, Joe turned his head and continued staggering ahead. 'Charlie? Are you helping me to my room?' he said, lurching to one side.

'Here, let me help.' She lifted one of his arms and put it over her shoulder, then guided him in a straight line.

Miraculously, he still had a firm grip on the bottle of whisky, and he swung it into the silver light of the moon. 'The doctor gave me a different type of medicine,' he said, giggling at his joke.

'It looks like he did. How is the doctor?'

'I don't think he can handle his whisky. He went home early.'

Charlie turned her head and stared at him for a moment to check he wasn't acting drunk.

'Charlie, I think I'm in love.'

Charlie's cheeks coloured.

'But she's on a different planet.'

Joe didn't see Charlie's mouth tighten. 'Is this your door, Major?'

He focused on the door. 'I think so,' he answered whilst thrusting his free hand into his pocket. Not finding the keycard on one side, he twisted his body and struggled to put his hand in the pocket on the opposite side.

He managed to swipe the card, and the door swung open. Again, rather than putting the bottle down, he twisted and stuffed the card in the pocket he'd just retrieved it from. He started falling forward. Charlie struggled to keep him upright. The pair of them fell through the doorway into the dark room, unaware that someone was watching them from the shadows.

Falling face-first onto his bed, Joe finally let go of the whisky bottle, which fell to the floor with a dull thud. Charlie stood up, seeing a beam of moonlight light Joe's hair. She checked that Joe was still breathing before picking the bottle off the floor and placing it carefully on the bedside cabinet.

At the doorway, she turned to look at Joe one last time before leaving.

***

Joe opened his eyes and groaned. A whisky bottle containing a finger of the amber liquid stood accusingly on the bedside table. He staggered to the sink and turned the cold faucet on full. The jet of freezing cold water thundered its annoyance at him. The shaver pulled at his hair, and he slowed down to prevent any bloodshed during the daily battle. After brushing his teeth, donning some clothes, and opening the door, Joe felt some semblance of normality filter through his consciousness.

He saw Jameson first and turned to avoid eye contact on his short walk to his office.

Solitude, silence, and time in a comfortable chair will help in my recovery.

Joe sat down and saw a folded piece of paper on the desk in front of him.

She is not as good as you think she is.

Joe blinked and reread it. He glanced at the doorway and then around the room. Unsigned and in unrecognisable handwriting, there was nothing to suggest to Joe who could have written it.

'Do you want my deputy job that badly, Jameson?' Joe whispered. 'It answers the question of who I should pick.'

He picked up the phone and was dialling the three numbers for the security staff room when he saw Fowler walk past his open door.

'Charlie!' he shouted.

A second later, her head popped around the doorway. 'Yes, sir?'

'Uh, Fowler, please come in.'

They both glanced down at the unfolded piece of paper, and he grabbed it and slung it into a drawer.

'Sir?'

'You may have realised that I have yet to choose a deputy.'

'Oh?'

'Yeah, and... well... You are top of my list.'

Charlie sat and stared at him.

'I want you to be my deputy.'

'Really? Why?'

'Do you want the promotion?'

'Uh, yes. Sure. It's just that I don't understand why.'

'The main reason is trust. I trust you more than anyone else here. We've both been through the Russian riot.'

Charlie slowly nodded and frowned, remembering the incident.

'Will you?'

'Yes, sir.'

'I shall log the records with your promotion to lieutenant with immediate effect. I'll inform the site director and will see about what office you can have.'

'Lieutenant,' she said softly to herself.

'Congratulations.' Joe held out his hand, and she shook it in a mild state of shock.

Chapter Eleven

'You'll be fine running this morning, sir,' Lieutenant Charlie Fowler told him whilst leaning out of the open doorway. 'No need for a mask until probably about 1300 hours.'

Joe nodded, continuing his stretches. 'Thanks, Lieutenant.'

He looked up at the grey, unmoving sky. *So much for it being spring! I would be impressed if the temperature got above ten degrees Celsius.* He set off at a slow jog towards the main gate.

Corporal George Swift raised the barrier before Joe got too close, snapping off a salute.

He recognised me with my hood up, Joe realised as he pushed back the fabric and felt the chilled air around his face. His all-black tracksuit would hopefully soak up any sun that Scotland could provide. Charlie had smiled briefly when he mentioned his choice of running gear.

He leapt over a puddle covering the full width of the lane and felt the strength in his legs despite the lackadaisical fitness regime he'd fallen into. A gap opened up on his right, and he turned off the track to begin the long loop parallel to the fence line.

Charlie has taken on the role of my deputy like a duck to water. He frowned at the memory of the anonymous note. *I have yet to speak with Jameson and tell him that the note he left had the opposite effect that he'd planned.*

Joe veered around a patch of dark pellets, which Charlie had mentioned were rabbit droppings—another patch and another turn away from the fence line. The incline slowed his pace enough for him to puff out with exertion. A sideways glance showed the horizon dominated by the growing monstrosity that was going to be Tower 17. He stopped jogging for a moment to appreciate the gigantic legs that were slowly writhing around each other as they grew towards the heavens. The underside of the clouds appeared to be teasing and enticing the tower higher.

Starting again, Joe continued his slow, comfortable pace.

A straight edge amongst the vegetation caught his eye. Joe slowed further and turned to investigate a human-made shape. Someone had set up a bivouac between two silver birch trees.

'Hey, anybody here?' he asked, bending down to find the inside of the tent empty except for a rucksack.

A campfire was loaded with firewood but had yet to be lit.

Just arrived and set up camp, or starting the fire in the evening to avoid everyone seeing a smoke trail. Shall I wait for the camper's return?

Joe looked around and saw nothing but shrubbery and rolling hillsides.

Although suspicious, given its proximity to the site, no illegal activity has been committed.

Joe had one last look around all 360 degrees, then set off again into his slow, loping jog, a comfortable pace that ate up the ground just as a cow would eat the grass. Within seconds, he was back to focusing on the ground and the tiny, round presents left by what must have been numerous rabbits.

***

The path, if it could be called that, was more of a line of well-trodden ground with clumps of grass sprouting randomly along the route. It wound past saplings and in between aged trees, always within a few metres of the fence line, and Joe was surprised when it led him out onto an open meadow. As he followed the flattened wild grass, he was aware of dark shapes at the northern end of the meadow. As he approached, the shapes coalesced into artificial structures—lots of artificial structures. It didn't take long before Joe was close enough to realise what the shapes were. Multiple solar panels stretched out in rows, standing uniformly for the daylight to be at its optimum angle, which in this case was due south.

Joe slowed again, this time to take in the impressive sight of the rank upon rank of solar panels crouching silently in anticipation of the sun's rays. He couldn't see any cabling or any sign that this solar panel array was part of the Tower 17 site or had been coincidentally located close to the perimeter fence. He continued his jog, pondering whether there would be any more surprises on his journey today.

He felt his stomach muscles tighten into a stitch and immediately regretted having a cooked breakfast only an hour ago.

The canteen was more of a restaurant. In Joe's estimation, it had offered the local speciality of a full Scottish breakfast. A fried egg with a yolk so golden it was almost orange lay on top of two rashers of thick back bacon. The bacon had been grilled until the fat had browned, and the meat was cooked well but not so well that it would have been the texture of a sliver of leather. There was a tomato and a ladleful of baked beans next to what he now knew to be a tattie scone. The star of the plate was, at first glance, a hockey puck. The slice of haggis was a dark grey, well-spiced, and after trying to forget what the chef had told him about its ingredients, Joe found it not just palatable but tasty.

It was more delicious than the browned sausage that finished off the filling meal.

How does anyone eat the full Scottish breakfast daily? I don't know.

The ground opened up once more, and Joe saw it drop away in the distance, marking the edge of the cliff. As he neared it, he stopped completely, paced slowly to the edge, and peered down at the river below. The fisherman's tent was back, and the man was tending to his rod. He glanced up and waved. Joe automatically waved back and smiled.

Looking at the time on his digital watch, he sighed and took several steps backwards before turning around and jogging once more. The fence line stretching to the top of the cliff prevented him from completing a complete circuit. Instead, he had to find the gate and press a buzzer to gain access. Joe cut inwards and followed the fence line closely. The wrought iron fence stood tall whilst the circular monocle of the camera looked down upon him.

He lifted the square flap on the post and pressed the button, then looked directly at the camera. That simple action took him back in time to another place.

***

Joanne Stravanski opened the door after a long pause.

Joe felt that she'd taken the time to check he was alone as he'd promised.

'She doesn't know you came, does she?'

'Melanie? No.'

'I'm worried about her.'

Joe said nothing, as he'd found keeping quiet almost always made the other person fill the silence with more words.

'I tried to raise her properly, but something was always off. As a child, she made up stories. She told anyone anything to keep their attention. I think deep down she knew that I wasn't her mother... her biological mother.'

'Do you know who was?'

'Not for certain. I was never told. But I had access to everyone's medical records. I worked it out.'

'Did Melanie ever look through the records?'

'No. Well, if she tried, she wouldn't have found them. I made sure they were beyond her security level.'

Joe nodded.

'Recently, though, she has been worse. When you were in hospital with the sickness, she made up stories again. She told Jameson that I was being blackmailed to keep quiet.'

'About what?'

'I think she'd twisted it in her mind that I was being forced to keep quiet about who her true mother and father were.'

'She told me that someone was using you to keep her quiet.'

'I'd planned to visit you when you had got through the sickness and let you know about her... her imagination.' Joanne had a tear running down her cheek. 'I'm sorry. I did my best for her. But my patience has gone. I'm too old now for this.'

Joe noticed her posture was slumped, and for the first time, she looked frail. With bags under her eyes, he could tell that she'd been worried about Melanie for a long time.

'You must be tired. I have to leave New Trinidad for a while.'

'But...'

'I have to escort someone to map more of the land.'

'Can't you get someone else to do it?'

'I need to get away myself.'

Joanne nodded. 'Will you speak to her when you get back? She has talked about you a lot. I think she has feelings for you.'

Joe remembered waking up to find Melanie straddling him. 'I think you're right.'

'Do you have feelings for her?'

'Not in the same way.'

'That's what I thought you would say.'

'I'm sorry.'

***

Joe blinked as the intensity of the memory receded. The lock clicked, and he pushed open the gate, which squeaked a protest. He glanced up at the glinting light reflecting off the razor-sharp barbed wire at the top of the fence. The gate clanged shut behind him as he set off jogging once more.

Tower 17 reached into the clouds like a modern-day giant beanstalk, and Joe was already accustomed to its size. As he reached the top of a rise, the buildings lay down, which looked like, from Joe's distance, a naturally formed basin.

Joe headed straight towards the security office.

'Told you that you didn't need a mask this morning, sir.' Lieutenant Fowler smiled as she looked up from her desk.

Jameson stood beside her as a holographic map lit up the surface of the desk in front of them.

'Someone is camping outside of the perimeter fence, southeast of the main gate.'

Fowler and Jameson stared at him, both open-mouthed.

'Jameson, mind checking it out?'

'I'm on it.' He grinned. 'Sorry, Lieutenant, but this seems more interesting than utility lines.'

Fowler nodded.

'Utility lines?' Joe asked as Jameson left the building.

'Making sure that we know what we're dealing with should crowds start appearing.'

'Any intel on that happening?'

'Nothing from the local police. Not that they're particularly bothered with us. They have their hands full with increased looting.' Fowler rubbed her forehead. 'But we never got intel before the riot in Russia, if you remember.'

Joe nodded. *Any intel would have gone to the major's desk and stayed there long enough to lose any tactical advantage.*

He pursed his lips. 'Have you checked out the solar panels?'

'Yeah, all the cabling is subterranean.'

'So, it's for Tower 17, then?'

Fowler nodded.

'What does it power?'

'All of this site, including powering machinery, offices, accommodation, catering, and the labs.'

'There are a lot of panels.'

'Any excess power is stored in a bank of batteries.'

'Are they secure?'

'They're deep underground, so fingers crossed any rioters don't have giant diggers,' she said with a grin.

Joe smiled back. 'Have you thought about them damaging the panels? Won't that cause a problem?'

Fowler raised her eyebrows. 'Yeah. I was thinking that they would want to steal the power. Of course, a mob would probably want to cause chaos and destruction.'

'What about expanding the fence to include the solar farm?' Joe slowly nodded. 'That is, assuming the land the panels are on is part of this site?'

'I'd have to check, but yeah. That would be the simplest solution.'

'How about I ask the site director?'

'That would be appreciated, sir.'

***

'Helen? We have found a gap in the security of the site.'

Helen Ogilvy sat down and indicated a chair for Joe. 'Oh? I thought that the fence Lieutenant Fowler ordered surrounded the entire site?'

'It does.'

'But then, I don't see how there can be a gap.'

'It isn't in the fence. Not as such anyway.'

'Joe, you're confusing me. We spent a fortune on surrounding the site on a fence. Is the fence not good enough?'

'It's not the fence. It's the solar farm.'

Helen Ogilvy blinked.

'If a group of rioters found the solar farm, they could destroy or seriously damage all the panels.'

'What group of rioters? We haven't even had a visitor, have we?'

Joe paused.

'Well, have we?'

'No, ma'am.'

Her mouth tightened. 'Ma'am, is it? You must be serious.' A finger touched the front of her chin. 'The fact that you experienced a riot in Russia has nothing to do with it, does it?'

'No, ma'am.'

'There you go again. What is your proposed solution?'

'An extended fence line to include the solar farm.'

The site director looked to the heavens and breathed out heavily.

Joe kept quiet.

She looked straight into his eyes, seeing how steady they were. 'Well, if you think it's essential for the future security of the site...'

'I do.'

'I shall see if we can get the additional funding. Given what you managed to achieve, I'm sure they'll say yes.'

'What I achieved?'

'The professor does talk to me, you know.' She smiled.

'Ah, yes. Who do you need to say yes?'

'Nobody you need to worry about.' Helen Ogilvie nodded at the door.

Joe didn't move.

'Have you got any other requirements?'

'Uh, no. Thanks, Helen.' Joe stood up and moved to the door.

'Joe.'

'Yes, ma'am?'

'Thank you for asking for the "favour."' A brief smile flitted across her face. 'And stop calling me "ma'am." It makes me feel so old.'

'You're welcome, Helen.' Joe winked.

***

When Joe reached the security office, Jameson waved him into the room.

'What is it?'

'Look what I found.'

In the centre of the floor was a pile of scrunched-up plastic sheeting. It appeared to be the same plastic sheeting that made up the bivouac tent on the ground outside the fenced-off grounds.

'Is that what I think it is?'

'Yes. I didn't find the guy, but hopefully, he'll go home now that we have his tent.'

'What if he was an innocent tourist?'

'Tourist? Out here? You gotta be joking.'

'Did you find anything else? Anything that might identify the... camper?'

'Nope. So, you were right. Someone was camping outside the site.'

'Let's hope he or she leaves now.'

'I'll go out again at dusk. The clouds should have passed by then.'

Corporal Swift came in through the door at the end of the corridor and removed his face mask.

'Swifty, anything happen on your shift?'

'Uneventful, Sarge.' Swifty saw Joe and was about to salute.

'No need to salute, Corporal.'

'Yes, sir.'

'Did you happen to see anyone on foot?'

Corporal Swift looked quizzical for a moment. 'Uh, no, sir. There were only deliveries of ore and supplies. Both vehicles.'

Joe nodded. 'Thanks. You back on shift later?'

Jameson cut in. 'He's back on in two hours, sir. Aren't you, Swifty? Best go and take your break.'

Swifty looked from the face of Sergeant Jameson to that of Major Wolfe and back again. 'Yes, Sarge. Of course,' he said before passing them in the corridor on his way to another room.

Chapter Twelve

'Trespasser apprehended, over.'

Joe looked from the holographic computer screen in front of him to the walkie-talkie in the charging dock on the side of his desk. He picked it up and turned it over in his hands, marvelling at how different it was from the original model he'd used in the army. The shape fitted perfectly in the palm of his hand, and the screen was completely smooth. Just like a cell phone, there was only an On/Off button barely visible on the right-hand edge of the device. Joe had no idea how to operate the walkie-talkie, so he decided to put it back on its stand and find out what was going on the old-school way—on foot.

'Say again, Sarge?

'Trespasser. Apprehended. I'm bringing him in for questioning. Clear out the spare office. I shall interrogate him in there, over.'

'Will do, Sarge, over.'

Joe stepped out of his office and into the corridor. The female radio operator was momentarily taken aback to see him standing in the corridor, waiting.

'Sergeant Jameson is bringing in someone for questioning, sir.'

'I heard. Thanks. Do you need any help clearing the spare office?'

'Uh, no, sir. Thanks for the offer. I only have to move some of the sergeant's stuff.'

'Sergeant Jameson's stuff?'

'Yes, sir.'

Joe nodded as if he knew exactly what was going on. 'Let me know on the walkie-talkie when he arrives with the trespasser, would you?'

'Of course, sir. I shall call it in as soon as he arrives back.'

Joe returned to his office and paced back and forth.

Who has Jameson caught, and why? Will he manage to bring in the trespasser unharmed?

Joe was out of his office when he heard the first syllable on the walkie-talkie, but he stopped in his tracks when he saw who the trespasser was.

He recognised Sergeant Denison out of uniform. The man was wearing washed-out green fatigues, old, scuffed, and worn jump boots, and a hat that reminded Joe of the fisherman he'd seen when out on his jog earlier.

'Sergeant Denison?'

Jameson did a double take. 'Sir? You know this man?'

'Sergeant Jameson, you have brought in Sergeant Denison, whom I met at the Russian tower. Kindly remove the restraints and tell me what you found Denison doing.'

Jameson lifted Denison's hands, which were bound at the wrists by a slim, dull, metal grey ring. He pressed the side of the restraints, and they fell into an open palm.

Denison massaged his wrists. 'Thanks, sir.'

Jameson looked at his captive and then back at Joe. 'Sir, this man...'

'Sergeant Denison,' Joe confirmed.

'This Sergeant Denison was found skulking near the fence line. He wouldn't give any reason for being there and wouldn't give any information like who he is and where he's from.'

'So, you took him in?'

'So, I brought him in. We can't be too careful, sir.'

Denison was looking at the floor.

'Sergeant Jameson, please take Denison to the office used for interrogation and get him to explain himself.'

'Sir? Do you want to conduct the interview, as you know him?'

'You start. I need to speak to Lieutenant Fowler,' Joe said, watching a range of emotions flash through Denison's eyes.

The man was a shadow of his former self. With sallow skin and bags under his eyes, the sergeant from Tower 3 clearly hadn't been looking after himself since the riot.

Self-sabotage? Guilt?

Denison dropped his gaze, and he was escorted into the office that only minutes earlier had housed Sergeant Jameson's possessions.

***

'Have you heard, Charlie?' Joe asked as he stood in the doorway to Lieutenant Fowler's office.

'Mmm?' Charlie stared at the holographic screen in front of her.

'Jameson has brought in the trespasser. And we know who he is.'

Charlie looked up. 'Who?'

'Sergeant Denison.'

Charlie's mouth dropped open.

'He looks...' Joe pictured the man in his mind's eye. 'He looks not himself.'

'What do you mean?'

'He looks worse for wear.'

A look of compassion flashed across her face, leaving it blank and with a tight line of a mouth.

'How was he when you left? Do you remember?'

Charlie looked downwards, apparently remembering back to Russia. Back to the time when she'd told him she was leaving him.

'Was he okay? Mentally, I mean.'

'He was hurt that I was going. But he'd been sort of off ever since the riot, anyway. I couldn't say whether he was okay or not. The riot changed everything. For him, for us, and for...'

Joe understood that Charlie couldn't say the Frenchman's name.

He found himself nodding. 'For me too,' he whispered subconsciously, rubbing his leg. 'Are you wanting to see him? I'm going to join Jameson in the interview, but I wanted to make sure you were aware of what's going on.'

'What? Why was he brought in? I thought you said the tent was far enough away from the fence line not to be a threat?'

'I'll find out why Jameson brought him in. Then I shall find out why he's here.' Joe looked up thoughtfully. 'Are we fully manned?'

A look of horror descended over Charlie's face.

'No. No, it's a stupid thought. Forget I ever asked about it,' Joe said quickly and noticed Charlie slump down in relaxation. 'I shall get some answers, then get him off site.'

'Thanks, Joe.'

Joe walked slowly along the corridor, thinking about Charlie, Russia, and the Frenchman who had died. He'd been a member of the team, although his overbearing misogyny had created a chasm between him and every other person on the security detail. Did he deserve to die for chasing anyone in a skirt? No. Did he deserve to die for making a pass at someone else's girlfriend? Definitely not. Maybe he should have been transferred to somewhere else. But wouldn't that have just been giving the problem to someone else?

Joe shrugged, breathed deeply, and stepped into the office cum interview room.

Denison was hanging his head, and Jameson was sitting back in his chair with his arms crossed over his shoulder.

'He said he isn't answering any questions. He'll only talk to you.'

Joe saw mud up the side of Jameson's leg. 'Sergeant, why don't you get cleaned up?'

'Sir, I'm okay.'

'Go for a coffee then, please.' Joe stared Jameson down.

Denison looked up into Joe's eyes when Jameson left the office.

'So, how are you, Denis?'

'I've been better, sir.'

'Call me Joe.'

'Thanks for asking, Joe.'

'So, what brings you here?'

'I was at a loose end.'

'Oh?'

'Well, to be honest. I haven't been too great... since Russia. I heard that you were here and thought, well, maybe I could be a part of your team again, sir.'

Joe pursed his lips. 'I'm afraid I can't give you a job.'

'I know. I mean, I guessed.' Denison looked at the desk. 'Charlie is here, isn't she?' he asked without wanting an answer. 'How is she?'

'Lieutenant Fowler is good. She hopes you're okay and are just passing through.'

Denison nodded slowly. 'She's always classy. Knows exactly what to say and when to say it.'

Joe nodded. 'So, why camp outside the fence line?'

'I dunno. I was too embarrassed to go straight to the front gate. Maybe I needed to build up my courage.'

'And what happened when Sergeant Jameson found you?' Joe asked and was surprised to see a slight smile on Denison's face.

'He grabbed me when I was in my tent. When he pulled me backwards, I resisted. He must have lost his grip and went flying and landed on his ass.'

Joe looked at the man. Denison wouldn't look directly at him. *Is he hiding something and feeling guilty about something, maybe?*

'So, where are you gonna go now?' Joe asked

'I dunno. Maybe I can hitch a ride back to civilisation.' Denison looked up. 'Do you think I can go and grab my stuff?'

'I'm sure that will be okay.'

Denison visibly relaxed.

''Tell you what. I'll walk you back there.'

Denison looked puzzled for a moment. 'But you're a captain?'

'A major now.'

'Sorry, sir. Congratulations.' Denison stared into the distance for a moment. 'I'm glad that something positive came out of... out of the riot.'

Joe nodded, then stood up. 'Come on then. Let's get your things.'

***

'Is that all you have?' Joe asked, seeing Denison pack his belongings into the rucksack.

''It's all I need.'

Denison untied the rope from one shrub, and they both watched the tent breathe out slowly as it sank to the ground. Joe watched as the sergeant he knew from his time at the Russian tower wrapped the rope around the top of his shoulder and down under his bent elbow. When the rope was coiled into a large bow-tie shape, the man folded and rolled the plastic sheet. He placed the rope into the midst of the sheet, and both items were secured into place at the base of the rucksack.

Joe nodded, admiring Denison as he looked after his camping equipment.

'Are you gonna be okay?'

'Yeah, I'll be all right,' Denison answered without looking Joe in the eye.

'You know, if it wasn't for Charlie... Lieutenant Fowler,' Joe quickly corrected himself. 'I would have found something that you could help with.'

Denison nodded and swung his rucksack up and onto his back, simultaneously putting his arms through the shoulder straps. With a quick check that the rucksack was on securely, he looked up, and Joe stepped back at the flash of fury in the man's eyes.

'Charlie isn't as good as you think she is.'

Joe, at first, didn't realise what Denison had said and nodded.

'What? What did you say?'

But Denison didn't reply. He was already striding away towards the road that the ore supply came in on.

It took Joe a moment to recover from the surprise. He remembered the note on his office desk. Denison had said out loud exactly the same words.

Surely not a coincidence.

Joe walked towards the main gate in the same direction that Denison had gone on the way to the main road. Being only seconds behind, he was surprised that he didn't see Denison at all.

***

The young, drunken Joe staggered as the boy who had called him chicken mumbled something. Joe shifted his grip around the back of what he could loosely describe as his friend, and they moved together in a zig-zag line towards the house. The sun had gone to bed, and the moonlight picked out the paved path to the front door.

Joe pressed the doorbell and shifted under the other boy's weight. A light was switched on downstairs, and the door flew open to reveal anger on the face of his friend's mother.

'Is that you, Joe Wolfe?'

'Yes, ma'am.'

The anger disappeared as quickly as the light had blinked on. 'Thank you, Joe. I guessed he'd taken the bottle; I didn't know where to,' she said softly. 'Do you know why he took it?'

Despite being drunk, Joe still had enough wherewithal just to shake his head.

'Well, thank you for bringing him home. He will surely feel bad in the morning.'

Joe nodded and only turned away when the front door closed. Thankfully, she didn't see him stagger away.

***

Joe shook his head free of the hazy memory, unsure of why his mind had shown him that event. *Am I still recovering from the suspended animation sickness I experienced during a four-month journey almost two years ago?*

He was still bemused when he walked through the main gate back onto the site, but when he saw Jameson, Joe took a deep breath and steeled himself.

'Sir?'

'What is it, Jameson?'

'Where is Sergeant Denison?'

'I sent him away.'

'You what? Sorry, sir, but I don't find that funny.'

'It wasn't a joke, Sergeant. Denison is a troubled man who is battling his own set of demons. He isn't a threat to this site, nor any of us working here.' Joe paused as he remembered the note that had been left on his desk and the exact words told to him by Denison.

Jameson's mouth dropped open.

'We have no reason to keep him here and, to be frank, we don't need to waste our time looking after him,' Joe said as he opened the door and entered the security building. He held the door ajar to allow Jameson to follow him in.

Lieutenant Fowler popped her head out of the doorway. 'Sir, the minister for transport is making a statement to the press about the tower of the United Kingdom.'

'Frickin' hell. It's too soon,' Joe said under his breath.

Joe, Jameson, and Fowler watched the hologram of Lord Anderson, the Minister of Transport, step behind the podium and fill the screen.

'People of the United Kingdom, it is with great pride that I announce that the Tower, our tower, is under construction....'

The rest of his statement was drowned out in a cacophony of questions shouted by members of the press.

The minister of transport raised his hands in an attempt to calm down the room full of journalists.

As Lord Anderson answered questions as best as he could, Joe took in the scene. The minister was as white as a sheet and looked as if he would fall over if someone were to sneeze in his general direction. The man wasn't happy, despite issuing the biggest news to the people of the United Kingdom since the announcement of the worldwide exodus.

'Minister, why has it taken so long for the construction of the tower to get underway?'

'We had to get the right team together and select the right location.'

'Where is it?' numerous journalists shouted out at once.

'In Perthshire, Scotland.'

Joe wondered how many of them needed confirmation that Perthshire was in Scotland.

'Minister, is there any truth that your wife has left you following your previous statement that you would not be taking your allotted exodus ticket when the time came?'

Joe cringed and felt for the man.

'I can confirm that I am currently residing in my family home alone,' Lord Anderson said, looking at the ground as if wanting it to swallow him up.

'Why did you do it, sir? Why did you give up your allotted ticket?'

'Having been a Lord of the Realm since my father passed away thirty-five years ago, I do not feel it right to have an exodus ticket because of the position I am in nor the status I have.'

Joe nodded. Lord Anderson looked as if he was in his eighties. With no colour to his face, completely white hair on his head, and the bags of stress hanging under his eyes, it was obvious that the minister had been sorely affected by the fallout of his stance on Project Exodus.

'I have to speak with the site director,' Joe told Fowler and Jameson, who couldn't tear themselves away from the hologram of Minister of Transport Lord Anderson.

***

Joe rapped his knuckle on the inside of the site director's open door.

The antique phone was slammed down.

'Bastards,' she muttered before looking up and seeing Joe at her doorway. 'Major Wolfe—Joe—how are you? I'm guessing you've heard the wonderful news. The whole world now knows that Tower 17 exists, and who knows who will come knocking.'

Joe saw the flash of anger fade in her eyes.

'Director, you had no warning that this announcement was coming out today?'

She shook her head. 'None whatsoever. I was only just told, which I'm guessing was after the press were told where you heard about it?'

Joe nodded.

She looked out of the window. 'So, how are we? How secure is the site?'

'Same as we've been since production began. Nothing to worry about.'

'Major, you probably haven't understood the ramifications of the statement to the press. Everyone now knows where we are. Everyone in Scotland will be wanting to see for themselves this tower of ours. Crowds will appear as if by magic.'

'But?'

'What do you think I was doing in Russia before you started here? I came back on the same flight as you. I was researching what went on when the Russian tower was built and how long it took for groups of people to visit the site of their tower.'

'Oh.'

'Yes. By the way, I signed off on the fencing to enclose the solar panel farm as requested. And if you need any more staff or defensive measures to shore up our security, just let me know.' She looked out the window again. 'Best you go and get things organised, Major.'

Joe nodded and left the office without another word.

Chapter Thirteen

They came in dribs and drabs at first. Then, like scenes from a zombie movie, the walkers coalesced into a mass of amoebas. The more walkers who arrived, the more noises the growing group made. And the more noises the group made, the more walkers it attracted. Within a day, there were a dozen tents dotted around the west side of the main gate. Within three days, over thirty tents were pitched outside the fence line. After a week, even Jameson gave up trying to count.

The team are looking to me to come up with an idea of what to do.

Joe glanced at Fowler and Jameson and saw a couple of paces behind them was George Swift. George had proved himself to be reliable and was always there, ready to lend a hand. But to Joe's sensitive gut, something didn't feel quite right. He looked again at the burgeoning potential problem and quickly forgot about George Swift's presence. The group was placid at the moment, with no undertones of malice or mischief, but given Joe's experience, a group this large could change in an instant. He knew he had to do something. He had to guide the growing crowd of visitors somehow and resolve their evident curiosity about Tower 17 and the site on which it stood. But what could he do with the visitors?

Visitors? Joe smiled to himself.

'Did you ever go on a school trip, Jameson?'

Jameson shook his head.

'Lieutenant Fowler, did you?'

Fowler nodded and looked at him quizzically.

Joe walked into the tented land, just like a reservation, where some tents were situated on higher ground, allowing dampness to drop below the occupants. Some campers weren't so lucky or clever and had set up their tents in dips, drops, and basins and would no doubt be wondering why they took longer to dry out in the mornings.

'Hi, how are you doing?' he said, walking past some bewildered campers. 'I hope you're enjoying your stay,' he said to another pair who looked up at him.

Lieutenant Fowler and Sergeant Jameson gazed on in horror as Joe was soon lost from their view in 'enemy' territory, in Jameson's humble opinion.

Joe squatted down at the fireside and rubbed his hands together. The people dotted around the fire stopped talking and stared at him.

'Warmer days are on their way,' he offered to nobody in particular.

'Aye, changeable weather this season,' a bearded old man replied.

'Has anyone seen the tower close up?' Joe asked whilst staring into the flames.

'Nah, we haven't been allowed onto their site.'

'We can see it from here, though,' another camper said, pointing over the fence at the base of the tower rising above the buildings and visible through the vicious-looking barbed wire topping the fence.

Everyone paused in conversation and stared at the gigantic edifice reaching for the heavens.

'Would you like to?' Joe posed the question.

The older man recovered from surprise the quickest. 'What?'

'Would anyone like to come onto the site and take a closer look at the tower?'

Whispers and muted conversation rippled through the grounds, all discussing the same thing. Who was this man in a plain green uniform? Who was he to ask this question?

'I could arrange it. Of course, it would have to be in manageable groups. Say, a dozen people at one time. Anyone up for it?'

'You could arrange it?' the old man asked.

Joe nodded.

'Who are you?'

'I am Joe Wolfe.'

'No. What do you do in there? How come you can sort out us getting in to see it?'

'Oh, didn't I say? I'm Major Joe Wolfe, head of security of Tower 17.'

There was a moment of stunned silence.

'You? You're in charge of the security?'

'What are you doing with us?'

'Just being friendly. I thought you might like to see it close up. That's all.' Joe stood up and dusted off his clothes. 'Well, if anyone is interested, organise yourselves into groups of twelve. Then tomorrow and every weekday onwards at 9:00 a.m., I'll be at the front gate waiting to show a group of you around.'

He turned. 'If nobody turns up, I guess nobody wants to see it. Nothing ventured, nothing gained,' he said before walking back towards the front gate to meet up with a pair of concerned colleagues.

***

'You offered to do *what*?' The site director was incredulous.

'I offered to show groups of twelve of them around the site tomorrow morning. Nine o'clock a.m., to be precise.'

'Nine a.m.?'

'Yeah. The earlier, the better for us. The group should be calm, being sleepy and all.'

She smiled despite herself. 'Well, I suppose you are head of security here. As long as you know what you're doing.'

'Would you like to talk to them?' Joe looked at the mobile in the corner. 'You could talk about the heavens, what is up there in the stars.'

The site director frowned. 'Joe, although I love the science of space, there is no way that I will give a talk to stinking campers who are just waking up in the morning. Just make sure they don't cause chaos.'

Joe grinned and nodded. *I think I know what I'm doing. Anyway, what could go wrong?* He left a stunned site director and walked straight over to Lieutenant Fowler and Sergeant Jameson.

'So, tomorrow morning, I don't want anyone showing off their firearms.'

'But...' Jameson began to protest.

'No firearms, Sarge. That is an order.' Joe smiled. 'We're going to show them to the base of the tower, and with any luck, the spare printer will be down for repairs, and they can see that too.'

'What if they're spies?'

'From where? Every major power has at least one tower, if not more. Who would want to spy on ours?'

Jameson tried to find holes in the plans and, in the end, couldn't find any. 'I just don't like it,' he offered at last.

'I shall see if Professor Viggenson would like to speak to them,' Joe said mainly to himself. 'After all, he may still owe me.'

Fowler smiled. 'I think he still worships you for being able to get all the ore from Planet 27 that he could ever want. Would you like me to come with you to see the professor?'

Joe smiled. 'That would be good. It would save me from getting lost in the underground labyrinth.'

Fowler laughed and then started up her computer to check on the weather conditions. 'Mmm.'

'Problems?'

'No, not really. A storm front is moving westwards and bringing with it the poisoned air from the east of Scotland.'

So, masks it is then, when we go outside.'

'Masks it is. Could last longer than a day too."

Joe frowned. 'The visitors tomorrow,' he murmured. 'They may not be safe.'

'You aren't responsible for them, Joe.'

'Humph.'

***

Joe stood in front of the camera wearing his mask and couldn't understand why the door wasn't unlocking as it had on previous occasions. Fowler pushed him out of the way and tapped the code into the keypad. The door clicked loudly enough to be heard through their face masks.

She pushed open the door, and only when he was safely inside did she lock the door behind him and remove her face mask. Joe followed suit and had to lengthen his stride down the corridor as she walked quickly to the professor's office.

'Major Wolfe, my favourite head of security. To what do I this pleasure?'

Joe smiled. 'I don't know if you've heard yet, but Minister for Transport Lord Anderson told the press that Tower 17 existed and it was located outside Perth. Since then, the curious have travelled to our location and are camping on the other side of the fence. The numbers have increased, and the group has grown to some size. I've invited a dozen visitors to come by tomorrow morning to have a guided tour around the place and to see the base of the tower.'

'I hadn't heard about either. I have been studying the.... I have been busy.' The professor caught himself from saying too much. 'So, why did you invite them?'

'To get ahead of the curve. I would rather have the visitors see what the site is like before they get angry and cause a riot.'

The professor nodded. 'Good plan.'

'So, I was wondering...'

Fowler gave Joe a nudge.

'Sorry, WE would like to know if you would give a talk tomorrow.'

Professor Viggenson rubbed his chin. 'A talk, eh? It has been a while, but it does sound interesting. A captive audience of twelve.' He smiled. 'Yes. That sounds good.'

'You'll do it?' Joe asked in surprise.

'Of course. How could I refuse a request from Major Wolfe?'

'The only possible change to the plans would be the weather. There is a weather warning out now that could still be in place in the morning.'

'How bad is it?' The professor looked between Joe and Fowler.

'Category six, Professor.'

The bespectacled professor nodded slowly.

'What would happen if they weren't protected during a category six?' Joe asked.

'They would have difficulty breathing. They would likely feel nauseous and, if outside long enough, would experience D & V.'

'D & V?'

'Diarrhoea and vomiting,' Fowler answered.

'What can we do to stop that from happening?' Joe asked with a grimace.

'Well, we can't change the weather, so the only thing would be to make sure the people outside of the fence line had their masks.'

'And if they don't?' Joe looked from Fowler to the professor.

'We don't have enough spare masks,' Fowler said.

''Actually,' the professor said slowly. 'Follow me.' He took them down to the end of the corridor and slotted a card into a slot in the wall that neither of them had seen before.

With a pneumatic hiss, a door popped out of the wall and opened to show a room full of 'easy breathing' face masks and rows of clothes rails covered in chemical defence suits.

Joe stared at the professor.

'For any eventuality,' the professor said at last. 'There is a lot more in this bunker to preserve the human race.'

***

Joe staggered out of the bunker with his face mask securely in place. He tightened the straps to ensure no gaps were left to allow the poisoned air in. Fowler was behind him, and both of them walked slowly, still struggling to accept what they'd learnt in the bunker. Although the professor wasn't opposed to handing out face masks and chemical defence suits, he'd drawn the line when it came to allowing non-site personnel access to his domain.

'I can't believe he had that much safety gear,' Joe admitted.

'I can't believe he's lending it out to—'

'Visitors?'

Fowler smiled. 'Yes, visitors. I'm starting to like Professor Viggenson.'

'Starting to?'

'He's too secretive for my liking. But, well, I see another side to him. A caring side.'

Joe nodded. 'So, you can arrange for thirty masks for tomorrow morning?'

'Yes, sir. But there are more than that camped outside the fence line.'

'Yeah, but most of them will have their own masks.'

'And you think that there will still be visitors turning up for your tour?'

'I think so. They put up with camping up here, far away from running water and a proper washroom. They'll want to see what we have on site and the tower. Yeah, they'll want to see the tower up close.' Joe nodded. 'I shall leave it in your capable hands and see you in the morning.'

Fowler smiled. 'Yes, sir.'

Joe watched her walk away for a moment before heading to his own office. As soon as he entered the building, he ripped his mask off and saw the slick of perspiration on the rubber seal. He stepped into the clean room and closed his eyes as a cloud of fine dust was blown at him from all directions. He kept his eyes closed as an automatic vacuum cleaner removed all of the dust. Only when the clean room went quiet did he open his eyes.

It's never too safe.

He looked at his bare-walled office and thought about the day. Sitting down, he rubbed the bridge of his nose and then remembered the computer.

'Computer—on.'

The holographic screen appeared above his desk. 'Voice of Major Wolfe recognised.'

'Computer, open personnel files of Lieutenant Fowler and Corporal Swift.'

Two files appeared before him. Joe flicked through Charlie Fowler's file, basic details he barely took in. She was twenty-eight and single. Born in Carlisle, Cumbria in England, she'd passed security checks with no red flags. She'd been in the British Army until it downsized, an effect of the worldwide Project Exodus. Her military experience had landed her straight in the tower security force and posted her to Russia as a sergeant. With no children and no mention of Denison, her file was very empty.

Too empty?

Joe tapped the one entry field he was looking for: Sponsor.

It was empty.

He frowned, then tapped the screen to close her file. Corporal George Swift's file was as equally empty of history. Joe's eyebrows arched briefly as he noticed George's date of birth field was empty. The sponsor was Coben Engineering, as to be expected. On the few occasions he'd spoken to George, Joe had detected an American accent.

Two enigmas.

Joe's thoughts were interrupted by a red light flashing above him. He put his head out of the doorway and saw a corporal putting on a jacket.

'What's going on, Corporal?'

'Oh, hi, sir. The fence alarm has been tripped.'

'Which section?'

'The north side, sir. Near the cliff.' The corporal put on his face mask and dashed out of the building.

Chapter Fourteen

Joe watched the screen as the feed from the head cam showed the corporal's team accompanying Sergeant Jameson and heading to the north side of the site. What he saw was beyond believable.

Three people were standing inside the fence line. Their eyes were red-rimmed, and mucous dripped from their noses. They were foaming at the mouth and scrabbling at their throats.

'Control, this is Jameson. We have a situation here, over.'

'What is it?'

'Switch on the video signal from our head cams, control. Three intruders are very much worse for wear, over.'

Joe listened to the pregnant silence and imagined the controller bringing up the headcam footage on the computer screen.

'They aren't wearing any face masks,' the controller uttered.

Joe thought about the lack of masks. *If they've been out of contact with anyone, they may not have known the bad weather was coming. Their ignorance could have cost them their lives. If they hadn't got through the fence today, they may not have survived their visit.*

'What do you want us to do with them, control?'

'How should I know?'

'What is the procedure?'

'Sorry, Sarge. Wait one.'

There was another pause whilst the controller turned off the audio to ask the computer for guidance.

Joe looked at the three people on the screen. From where Jameson stood, he couldn't tell if they were men or women. They appeared to be Caucasian, but again, he couldn't be certain as there was so much froth at their mouths and tears streaming from their eyes. They were all wearing dark clothing. Matching dark clothing—just like uniforms.

Military?

'Sarge, there are no procedures for this type of event. Sorry.'

The head cam microphone caught all of the syllables of Jameson swearing under his breath.

Joe looked at his walkie-talkie and turned it in his hand. He pressed the single button and tapped the screen once.

'Jameson, this is Major Wolfe. Bring them in.'

'Sir, say again, over.'

'Bring them in. Take them to Medical.'

Joe saw Jameson and the corporal step towards the three intruders.

'No can do, sir.'

'Are you disobeying a direct order, Sergeant?'

'No, sir. Look behind them.'

Jameson used his head to pan the camera across the fence. Barbed wire hung down over a large area where the mesh of the fence once was.

'I don't want to leave the site insecure.' Jameson flicked off the safety catch of his weapon, causing a metallic click.

'Sarge, maintain your position and send the corporal to bring the intruders back.'

'But sir...'

'I don't think the intruders are in any fit state to be difficult, do you? Get the corporal to take them to Medical.'

'Yes, sir.'

The screen flared brightly before the computer compensated for the contrast as Jameson's head cam swung towards the site buildings and the floodlights.

'Sarge, turn back to face the fence.'

'What, sir?'

'Turn to face the fence. You won't be able to see it now. Your night vision will have to recover.'

'Oh, yeah. Sorry, sir.'

'Control, this is Major Wolfe.'

'Yes, sir?'

'Inform Medical that the corporal on shift is bringing in three intruders with category five or six sicknesses.'

'Yes, sir.'

'Oh, and control... Get maintenance out to repair the fence.'

'Now, sir? They'll be in the bar.'

'What?'

'Yeah, they're celebrating the printers working through and above cloud level.'

'I don't care if they're celebrating. The fence needs fixing tonight. Just get them on it pronto.'

'Yes, sir.'

***

Joe and Dr Wardle stood in the corridor outside of the medical bay.

'What do you think, Doc?'

'They should be okay to answer questions now. The shower will have washed away all the toxins.'

The two male intruders sat on the edge of two bunks. They looked away as the female intruder wrapped herself in a large towel before sitting down on a bunk on the opposite side of the ward.

Joe pushed open the door and stepped inside. The three intruders stared at him.

'What are your names?'

There was no response.

Joe frowned. He tried to remember the language courses that he'd listened to on the computer.

'Are you Russian? Can you speak English?' Joe said in Russian.

There wasn't a flicker from any of the three.

'Can you speak English?' Joe said in Korean.

Still nothing.

'Can you speak English?' he said in Mandarin.

The woman looked at the shorter of the two men.

Joe noticed one of the men's jaws clenching, but that was the only response to the only words he knew in Mandarin.

'Well, if you don't tell me who you are, I won't be able to tell the consulate that you're here,' he said conversationally in English.

The smaller of the male intruders glanced at the other man, but the three of them didn't say a word.

Back out in the corridor, Joe shrugged as the doctor looked at him. 'Chinese military is my best guess. Do you know if we have any Mandarin speakers on site?'

The doctor shook his head. 'Even if there was a Mandarin speaker here, I don't think we would get anything out of them.'

'Humph. Can't we do anything?' he muttered.

The doctor shook his head again. 'We can't interrogate them in their language, and we can't force them to speak either. We aren't exactly set up for this eventuality like a spy movie, are we?'

Joe frowned, turned, and was about to walk away.

'What are you going to do, Major?'

'Inform the site director. Where are you going, Doctor?' Joe asked.

'To inform the professor.'

'Why? Why does the professor need to know?'

'The professor looks after some sensitive data. His research is confidential.'

'What is he researching?'

'I'm not allowed to say.'

'You can tell me. I'm in charge of the site's security.'

'You don't have security clearance for this, Major.'

'What? What level of clearance do I need?'

But the doctor was already walking away.

***

'Chinese, you say?'

'That's my best guess. It was only when I asked them if they could speak English in Mandarin that they made any movement. I asked the same question in English, Russian, Korean, and Mandarin. There was only a response to the Mandarin.'

'You speak Russian, Korean, and Mandarin?'

'I can only say "Do you speak English?" I'm still learning.'

The site director pulled a face. 'Of course, Mandarin is the only language that nobody on site can speak.'

'Yeah, that's what the doctor said too.'

'Of course, if they're Chinese, then this goes above and beyond both our heads.' The site director tapped a finger on her chin.

Joe didn't say anything further.

Helen picked up the phone and dialled a number she apparently knew instinctively.

'Sir, three intruders. Suspected to be Chinese.' She listened intently to the response. 'Uh-huh. Yes, of course.' She turned to Joe. 'They're ill, you said?'

Joe nodded. 'Yeah. They were in the poisoned air without masks.'

'What did the doctor say?'

'They should recover in a couple days.'

She nodded and put the phone back up to her face. 'Yes, sir. Poisoned air sickness. Forty-eight-hour recovery expected.' She shook her head. 'What? Sir? Okay.' She looked at the handset as the other person clicked off.

'Who was that?'

'My boss.'

Joe raised his eyebrows.

'The Minister for UK Transport and Head of the Council for Project Exodus.'

'What did he say?'

'That when the intruders have recovered, take them to the front gate and let them go.'

'You must be joking. They cut through the fence. Who knows what they would have done if we hadn't stopped them.'

'Not much, as they're sick,' she said matter-of-factly.

'But they're intruders.'

'They did nothing more than cut the fence. We aren't to cause an international incident.'

'But—'

'That is an order from the top, Joe. We have to do what we're told in this instance.'

Joe frowned.

'Please, Joe.'

Joe's face softened and he shrugged. 'You're the boss, Boss.'

'Thanks. Sometimes I wonder.'

She said it so softly, Joe didn't know if she'd actually said what she said.

'Are you still going ahead with the group visiting tomorrow?'

Joe nodded. 'If anyone turns up, we shall show them around.'

'But not the broken fence.'

'No, not the fence. If the weather is still bad, we shall take spare face masks to the campsite and see if anyone needs one. It's the right thing to do."

The site director slowly nodded. 'I knew you were the right person for the job.'

Again, she spoke so softly, Joe wasn't sure he'd heard right. 'Good night, Director,' he said with a nod.

'Thanks, Joe.'

Joe went to his room, lay down on his bed fully dressed, and stared at the ceiling. The questions kept on swirling about in his head.

Why did the Chinese break onto the site? What did they expect to find?

Should I cancel the guided tour for the morning? Will anyone turn up?

Joe undressed and stood in the shower, taking full force of the water on his head in an attempt to clear his mind.

The memory of one of his first conversations with Trent on Planet 27 resurfaced. They were admiring the sunset, and Trent had told him in no uncertain terms not to trust anyone. Their very conversations were being monitored. At the time, he'd taken the warning at face value. Only afterwards did he realise Trent wasn't to be trusted either.

'Fortune favours the bold,' he whispered.

Wearing only a towel wrapped around his waist to cover his modesty, Joe stepped slowly over to the lamp, careful not to make a sound. He tapped the base, and the light ceased. He lifted the lamp and turned it over. Something fell onto the floor, and he returned the lamp to its position before bending down and eyeing up what appeared to be a button.

The button was ear-like. Miniature folds of the soft membrane formed several rings, one within another, within another. Joe shrugged, picked up the odd, button-shaped device, and put it on the table next to the base of the lamp.

He turned slowly on the spot, looking at his room with fresh eyes. A black dot in the corner where the walls met the ceiling caught his attention.

What the....

Joe smiled to himself, tugged the corner of his towel, and allowed it to drop to the floor. He'd been brought up never to be ashamed of his body and now was no different. With no idea of who might be watching the footage from the miniature camera, he turned, bent over, and picked up the towel, sending the viewer a cheeky sign that he knew there was a camera in his room.

Chapter Fifteen

Joe tightened his face mask and then the hood of his chemical protection suit. He dusted off his name badge and admired it in the mirror.

Major Joe Wolfe—Security

Prepare for the worst and hope for the best.

Joe opened the door and stepped into a new adventure. The air was thick with poison, and he hoped that everyone who had camped outside the site's fence line was protected.

Jameson was standing a couple of metres back from the open front gate, holding a pistol in his gloved right hand. The trio of Chinese spies stood before him, all wearing protective gear and masks. They were facing the open gate and waiting.

'Sarge, I'm guessing they never said anything.'

'Oh, hi, sir. No, nothing. Not even a thank you for saving their lives.' Jameson and Joe looked at the thick, scudding clouds. 'I still can't believe we have to let them go. They broke into the site, for chrissakes.'

'Not my decision. The government decided it.'

'Humph.'

They heard the vehicle before they saw it. An antique military five-tonne truck trundled around the corner and up to the front gate.

The guard had words and indicated that the driver wasn't allowed on site. The truck had to either reverse or make a five-point turn.

The Chinese stepped forward a pace before Jameson waved at them with his pistol to stand where they were. Everyone watched as the vehicle went back and forth several times until it managed to turn around on the one-lane track.

Jameson waved the Chinese intruders, and they needed no further instructions. The three of them jogged to the back of the truck, climbed up, and piled into the safety of the cover provided by the taut canvas roof.

The last Joe saw of them was their profiles sitting with bent heads, no doubt with the weight of a failed mission on their slumped shoulders.

'So, why didn't you tell the guard to let the truck turn about here?'

Jameson grinned under the face mask. 'We didn't want to make it easy for them. After all, they were still the ones caught in the act.' He pointed to the front gate. 'Here are some of your new friends, sir.'

Twelve people wearing an assortment of clothing had one thing in common: they were all wearing new face masks supplied by the professor.

'I'm guessing Lieutenant Fowler took the masks out this morning?'

'Yes, sir. She was out bright and early. I understand she took out almost fifty masks and even managed to persuade the head of catering to donate some tinned food and bottled water.'

Joe nodded and stared at Jameson's pistol. Without a word, Jameson holstered his weapon under a flap of his jacket so it was nearly invisible.

'Major Wolfe? It is, isn't it?'

'That's me.' Joe smiled. 'What's everyone's name?'

The man closest to Joe, who must have been the appointed spokesperson, shook his head. 'Sorry, Major. But we'll be keeping our names to ourselves, if it's all right with you.'

Joe inclined his head. 'Come on then,' he said, waving forwards the deputation onto the site of Tower 17.

He noticed Jameson's hand reaching inside his jacket to grip the pistol. He gave a hard stare until the sergeant dropped his hand down to his side.

'So, friends of Tower 17, welcome!' Joe shouted through his mask. 'I wish we had better weather.' He looked around and saw several nods. 'As you may know, we have the best technology to build the tower...'

'Can we see it?'

'Unfortunately, the devices are all in use.' Joe gave the white lie as he was unwilling to show the spare printer undergoing maintenance in the workshop. 'And I can't let you go up there,' he said, pointing to the heavens.

There was some laughter this time, and almost everyone stared upwards. The eight octas of cloud cover appeared to hang back away from the tower. The poison-infected cumulonimbus clouds surrounded Tower 17 menacingly, but Joe could swear that if he stood right next to the base, he would be able to see all the way up the side.

I need to speak to the professor about that.

Joe looked at the group and saw that two of the twelve were staring straight at him while the others were still craning their necks. He tapped Jameson on the shoulder.

'Sarge, keep an eye on those two visitors at the back of the group, would you?'

'Yeah, sure. Whatever you say, Boss.'

'How high is it gonna be built?' the old man whom Joe had met at the fireside shouted out in his raspy voice.

'As high as we can go. As close to the Karman line as possible.'

'What is the carping line?' the old man asked.

'The Karman line,' the visitor next to him said loudly.

Joe couldn't help but smile.

'Why?' another visitor asked.

'The purpose of the towers is to provide an economical method of launches. The closer to the Karman line, the less fuel is needed for each launch,' the professor shouted as he walked over to stand beside Joe. 'Sorry I am late, Major.'

Joe smiled. 'Just in time for the... technical questions, Professor.'

'If you would like to follow me, I am the chief of science here on site. We don't want to tax the major's grey cells, do we?'

More laughter.

Joe didn't know whether to smile or not.

'Why is the tower so smooth?'

'I am glad you asked that,' the professor answered, pointing at the smooth surface. 'Our technology has been designed to be so efficient that nothing is wasted in building the tower. Some of you may have heard of Tower 1 and its horrifying collapse. The smooth surface of Tower 17 ensures that the pressure from the weight above is evenly distributed. There is, therefore, less chance of fracturing and less chance of collapse.'

'What is it made of?'

'It is made of a mix of iron and ore from Planet 27. You may not know that the major here has completed a tour of duty on Planet 27 and knows the ore very well.'

Everyone turned to stare at Joe, who was frowning behind his mask.

What the hell, Professor!

'Doesn't it take a long time to travel to that planet and back? You must be ancient.'

'Come now,' the professor attracted their attention once more. 'We have much more interesting facts than the major's age.'

'What is the mix of the ore?' someone shouted.

The professor smiled behind his mask. 'Now, that is one thing I will not tell you. I have to have my trade secrets.'

Joe saw Jameson standing directly behind two visitors who were now trying to blend in with the other visitors.

There is something about those two that is different. Yes! They have really impressive-looking masks. Their masks are of a better standard than those issued out from Tower 17 stocks.

Joe tried to catch a glimpse of what they looked like behind their masks, but they were either standing at the wrong angle for him, or there were too many other visitors blocking his view.

The professor was describing the power of the pump needed to transport the ore up to the manufacturing platform, which was located high above.

'What is that?' Someone pointed at a metal pole next to one of the tower's two legs.

'That is to protect everyone and everything during storms. It is a lightning conductor or, as we call it, the ground rod.'

'Why is it so thick?' the same person queried.

'It has to be thick enough to withstand the charge of electricity from the lightning and not explode.'

Joe's eyebrows rose in surprise. 'That should be enough shocking information from our head of science,' he said loudly. 'Please join me in thanking the professor for his time and knowledge in answering our questions.'

There was a smattering of applause.

'Let's now go back to the front gate and allow the professor to get back to his day job of doing science stuff.'

More laughter.

Joe saw out of the corner of his eye that Jameson was guiding the two visitors at the back to leave the site along with the rest of the group.

The old man had stayed back as the visitors were strolling out of the open gate.

'Major, please thank Charlie for all the food and water this morning.'

'Lieutenant Fowler, you mean?'

'Aye, her too.' The old man laughed and sauntered off.

***

'Well, how did it go?' Lieutenant Charlie Fowler asked as Joe and Jameson took off their masks.

Jameson grunted.

Joe patted down the rivulets of sweat on his neck with a towel before dabbing his face dry. 'I think it went okay. The professor did the heavy lifting, answering all the technical questions as he did.'

'He dropped you in it. Why do you think that was, sir?'

'I think he was rambling. He was probably nervous too.' Joe rubbed the back of his neck. 'The old man has a soft spot for you, Lieutenant.'

'Oh?'

'Yeah, he called you by your first name,' Jameson grumbled. 'And those two idiots. I almost had to force them off the site at the end.'

'Did you get any idea of who they were? Male or female? Young or old?'

'Sorry, sir. I have no idea, but I would guess that they're both male.'

Fowler looked at Joe.

'Two visitors who had better face masks than we do were different, I suppose. Different to the rest of the group, that is.'

She nodded. 'Oh, by the way, you'll be pleased to know that the air quality will have improved in half an hour.'

'Great, no more masks for the rest of the day,' Jameson said, still grumbling before leaving them alone.

'Was it that bad?' Charlie asked.

'I felt it went okay. For the first time, that is. I got them laughing a little, and then the professor got them laughing even more.'

Joe scratched his head. 'Yeah, a good first time.'

***

'So, Professor, what is it that I should know about?'

'I don't know what you mean, Major.'

'Well, we've had Chinese spies break onto the site. Then we had two men overly interested in our site who didn't want to leave. They had protective equipment better than the average person.'

'Oh?'

'Yeah, their face masks were probably better than ours.'

'They will be Americans, I would guess,' he said thoughtfully. 'Thanks for letting me know. I will be even more vigilant.'

'Vigilant about what?'

'I can't tell you. You haven't got clearance.'

'But I'm the goddam head of security. If I'm not allowed to know, who is?'

The professor just shook his head. 'I'm sorry, Joe.'

Joe tried a different tack. 'Do I need to know? Will not knowing prevent me from doing any part of my job?'

The professor thought for a moment. 'No, it won't.'

'Are you going to talk to the visitors tomorrow?'

The professor nodded. 'Are you expecting a full group?'

'As the weather has improved and the poisoned air will have gone, yeah. I'm guessing the full dozen.'

Joe and the professor's heads snapped around to face the doorway as a man in a full protective suit and mask appeared in the corridor.

'Sorry, Professor. I didn't realise you had a guest.'

'No worries. Nathan, this is Major Wolfe.'

'*The* Major Wolfe?' Nathan asked unapologetically, enthusiastic. 'Thank you so much, sir.'

Joe's eyebrows furrowed in confusion.

'You don't know what your favour did for us.'

The professor coughed. 'That is enough, Nathan.'

Joe saw that the professor was frowning.

Did I miss something there?

'So, what did you come to see me about? I thought you were conducting that confidential series of tests?'

'Yes, Professor,' Nathan replied, looking from the professor to Joe and back again. 'Erm, one of the results is beyond what we'd predicted.'

The professor's face lit up with a beautiful smile. 'Okay, okay. Well done for letting me know. It's best you return to the lab and record the results. I shall be with you shortly.'

'But I've recorded my results.'

'I shall be right with you,' the professor told him, nodding towards the corridor, seeing Nathan had stepped closer to Joe.

Nathan nodded once and slowly paced backwards without turning about. He was eking out every last moment in the presence of Major Joe Howling Wolfe.

'Sorry about that, Major.' The professor grinned. 'I'm sure you're getting used to being famous by now.'

'Famous? Why?'

'You are famous for being the oldest man on Earth. You have been to Planet 27 and back on several occasions and you have ensured an unending supply of ore 27.'

'H-how? What?' Joe stammered. 'Who told you about me?'

The professor stepped back a pace. 'I'm sorry, Joe. The doctor told me, or was it the site director? I can't remember much as it was after a few drinks the other night.'

'I would prefer that my personal details weren't shared with anyone. Especially staff, not to mention not saying a word about me to visitors,' Joe said, his face burning as mild irritation mutated into low-level anger that he hadn't felt in some time. 'I hope to see you tomorrow, Professor,' he uttered with a clipped voice before leaving the office.

***

Joe sat in his office, staring out the window. He wasn't accustomed to adulation and certainly wasn't accustomed to those in charge discussing the contents of his personnel file and then releasing details to the public domain. With Chinese spies, ex-staff, and potentially untrustworthy current staff all in the mix, he just knew the less said about him, the safer he would feel.

'Dagnabbit, Professor,' he whispered. 'I don't want to be the centre of attention for anyone. I don't know who the details of my past will attract.'

He opened the desk drawer, eyed the bottle of whisky, and sighed. The picture of his father draining a can of beer and burping after scoring a touchdown came to mind, with the on-screen audience screaming and jeering simultaneously. He nodded, closing the drawer and the frighteningly delicious temptation.

'Hi, Major. Have you been to see the professor?' Lieutenant Charlie Fowler asked.

'Oh, it's you, Lieutenant Fowler.' Joe rubbed his forehead.

'Sorry, did I catch you at the wrong time?'

'No, no. I just came from the professor.'

'Was he asking you how it feels to be so old?'

Joe frowned. 'What? Has he told you about me too?' The annoyance which had settled in his gut came spewing out. 'For frig's sake. Is nothing confidential on this site? Anything apart from you, eh?' His eyes flashed with anger, and he knew he'd said too much.

'What? What do you mean, "apart from me"?' Charlie was visibly shaken.

'Somebody doesn't like you, Lieutenant Fowler.' The poison started to vent. 'Did nobody tell you? Someone left me a note not to trust you.'

Her eyes went wide.

'Yeah. Just before I offered you the promotion to lieutenant, a note was put on my desk telling me that you're no good.'

Charlie's hand shot up to cover her mouth.

Joe's emotions were fading, and a sense of deep regret was already filling the void that the anger had vacated.

'I'm sorry, Charlie.' He stared at her back as she was already escaping his wrath. 'It's been a long day with so much going on,' he said, his excuses losing volume with every word until he found he was only mouthing an apology.

Chapter Sixteen

Despite feeling the weight of the world on his shoulders, Joe pushed himself to complete an extra ten press-ups before his morning stretches.

Frickin' hell.

He remembered Charlie's white face, and his gut churned with a sickening shame.

Frick.

Joe finished his thirty sit-ups, the quickest he'd ever done, and found he was breathing heavily.

Another day, another visitors' group, and another chance for the professor to tell them some personal tidbit about me.

Frick.

He avoided touching his name badge, as if it were toxic, and wished he could hide behind a face mask. He breathed in deeply and pushed the door open.

Rather than Jameson waiting at the front gate, it was her, and Joe realised he couldn't hide from his emotions today. Charlie stared out through the gate and kept her back to him even when he coughed to get her attention.

'Lieutenant... Charlie... I have to apol—'

'Major Wolfe. A group of twelve visitors are approaching,' she informed him in a cold voice, cutting him off and confirming that she hadn't forgiven him for his moment of anger.

Joe turned and saw the new group of visitors in a variety of clothing. Some were in shorts and T-shirts, others were in jeans and T-shirts, and a few were in military-style green shirts and trousers.

'Good morning,' Joe said, adopting a false sense of bonhomie. 'Welcome to Tower 17, where we are doing our bit for the Exodus Project.' He saw their faces turn implacable and quickly realised that the visitors were highly unlikely to have been included in the draw for tickets. He coughed. 'Hopefully, you will see the progress that everyone here has made and see the amazing technology needed to build this tower.'

The group was now turning frosty, and Joe glanced at Charlie, who had softened with sympathy at the massive hole he was digging for himself.

'Visitors, I am Lieutenant Fowler,' she offered brightly.

'Are you English?' a Scottish voice shouted out.

'Aye'—she took on a Scottish accent—'but my grandparents were from Glasgow.'

'Are you a Weegie?' the oldest-looking member of the group asked with a grin.

'No more than you, by the sound of your accent. Aberdonian, is it?'

The group chuckled, and the older man nodded with respect.

'Major Wolfe here doesn't like to think that he's the hero of the riot at the Russian Tower. Do you know he jumped in front of a young woman to stop her from being shot? He took a bullet to his leg and one to his shoulder.'

Joe hung his head. *I'm not a hero. I was only in the right place at the wrong time.*

The group stared at Joe, ensuring he felt even more embarrassed for the attention.

'He doesn't realise that all the staff here admire him for what he did.' Lieutenant Charlie Fowler turned and gave him a wink and a grin.

'Enough of that, thank you, Lieutenant Fowler. You've got me blushing.' He raised his head and looked steadily at the group. 'Any questions?'

'Why did you save a Russian? You're American, aren't you?'

'A human life is a human life regardless of where the person is from,' Joe answered plainly. He was positive that the man who shouted out had a Russian or Eastern European accent.

The man who had asked the question nodded. Joe noticed that he was wearing a plain T-shirt and jeans. No clothing brands were evident.

Someone at the back pushed another forwards a step. The woman who had been pushed raised her head, and Joe saw she had a beautiful face framed with dark, chocolate-coloured hair.

'Excuse me, Major Wolfe. Can we take photographs today?' She held out a battered-looking digital camera.

Joe quickly reviewed in his mind what would be visible on the tour today. *That would mean they can't see the printer.* The printers used for producing Tower 17 were advanced versions of those used on every other site. He couldn't remember if any other space towers were being constructed at the same time as the British tower. *I could ask the site director. She would be the one person most likely to know the answer to that question.*

'Yes, you can take photographs.' Joe nodded and remembered where he'd heard a similar accent to that of the woman speaking. *Korean. I'm sure she has a Korean accent. Oh, my gawd. Chinese spies, Americans with better face masks, a Russian or two, and now a Korean.*

Tower 17 is attracting a global audience. Or are they here for something completely different?

Charlie grabbed his arm. 'Sir, are you sure we haven't got anything that would be sensitive?' she whispered in his ear.

Joe shook his head. 'I won't be showing the spare printer today.' he whispered back. 'Just be on the lookout for anyone straying off route.'

Charlie nodded.

'So, if you would all like to follow me.' Joe began walking towards the base of the nearest leg of the massive tower. 'As you can see, the tower is built so large that you can't get an idea of the shape.'

'What shape is it?' someone shouted out.

'I always find that is hard to describe. The best way I could put it is like two intertwining snakes spiralling towards the heavens.'

'Very poetic,' Charlie whispered.

'I try,' he replied quietly.

The Korean woman and a man stood next to the base of the leg and pointed their cameras straight upwards. Joe frowned as he saw that although the woman's camera appeared to be old and shabby, the man's device had a telephoto lens which was fully extended.

I wonder what distance that lens can discern.

He watched them snap happy and point at every little item that took their interest on the journey around the site. When the professor appeared and began his talk, Joe and Charlie faded to the back of the group, where they could see what every person in the group was doing.

Joe could swear that a few times he'd been photographed by both Koreans and the Russian-sounding man.

***

'Major Wolfe, I'm glad you popped in to see me. I was about to look for you.'

'Oh?'

'How are the visitors? Are they behaving themselves?'

'Yeah, they're okay, I suppose.'

'Are you not completely sure?'

'Well, I'm more concerned as to the range of nationalities.'

'How so?'

'I would have guessed that they would be locals. If not Scottish, then certainly British.'

'And they aren't?'

'There are some Scots, Americans, Koreans, Russians, and probably Chinese too.'

'Hmmm.' The site director steepled her fingers as her hands rested on her desk. 'I think I know why those nationalities.'

Joe raised his eyebrows.

'They're the nationalities of the companies that were involved in bidding for the contract to build the tower.'

'Who was awarded the contract?'

'Your friend's company—Coben Engineering.'

'That answers one question I had.'

'What was that?'

'Why did my friend agree so quickly to send us more ore?'

'You don't think it was due to your friendship?'

Joe's mouth puckered. 'That may have had some bearing on it. But I think more that he didn't want to leave any chance that this tower would collapse.'

The site director nodded.

'But why are they all so interested in this tower?'

'I shall ask them next time I see them.'

'What?'

'The reason I was going to find you today was to say that I'm going to another Space Tower conference. So, you will have to look after the site and the tower all by yourself.'

Joe smiled.

'Well, you and your team, of course.'

'Wait. How many of these conferences have you been on?'

'All of them.'

'How many is that?'

She looked upwards and did some mental calculations. 'About fifteen of them.'

'What? So many? What do you speak about?'

'Oh, this and that. Everybody gives an update on the status of their own tower.'

'What have you told them about ours?'

'I've told them how tall we plan to build ours. Oh, and about you, of course.'

Joe's mouth dropped open. 'What about me?'

'That I managed to get you on board. And then, you came up trumps and increased the quantity of Planet 27 ore that we could use.'

'So, none of that is confidential then?'

'What? No.'

'Tell that to the professor.'

She laughed. 'I know. He thinks the results from every one of his little science experiments are secret.'

Joe frowned. 'I've been shot, stabbed, and beaten up over information about ore... and you're telling me it isn't confidential?'

The site director's eyes widened. 'So, that's what's in the restricted section of your personnel file.'

'I don't know. I didn't realise there was a restricted section of my file. I would prefer that you didn't tell everyone anything about me at your conference.'

The site director stared at him with a stony face. 'If I know any information that would benefit the cooperative alliance for the Exodus Project, then I will say whatever I please, Major Wolfe.'

'I hope that I survive to see the first launch from Tower 17,' Joe said slowly. 'Pardon me, Boss. I have somewhere to go.'

Joe felt the site director's eyes on the back of his head as he left her office. The door closed softly behind him, and he leaned against the wall, rage pulsing through his veins.

'...I know, Kitty, your mummy is working very hard.'

Joe couldn't help but listen in to the one audible half of the conversation.

'But darling, you remember we talked about Daddy leaving and going to heaven.'

Another pause as the site director's daughter replied.

'I can't come home for a while. People in Russia want to hear what I have to say.' The site director must have held the handset away from her mouth as Joe heard her blow her nose. 'Mummy is okay. I know I don't sound fine, but I am. You listen to Maggie while I'm gone, and I'll be back as soon as I can. I love you.'

There was another pause before the handset clicked off.

Joe walked away in a daze. The anger had disappeared, and in its place was sympathy, complete and utter sympathy.

'Hey, Major Wolfe. Come here, will you?' Doctor Wardle was standing in his office's doorway and had spied Joe walking slowly down the corridor.

'What is it, Doc?'

The doctor held out a glass with a finger of whisky in it, offering it to Joe.

There was a moment's hesitation before Joe grabbed it and threw the alcohol down the back of his throat.

'Whoa, steady on, Joe. What seems to be troubling you? Are you still angry with the professor telling the groups something personal about you?'

'How did you hear about that?'

'He told us about your reaction the other day. He was mortified. He hadn't meant anything by it, by the way.'

Joe held out the empty glass and watched the level of the rising alcohol with grim determination.

'What is it? What's wrong?'

'I've just spoken with the site director.'

'What did she have to say?'

'Is she a widow?'

The doctor paused. 'I don't think so.'

'Is she a single mom?'

'What is this all about?'

'I'm curious. I don't know anything about the woman in charge of Tower 17. Do you?'

The doctor nodded. 'She is technically married.'

'What does that mean? Technically?'

'Her husband travelled to Planet 27.'

Joe's jaw dropped.

'He was, what did you call it? Oh, yeah. He was a lifer.'

'Which means...'

'Which means that by the time he arrives, it will be over twenty years from now, and the director and her daughter will probably never see him again.'

'He has gone to heaven,' Joe whispered.

'What? Heaven? Yes, you could call it that.'

'What does he do? What role will he be doing on the voyage?'

'Security specialist.'

The news hit him, and it took a while for words to form once more. 'Why didn't he... why wasn't he in charge of security here?'

'He was selected before the decision had been made to begin constructing this tower.'

'But...'

'He was already travelling to Planet 27 before the site had been chosen.'

Joe slumped in the chair. 'Why didn't he refuse? He has a young child, for chrissake.'

'Did you refuse?'

'No, but I didn't have a kid.'

The doctor nodded and poured another shot of whisky into the near-empty glass before topping up his own. 'Who knows what really goes on behind closed doors? What makes people decide what they do.'

'You think they were having difficulties?' Joe nodded slowly. 'Yeah, that would make sense. But going to Planet 27 and leaving a wife and child behind. That is...'

'Someone's choice. Shall we leave it at that?'

Chapter Seventeen

Joe opened a bleary eye and wondered why he was cold and why there was a blade of grass in front of his eye. Sitting up, it dawned on him that he'd been lying on grass in the lee of one of the buildings on site. The single malt hangover was creeping up the insides of his skull.

What the hell? What happened to me last night?

His left toe shifted, and the tinkling sound of an empty whisky bottle rolling over gravel answered his question.

'Oh, my head,' Dr Wardle whispered. 'I guess I couldn't carry you after all.'

Joe turned to face the doctor, and flashes of drunken moments made him cry out.

'You're not going to be sick now, Major, are you?' the doctor asked with a slight chuckle before groaning himself.

Joe rubbed his eyes, and movement caught his attention.

'What...'

'Shhh!' Joe pointed at a figure at the base of the tower.

They watched as someone wearing a hooded dark jacket crouched over the fittings of the ground rod.

'What the frick.'

'Shhh, you'll scare him or her. We won't find out who it is if you scare them off,' the doctor whispered.

'I don't think I'm up to doing anything anyway.' Joe massaged his temples with one hand. 'Why did we finish the bottle?'

The figure looked around and, for a split second, Joe recognised the young man in the hood.

'It's Nathan.'

'Who?'

'Nathan. You must know Nathan. He works for the professor.'

'Now that you know who it is, you can relax. You'll be able to talk to him at the lab.'

'What can you prescribe me for the pain, Doc? I'm in need of medical assistance.'

'Serves you right, Major. You were the one who couldn't slow down the drinking.'

'Oh, yeah. That was me; that was my fault. Why was I drinking so hard?'

'Something about a conversation with the site director, who, by the way, is off site.'

'One week before an exciting moment in this site's history.'

'And what would that be?'

'We're soon to be receiving delivery of the engineering pod, and then...'

'Don't keep me in suspense, or you won't get my medical opinion on what you should do to alleviate the hangover symptoms.'

Joe nodded as he tracked Nathan's scurry back the way he'd come. 'Shortly after the engineering pod, we'll be receiving delivery of the UK shuttle.'

'Really? You're not joking, are you?'

'Nope. I don't know yet what our shuttle will be called.'

'What about *Bottle of Macallan*?'

Joe snorted. Getting gingerly to his feet, he then held out a hand and helped the doctor up.

'So, what's your prescription, Doc?'

'As much water as you can drink and some multivitamins.'

'What? No aspirin or paracetamol?'

'No, they'll be no use to you. Rehydrate and top up your electrolytes. If possible, return to bed and get some better quality sleep.

***

Joe stood beneath the tower and looked at the ground rod.

Lieutenant Charlie Fowler pointed at the piece of metal that had been snipped by what must have been a large pair of pliers.

'You were right, sir. It looks like industrial sabotage. And by an insider, you say?'

'Yeah, despite my... despite my brief glance, I recognised the culprit. It was Nathan, who works with the professor.'

'Are you one hundred percent certain? We don't want to go down there and throw about wild accusations.'

Joe nodded. 'It was him, all right. It would be best if we got this over and done with. Let's find out what young Nathan has to say for himself.'

'After you, sir. Lead the way.'

Joe walked directly to the entrance to the subterranean labs, wobbling only once.

'Are you okay, sir? You seem to be a bit unsteady on your feet. And now that I come to think of it, you're very pasty this morning.'

'I'm okay, Lieutenant. What does "pasty" mean?'

'Pasty, you know. Pale. You're as white as a sheet.'

'Oh, I'm looking white-faced? Yeah, probably due to the poor sleep I had last night. I may have tweaked a muscle, or how do you say it? Oh, yes. I got out of the wrong side of the bed this morning.'

'Have you taken anything for it? Maybe you should see the doctor.' She saw his smirk and shook her head.

Joe tapped the correct access code onto the panel and breathed out in relief as the door clicked, and Lieutenant Fowler opened the door for him.

'After you, sir.'

'Why thank you, Lieutenant.'

They went straight to Professor Viggenson's office, and Joe slowed them down with a slight wave of a hand. As they neared the office door, they heard talking.

'Are you sure nobody saw you this morning?'

'I did as you told me to, Professor. I went and did it in the morning before anyone had gotten up.'

Joe walked around the corner and stood in the office door with Lieutenant Fowler at his shoulder.

'Professor! Oh, and Nathan. I need to speak to both of you.'

'Good morning, Joe. What seems to be on your mind?' the professor asked.

'I'm here on official business. I'm here to question Nathan.'

'Oh, why?'

'I saw him sabotaging our tower this morning.'

'Nathan, did you sabotage the tower this morning?'

'No, Professor. I haven't sabotaged anything.'

'Don't lie, Nathan,' insisted Joe. 'I saw you with my very own eyes. You cut the connection to the ground spike.'

The professor smiled.

'What seems to be so funny, Professor?'

'I instructed him to cut the fitting.'

'Why? Won't that make it useless during the next storm?'

'It's our little experiment, Major.'

'You do know that next week we have the engineer's pod arriving, and not long after that is the shuttle itself?'

'I shall be monitoring the weather every second until the next storm, Major.'

'And what happens if there isn't a storm between now and then?'

The professor's eyebrows rose. 'I hadn't considered that.'

'Well, best you do.'

***

Joe did his stretches and felt his hamstrings tighter than usual. It was a clear day except for a few small clouds scudding across the sky. Charlie, who was now his go-to for all weather forecasting, had given the day a clean bill of health. The next couple of weeks were looking good as well.

He breathed in deeply and set off at a steady pace. Through the gate, he nodded to the guard; although he didn't recognise her, he continued on his run, not wanting to stop for anything or anyone. He stared down the lane and wondered how they planned to deliver the shuttle. He shook his head of random thoughts and swung right along the fence line.

With the recent run of dry days, the bare earth was hard underfoot and was Joe's preferred surface. As he approached the edge of the campsite, he had to slow down to slalom between the tents.

'Morning, Major,' someone called out.

Joe raised a hand in acknowledgement and carried on.

'See you later, Major Joe,' shouted another.

Joe grinned despite himself. *I've been called worse. But it's good to feel recognised. These visitors could easily have felt resentment towards the site of the seventeenth tower being built in their back yard.*

After a dense patch of battered-looking tents and homemade bivouacs, Joe stretched out his legs, only to slow down once more as he negotiated a huddle of sharp-edged, camouflage-coloured tents. These were distinct from the others, both in terms of superior quality of the frame and the fabric, and they were set apart from the rag-tag and shambolic positioning of the main glut of tents.

Someone clambered out of their tent to stand and stare with their mouth wide open.

I wonder...

Joe paused mid-stride and snapped off a salute. The person automatically saluted in response.

I thought so—a member of the military. Judging by the cheekbones and the pale skin, I would say ex-GRU Russian Main Intelligence Directorate or even Spetsnaz.

Joe nodded and gave the Russian agent a smile before continuing on his route. He glimpsed the confusion on the man's face before a turn changed his view to shrubs. There were more tents dotted about, and he took care to avoid all personal possessions and the evil spikes of the gorgeous-smelling gorse bushes.

Onwards he went, and when he reached the solar farm, he was pleased to see that all of the structures and lines were enclosed within the new fence line.

The site director was true to her word.

Whilst the shrubbery petered out, the rise caused a stitch to slice through his gut.

Damn alcohol. That doctor is leading me astray.

Joe knew deep down that it was his responsibility for his repeated drops out of sobriety, but it was so much easier to blame the doctor. The clifftop came quicker than expected, and Joe tapped his finger on the face of his watch to cease recording his pace. He carefully took a few paces to the edge of the cliff and sat down with his legs dangling over the abyss. The stitch faded dramatically.

Sunshine caressed the back of his neck, and he reminded himself to put sunscreen on before the next run. For today, aftersun lotion would have to suffice. With the landscape gloriously spread out in front of him, he looked east to see the pall of gunk hanging over the city of Dundee. With more heavy industry than its sister city of Perth, Dundee was suffering now due to its past success.

Joe glanced over at Perth and saw a shadow of a poisonous cloud in comparison. Its history seemed to be more illustrious, and up until the realisation of Earth's frailty and subsequent creation of Project Exodus, the Stone of Destiny had been housed in a Museum in Perth.

The destiny of Earth seems to have shortened, and its population is splintering as numerous launches from around the globe occur each month, taking batches of the rich and powerful to other worlds.

'Major?' A pair of Koreans were holding their cameras up and nodding at him. 'Pictures, Major?'

Joe shrugged and then turned on the charm. He straightened his back, pulled his shoulders back to pronounce his pecs that multiple daily press-ups were defining, and smiled into the camera lenses.

'*Gam-sa-ham-ni-da*,' they both said, nodding numerous times.

'Thank you,' Joe repeated in English. 'What are you doing in Scotland?' he asked conversationally.

One of the Koreans looked at him quizzically whilst the other frowned momentarily and then considered what to say and how to say it in English.

'We are enjoying the holiday,' came the stilted response.

'From the army?' Joe pressed.

The English-speaking Korean stared at Joe and slowly shook his head. 'Thank you, Major,' he replied whilst pulling his colleague back away from the cliff edge and towards the path which led around the site.

Joe stared after them long after they'd disappeared from view. Although he wasn't one for feeling stressed and under pressure too often, he did feel the need to ensure the run-up to the arrival of the shuttle went smoothly. To date, nothing seemed to be in line with the Launch Prep Plan and Shuttle Arrival Plan.

With eased muscles cooling too much, Joe scrambled to his feet and stretched his hamstrings before walking quickly away from the cliff. He jogged over to the northern gate of the site and stood for far too long beneath the security camera.

Eventually, and just as Joe was feeling his neck muscles cramp from staring upwards, the door latch clicked. He pressed it, and the door swung in a big arc, allowing anyone interested at the north side of the site free access to Tower 17.

***

'So, you're saying that we have spies from all over the world watching us?'

'Spies from all the multinational companies which have stakes in different towers.'

'Americans, Russians, Chinese, Koreans?'

'Yes, yes, yes, and yes. I think they're all from military backgrounds as well. The question I haven't been able to answer is why us?'

'What do you mean?'

'What makes Tower 17 so special? Why are they all so interested in our site?'

'What makes you think that they weren't interested in the building of every other site?'

Joe's eyebrows rose and he nodded slowly. 'You're right. I don't. This is the first tower I've ever been around during its building stage.'

'Does that make it feel any better?'

Joe looked at Lieutenant Fowler, sitting opposite him in his office with her arms crossed.

'Sort of. If there is a logical reason for them all being here, rather than they're out to get me or destroy the tower, then, yeah—it feels better. He paused. 'I'm sorry for the other day.'

Charlie Fowler's mouth tightened into a slit.

'Everything had been building up, and Edison showing up like he did and saying what he said. I should have trusted you.' Joe scratched his head. 'I mean, I do trust you.'

She looked at him.

'I'm sure he said what he said just to... feel better about himself. He felt wrong deep down, so he just threw that at you. Maybe he was trying to get back at you for not trusting him.'

Charlie sat there and nodded. 'Thanks.' She got up, nodded once more, and left Joe alone in the office with his thoughts.

Chapter Eighteen

The first of the two flat-bed trucks roared in the distance as the driver down-shifted the gears to get extra torque to power up the incline.

The professor was standing next to Joe, and they both stared down the lane from the front gate.

'Where is Nathan?' Joe asked as a way of passing the time.

'He's doing more tests.'

'Well, we didn't get the storm you wanted.'

'Not yet. There is one expected tonight.'

'If either of the engineering pods are attached to the tower today, I expect you to sort the ground spike.'

The professor gritted his teeth. 'Yes. If they do, I will.'

The truck trundled between the gates with its tarpaulin-covered cargo, narrowly missing the fence at both sides.

Joe eyed the multitude of ropes securing the covering over what he knew to be half of the engineering pod. 'And what is the pod used for when the tower has been completed?'

'To transport the passengers up to the ship.'

Joe nodded. 'I'm glad I called off the visitors' site tours for the foreseeable. They don't need to see this and would only get in the way.'

He thought about his conversation with the site director, who had realigned his priorities for the site.

The future of the human species relies on Project Exodus, and Project Exodus relies on communication between all interested parties involved in the space tower. Joe shook his head. *The question of why many parties are interested in Tower 17 is the one I would like an answer to.*

Professor Viggenson had already turned away and was walking in the general direction that the first truck had gone. It was only after the third truck of the convoy had passed him that Joe went searching for the professor.

***

Although it was the duty of the security team under his command to ensure the security of both the site and Tower 17, Joe and his team couldn't help but stare at the group of international misfit specialist engineers crawling over and around the engineering pod. He glanced to his left and saw his deputy the lieutenant, and when he glanced to his right, he saw Sergeant Jameson and Corporal Swift a couple of metres further back.

Joe had agreed instantly to any member of staff who was off shift and who wanted to watch the two engineering pods being assembled. The event would be only third in the list of pivotal events at the site. The second would be the arrival of the shuttle, and the first would, of course, be the maiden launch.

It was amusing how there was a disparate selection of spies on the other side of the fence. Yet the engineers putting together the pods were from the same nationalities, all trying to understand the project leader's Mandarin. The leader was coping with varying language barriers, aided by a digital tablet and glowing blueprints displayed on the screen.

As the engineering pod began to take shape, clouds in the heavens above came to take a look.

'Let's hope Lieutenant Fowler is right with her estimate of the timing,' Joe said, nodding at the distant skyline.

Jameson glanced at Joe and then returned his attention to the pod. They were all startled as, one by one, the engineers shouted out in their language that their tasks had been completed. The Chinese project manager put a small, brass-coloured object to his lips and blew a shrill whistle, deafening all nearby.

A klaxon rang out, and a moment later, a chain was wound up and tightened in a straight line between the enormous legs of the tower. All security staff and engineers watched as the engineering pod was winched infinitesimally on its inexorable journey towards the base of the tower.

To Joe and probably others, it felt like hours by the time the pod reached the tower. He could only stare with his mouth hanging open as it clicked into place. The chain dropped away, and electric motors dragged it up the outside of the tower's leg.

Someone tugged his arm. 'Sir, we better get everyone inside.'

Joe saw Jameson's face showing a hint of fear. 'Good idea.' He turned and stretched an arm up into the sky, pointing at the ominous clouds crowding in on them. 'Everyone,' he shouted. 'Get undercover now!'

The engineers, despite the warning being in a different language to their own, understood the urgency and fled.

Joe turned and saw that only his security team remained.

'Come on then. Everyone in, now.' Joe waved his arms, cajoling them towards the nearest building. Darkness crept over the site as the poisonous rain clouds blotted out the sunlight.

Joe was the last to burst into a run and caught up with Jameson and then Swift, who gave him an odd look. It was only when he reached the sanctuary inside the head office block that he looked back and shuddered. The professor was sprinting to the ground spike that they'd all forgotten about in the excitement of completing the engineering pods.

The scientist slipped and went sprawling onto the ground on all fours.

Joe pushed Corporal Swift's back, shoving him through the doorway to safety. He then turned and sprinted over to the professor's side. He plucked the man out of the mud and together, they went to repair the ground spike.

As Joe looked up at the poisonous cloud cover, a droplet of rain landed on his cheek.

'Shit!' He dropped his head and watched the professor connect the metals and bring out a miniature electric welding tool.

'I'm almost done, Major.'

Joe felt the large raindrops on his scalp. 'Shit.'

'Nearly...' The professor coughed and spluttered.

'No need to say anything,' Joe managed to say before a cough tried to clear the glutinous phlegm that was now coating the back of his throat. He wiped at his streaming eyes. 'Shit. Move, Professor.'

'Done!' The professor was overcome with a coughing fit and fell over.

Not now, professor. Joe pulled the professor onto his feet and put his shoulder under the older man's arm. He felt the poisonous air coat the back of his throat just as the weight of the professor was taken from him.

Corporal Swift stared at the major through the toughened glass of his face mask. Pain shot through Joe's nervous system, and his eyes were streaming. He reached a hand out, and a fist punched his temple. Joe snatched at part of Corporal Swift's safety suit. Another punch to Joe's head brought the darkness of unconsciousness, and the last thing he realised was that he was grasping a handful of safety suit material which had come away in the struggles.

Crap quality material.

Joe's world went black as he passed out.

***

Joe looked up after vomiting into a bucket at the bedside and rubbed his eyes raw, trying to clear his vision.

'When can I go, Doctor?' a young male voice asked.

'When I say you can, Corporal Swift,' the doctor told him.

'Doc...' Joe managed to say through gallons of phlegm at the back of his throat.

'Major Wolfe, did you say something?'

Joe pointed at his eyes, then his throat, and finally his head.

'I shall get the nurse to tend to you.'

Joe grabbed the doctor's hand and stuffed the scrap of fabric that he still had in his clenched fist.

Dr Wardle looked at what was in the palm of his hand, then glanced over at Corporal Swift's safety suit hanging on the back of a nearby chair.

'I will inform Lieutenant Fowler of your status,' the doctor said without any change to the level of his voice.

Joe slumped back onto the bed and groaned.

'I know, Major. But the toxins you have ingested will soon be flushed away.' The doctor checked the drip line before nodding once and leaving the medical bay.

Within moments, the female guard Joe had recognised from last seeing guarding the front gate stepped into the room with a rifle held vertically. She was followed immediately by Sergeant Jameson.

'Corporal Swift, you are under guard now.'

'What, Sarge? What have I done?'

'Corporal Swift, you are suspected of causing Major Wolfe actual bodily harm.'

'What? What proof do you have?'

Sergeant Jameson opened his hand to show the piece of material. 'I think if we were to check your safety suit, we would find a hole in it about this size.'

Corporal George Swift glanced across at Major Joe Howling Wolfe, and Joe recoiled at the utter hatred in the young man's eyes.

'Why, Corporal?'

The young man looked away.

Joe sat up and felt his stomach heave. Luckily, he'd emptied the contents in the previous spasm of gut muscles, and all he tasted was sour, acidic bile.

'George? What did I do to you?'

George Swift turned. 'Nothing to me. You did it to my father.'

Joe raised his eyebrows. 'Swift?' he muttered. 'I cannot remember anyone else by the name of Swift.'

'You tracked down my father in South America, and he was lucky to survive the beating that you gave him.'

'What? Who?'

'My father is Benjamin Dawson. Do you deny tracking him down?'

Joe shook his head, speechless.

'My father is too big a man to seek revenge. But I have done it on his behalf. The rest of the squad was easy to manage. They were old.'

'But I stopped them.'

'Frickin' liar!' George shouted. 'You tracked him down. You almost killed him. If you're telling the truth, why didn't you tell anyone?'

'But... but I saved him. The rest of the squad beat me up to shut me up.'

'You kept quiet? My father almost died, and you didn't say a word?'

'It came out in the court martial.'

'What court martial? Never heard of such a thing.'

'Why do you think he changed his name?'

Joe saw a flicker of doubt creep in.

'Did you not speak to Ben? To your father?'

George stayed silent, staring at Joe.

'How old are you anyway? Where were you born?'

George looked away, and Sergeant Jameson came in with the doctor.

'The doc here says you're fit enough to be in jail. So, come on. Get out of bed. You're coming with me.'

George Swift looked all around the room but didn't move.

Jameson took out a pistol which had been tucked under his belt at the base of his back. 'Now, George. Move. It isn't a request.'

George made one last look around the room, and his eyes settled on Joe.

'Sir, I... I may have made a mistake.'

Jameson grabbed one of George's arms and yanked him out of the medical centre bunk. George stumbled and was about to land on his face when Jameson pulled him up with one arm again.

Joe was speechless as Corporal George Swift was hauled out of the room. After a moment, as everything sank in, he sat up and wobbled, almost toppling over.

'Woah, Major. You're still recovering. What are you trying to do? Kill yourself? You have to give yourself time,' the nurse said, having just entered the ward.

'I need to explain to George. I need to understand how he's my friend's son?'

'Not right now, you don't. You have to rest. The toxin flush we gave you will take a couple days to reset your system.'

Joe slumped back down and felt marginally better for it.

***

Joe opened his eyes and groaned. The pounding of his skull prevented any train of thought.

'You're awake at last,' Dr Wardle said.

'Hey, Doc. Good to see you. Please don't say you brought some whisky.'

The doctor laughed. 'No, I brought something better. But it's a secret. You can't tell anyone, not even the nurse.'

Joe nodded. 'My lips are sealed.'

The doctor moved to stand next to a table on the other side of Joe's bed. He took a small canvas bag out of his pocket and tipped some powder into the glass of water that was on the table.

'What are you doing, Doc?'

The doctor lifted the glass and moved it in a circular motion to swirl the contents. He briefly held it up to the light and nodded. 'That will do.' He held it out to Joe. 'Here, drink this.'

'What is it?' Joe asked, rubbing the bridge of his nose in an attempt to massage the headache away.

'Just drink it, Joe,' the doctor said, putting the glass to Joe's mouth.

Joe closed his eyes and gulped the liquid.

'Yuck. That was full of sand or something.'

'Or something.' The doctor smiled. 'Remember, don't tell anyone.'

'Will it make me feel better?' Joe rested back down on his bed and closed his eyes. 'Cos I could do with getting better fast. I need to speak to Corporal Swift.'

'Give yourself time, Joe,' the doctor said, already moving to the door. He turned before leaving. 'I shall see you tomorrow.'

'Yeah, yeah. Let me sleep, Doc.'

Chapter Nineteen

'Major Wolfe, what are you doing out of bed?' the nurse said in alarm after walking into the room.

'I feel fine.' Joe winked at her.

The nurse frowned. 'There is no need to pretend to be fully fit and well, Major.'

'But I'm okay.'

'You may say that, but I have to check your vitals. Now, sit down on the bed.'

Joe sat down in his flimsy hospital gown and arranged it to cover his modesty fully. The nurse pointed a pencil light into each of his eyes before tapping a tablet. She lifted his arm and held his wrist whilst looking at her watch. She shook her head and tapped at the tablet.

'Well?' Joe asked in good humour.

'Well, you seem to have recovered in record time. But you can't leave until we test your blood and the doctor discharges you.'

Joe rolled his eyes and climbed back into bed. 'I'm telling you, I feel fine. Better than fine.'

'Yeah, well, that may be. But rules are rules.'

Both Joe and the nurse turned as a groan emanated from the far end of the ward.

'Professor, I will be with you in a moment,' the nurse called.

Joe saw her tap some last details about his miraculous recovery before she walked away from the computer to see the professor. He stared out the window, saw the dark clouds, and shivered.

What would have happened to me if I'd been any longer outside in that?

As soon as the nurse left the room, Joe got out of bed and wandered down to the far end of the ward.

'Professor, how are you doing?'

The professor opened one bloodshot eye and cleared his throat with a cough that overflowed with mucus.

'I see.'

'Thank you, Major,' the professor rasped.

'What for?'

'For saving my life.'

'I think someone else would have come to your rescue if I hadn't.'

'But you did.' The professor cleared his throat in a loud, hacking cough. 'And at your own risk.'

'I couldn't have you missing the arrival of the first shuttle.'

'Was there any lightning?'

Joe dropped his head. 'No, no lightning yet.'

They both looked out the large window on the wall opposite the professor's bed. It was the only window with a view of one of the tower's legs.

'I'm sorry,' Joe said.

The room lit up as a bolt of lightning erupted outside. A rumble of thunder was short-lived, as the sound of the lightning ripping through the sky blocked out all other noise.

'It seemed that you were right,' the professor admitted.

The rumbling thunder returned, cancelling out any possibility of Joe's immediate response. The two men watched as the lightning bolt faded.

'Is it my imagination, or is there a gap in the clouds where the lightning went?'

The professor propped himself up on his elbows and groaned again.

'Don't worry, Professor. Rest back down.'

The professor stared out his bleary eyes for a moment longer and then sank back onto the mattress.

'I didn't see anything. But...' He professor paused as another wracking cough rippled through his upper torso. 'My eyes aren't as young as yours. Physically, at least.'

Joe nodded and stared once more out of the window. The clouds had returned to their normal blushing brown hue.

An alarm sounded out. Startled, Joe stepped away from the professor's bed.

The nurse was first in the room and knocked Joe out of the way.

'What's happening?'

'Professor, stay with us,' the nurse said, wiping phlegm from the old man's mouth and putting two fingers to his carotid artery.

The doctor rushed in, red-faced and out of breath. 'Status?'

'Patient was experiencing dyspnoea and now apnoea.' The nurse glanced at Joe. 'Major, back to your bed, please. Give us room.'

Ignoring Joe, Dr Wardle went straight to the bedside. He pulled out a hypodermic needle, tapped the IV tube, and stabbed it. The nurse placed a breathing device over the man's face.

'Doc, what about the magic dust?' Joe shouted.

The doctor shook his head. 'He's unable to ingest it.'

'But... You have to try. Do something, dammit!' Joe's voice grew more and more strident with every word.

'Major Wolfe, get back to your bed now!' the doctor ordered.

A high-pitched alarm rang out.

'Nurse, turn that off, please.' The doctor placed a device on the professor's chest, which began compressions.

With the alarms turned off, the room was eerily quiet, and only the exertions of the device were evidence of any activity. Time stretched, and Joe saw the doctor's white cheeks framing tear-filled eyes. The nurse's head was bent low, and Joe felt the chill spread through the room as the Grim Reaper made his call.

'Doctor? Has he gone?' Joe whispered, still standing a few paces away.

Ignoring Joe, the doctor said in a low voice, 'Nurse, make a note of the time for the records.'

The nurse raised her tablet and tapped out the word 'Deceased.'

***

Jameson knocked on the office door and gently pushed it open.

'Sir, I have something I need to discuss with you.'

Joe was staring out of the window into the distance. He was neither focused nor aware that someone had said anything to him.

'Sir?' Jameson took a step into the office. 'Major?'

Joe turned at last with a deathly pallor and red-rimmed eyes with no spark.

'Sorry, did you say something, Sergeant?'

'I have something I need to discuss with you.'

Joe stared at Jameson.

'It's about the lieutenant.'

A frown appeared on Joe's face.

'She has been up to no good.'

Joe's frown turned into a scowl. 'This isn't the time to air your personal grudges,' he hissed before turning back to face the window.

'But sir. It isn't a grudge.'

'Not the time.'

Joe didn't see Jameson's shoulders slump before the sergeant retreated out into the corridor without another word.

'I have to make decisions about a man's funeral. A man whose life I thought I'd saved,' Joe said softly. 'What about Nathan? I have to speak to Nathan.' He stood up.

The journey to the outside of the underground laboratories was made automatically. Only when he was standing outside and staring at the security door did Joe come back around and tap the correct access code into the panel.

But this time, the red light flicked on for a second and backed off.

Joe frowned and typed the code more slowly and accurately, ensuring there were no errors or mistyping of any numbers.

The red light flickered on and off.

His eyebrows rose. He jabbed at the call button and heard the microphone click on.

'Nathan. It's me. It's Major Wolfe. Joe. Let me in, will ya?'

He waited for an eternity of thirty seconds before firmly pressing the call button once more.

'Nathan, please. I need to speak to you about... about funeral arrangements. I need to speak to you, please.' The sentence was filled with raw emotion.

The security door stared down at him, silent and unmoving.

One last yearning look into the security camera, then a disconsolate shake of his head.

Joe stared into the clear morning sky and pulled a face. *What are you playing at, universe? Now you decide to be nice weather?*

On his return he pushed open the door to the security building and went in, out of the frigid air.

'Ah, Lieutenant, you're just the person I need to see.'

Lieutenant Fowler was standing in the corridor outside her office. 'Oh?'

'I went to speak to Nathan in the labs, and I couldn't get in. Has the code changed?'

Fowler's eyebrows shot up. 'Not that I'm aware of, sir.'

'Yeah, and he didn't respond to the call button either. Where is his accommodation? Do you know?'

'Have you checked the computer database? I guess not. Come in, sir. We can check on my computer.'

In Lieutenant Charlie Fowler's spartan office, she quickly brought up the computer screen and selected Nathan's personnel file.

'It seems that he has accommodation in the bunker,' she said, looking up at him.

'Is there a security code that overrides all other codes?'

'Computer, what is the current access code for the subterranean laboratory?'

'Security code for the laboratory is classified.'

'Computer, who has access to the classified security code for the laboratory?'

'Head of R&D, assistant to head of R&D, and head of site security.'

Joe stepped forward. 'Computer, this is Major Wolfe. Confirm what is the current access code for the subterranean laboratory.'

'Major Joe Wolfe's voice recognised. Security access code is one-seven-five-two.'

'Computer. Do not allow anyone but the head of site security to change the access code until I say otherwise.'

'Code access restriction confirmed.'

'Computer, turn off,' Fowler instructed. 'Shall we go and see what he is up to, sir?'

Joe nodded.

***

Standing outside the security door to the laboratory once more, Joe breathed in deeply and tapped in 1-7-5-2. The green light flickered on and off again, and the latch to the door clicked open.

'After you,' Joe said, waving his arm open wide.

Fowler nodded and stepped in first.

'I forgot to ask you... when is the next wave of poisonous clouds expected?'

'Next Tuesday, sir. I keep checking twice a day, every day now, sir.'

'Oh?'

'Yes. I thought you would want to keep track, especially with the funeral and then the arrival of the shuttle.'

Dammit. The funeral is planned for Tuesday.

'How long are the clouds expected on Tuesday?'

'That cloud formation is expected to drift slowly across the county all week.'

Joe frowned. 'We'll need to have the funeral all safety-suited up.'

Fowler nodded without saying a word.

They heard footsteps in the corridor ahead. Fowler looked at Joe, who nodded. The pair of them burst into a run down the corridor, only to see the back of Nathan entering a room. They heard the loud click of a lock being made secure.

Joe stood in front of another security access panel and pressed 1-7-5-2 again. He breathed out audibly as the security mechanism unlocked with a click.

'Nathan, it's Major Wolfe and Lieutenant Fowler. Joe and Charlie. We're here to talk with you,' Joe said loudly in a calm voice.

'Nathan, why don't you come out and speak to us?' Fowler asked.

'You killed the professor!' shouted Nathan.

'What? No, I saved him,' Joe shouted and immediately felt déjà vu with the conversation he'd so recently had with George Swift.

'Liar. You ordered him to see to the spike when there was no risk of lightning.'

'But there was.'

'What happened then? When was the lightning?'

Joe thought back and remembered who had given him the timings for the storm and the poisonous clouds. It had been confirmed confidently and with no hesitancy by none other than Lieutenant Charlie Fowler.

'I saved him. I pulled him in out of the rain.'

'Yes, the major risked his own life,' Fowler shouted.

'Don't talk to me about risking lives. He was only out there because you told him to be.'

'I'm very sorry. I did all I could to save him. The doctor and the nurse did everything they could to save him. I think he was too old.'

'He wasn't too old,' Nathan shouted angrily, his voice breaking with emotion. 'You killed him. I saw it all.'

Joe's eyebrows furrowed. 'What did you see?'

No answer.

'Maybe we should allow him to grieve?' Fowler said softly.

'Nathan. The funeral is scheduled for Tuesday, and we're expecting inclement weather. Make sure if you attend that you're in a safe suit and mask.' Joe cocked his head, hoping for an answer.

Fowler shook her head and gently pushed Joe back towards the door.

***

Joe tightened the straps of his mask, and the excess air sighed out of the sides. His legs swished as he walked out of his office in a complete safety suit. There was no point in risking his health by not wearing the full garb, and as he looked down, he saw the vague outline of his feet distorted by the opaque blue plastic. The black rubber gloves completed his personal security, and as he joined a throng of staff exiting the building, he realised he couldn't make out anyone in the androgynous attire.

Ground out past the solar farm was the only land suitable for a funeral, and when they walked along the inside of the site's fence line, they passed the tented encampment. Many of the camping visitors who had remained after the last storm peeked cautiously out of their tents and paid silent respect to the funeral procession.

The coffin was on the shoulders of volunteers from the security department. Many had only joined the weekend before, as Joe had had the foresight to increase his team's numbers with the imminent arrival of the shuttle. With luck, the first launch wouldn't be too far in the future. The only person he knew among the pallbearers was Sergeant Jameson, and Joe was pleased that no further mention was made of his gripe or issues with Lieutenant Fowler.

When the procession arrived at the burial ground, the pallbearers carefully laid the casket into the grave, a task made more challenging as each pallbearer was in a full hazmat suit and mask. The site staff formed a semi-circle, and the site director stood at the head of the group, alone and with head bowed. She only raised her head when everybody quietened down.

'We are gathered here to pay respects to the professor. He was a man of science through and through and died after sacrificing his own health to make the tower safe.'

Nobody saw the face Joe pulled. Although the guilt of demanding the professor reconnect the lightning spike kept returning to the outer limits of his consciousness, Joe knew that he wasn't really to blame. He looked at the sky and shuddered. The clouds looked more ominous, poisonous, and threatening than ever before.

The site director's voice floated on, but Joe didn't pay much attention until she uttered her last few words.

'...take a moment now to contemplate life and death in these times as we all work as a team to do our bit for Project Exodus.'

She bowed her head and, like a wavelet, the crowd rippled with head after head, bowing low in silent prayers. A lone piper played what Joe now knew to be 'Flowers of the Forest' in the distance via a contraption that kept him safe from breathing in poisonous air and allowed the sounds to emanate with no restrictions.

The crowd splintered away from the graveside, and Joe thought he may have seen the young face of Nathan behind a face mask. Watching everyone leave and wander at a gentle pace back towards the site's buildings, Joe was one of the last to move away from the open grave. Two members of the maintenance and engineering crew began shovelling dirt on top of the casket.

A movement amongst the crowd caught his eye, and Joe set off towards the main grounds. A slim figure in a full hazmat suit was staggering back.

One too many whiskies. Joe smiled to himself.

***

Jameson stood at the office door with an ashen face.

'What is it now, Jameson? You pick your moments, don't you.'

'It's about Nathan, sir.'

Joe looked up from his desk. 'What about Nathan?'

'He's dead.'

'What?'

'He was stabbed in the back. Probably at the service and died on his walk back.'

Joe's mouth dropped open. 'He was murdered on the day of the professor's funeral.'

Jameson nodded.

'Did anyone see what happened?'

'A few people saw Nathan staggering, but they thought he may have been drinking.'

Joe was speechless.

'What do you want me to do, sir?'

'I don't know,' Joe said in a whisper.

Chapter Twenty

'Murdered, you say?' the site director asked.

Joe nodded.

'How?'

'Somebody stabbed him on the walk back from the funeral.'

The site director stared out of her office window into the distance. 'You see that, Major?' She pointed outside.

Joe noticed she was wearing a diamond-encrusted wedding ring. Her fingernail was clear gloss varnished.

'What?'

'Tower 17.'

'Yes.'

'We're so close to achieving building the tallest space tower in history. Safer than the second Tower 1, and faster than they built Tower 7.'

Joe kept quiet.

'Tomorrow, the shuttle arrives. That means you need to maintain security for the next month. In a month, we'll have our first, hopefully of many, launches. So, Major, I don't want to hear of any alleged murders, deaths, or injuries. Do you understand?'

'But he was murdered.'

'So you say. However, I have the international press phoning me every day, and I have representatives from every nation watching my every move. I don't have time for your allegations, conspiracy theories, or downright lies.' The site director nodded towards her office door with a stony face.

***

'Sir, I think you should see something.'

Joe raised his head, which had been resting on his steepled hands.

'Do you think you know who murdered Nathan?'

'Just watch some security footage. May I use your computer?'

Joe nodded.

'Computer, this is Sergeant Jameson.'

'Sergeant Jameson's voice recognised.'

'Computer, bring up security footage from last week's medical ward, which I instructed had to be saved beyond the default retention period of a week.'

The holograph flickered to display the professor having a drip being set up.

'Computer, fast forward sixty times normal speed.'

The screen showed the doctor checking on the patient and then leaving, followed by the nurse completing hourly checks.

'Computer, fast forward to the night before the professor died.'

Figures moved on screen so quickly that their figures were ghostly blurs. Lighting transitioned from bright daylight to dim evening lighting and back to daylight.

'Computer, stop. Play from this point at normal speed.'

The lighting indicated it was late evening. The nurse had walked past the camera, unaware of being filmed.

'I'm trying to think of what stage I was at that point,' Joe said, scratching the side of his face. 'I'm guessing I was out for the count after being given... medicine from the doctor.'

Lieutenant Charlie Fowler walked into the ward, glanced once in the direction of where Joe's bed would have been, and then stepped carefully over to the professor's bedside.

Joe's eyes narrowed. 'Does this recording have audio?'

'Computer, increase the volume of audio.'

A faint buzz was heard, and Joe looked at Jameson with his eyes raised.

'It's probably interference from all the other devices in the room.'

Lieutenant Fowler bent down at Professor Viggenson's bedside and said something into the man's ear. Nothing but buzzing could be heard. The professor didn't move and appeared not to respond to what she'd said.

'Not much there,' Joe said matter-of-factly.

'Just wait.'

The lieutenant stood up and waited for the professor to awaken. She moved back to his side, grabbed the man's shoulders, and shook him vigorously. The man remained unconscious, not even showing a flickering of an eyelid. Fowler let go of him and, as he dropped back onto the mattress, a red blinking light could be seen on the IV line controller.

'The drip line must have been pulled out.'

Jameson nodded.

Fowler backed away from the bed, having seen the red warning light, turned, and fled.

'Does that warning light set off any alarm?'

Jameson shook his head.

'So, I need to speak to the doctor to confirm what effect that would have had on the professor.' Joe stood up. 'I'm sorry for doubting you,' he said, looking directly into Jameson's eyes.

'Wait, there's more.'

Joe raised his eyebrows and sat down again.

'Computer, fast forward half an hour.'

The background buzzing accelerated into a faint hum of a large swarm of insects and then, thankfully, reverted to a steady buzz when the footage returned to normal speed.

A figure in a full hazmat suit and mask walked past the camera and straight to the professor's bed. Whoever it was must have seen the warning light and gone to the IV line. The person pulled off their gloves to reveal two perfectly manicured hands. The hands had no distinguishing marks, nor were rings on any of the fingers, and the fingernails were an unpolished plain colour. But even at such a distance, on screen, they were noticeably a woman's hands.

The woman pulled out a hypodermic needle from a pocket, stretched up, and injected something into the top of the drip bag. She carefully tucked the spent needle back into the pocket, retrieved the end of the drip line, and reconnected it. Instantly, the red light stopped flashing. The woman carefully put her gloves back on, took one step away from the bedside, and left the ward, all without her face appearing in the full shot and being recognised on camera.

'Was it her? Was that Fowler, and what was that she injected into his drip?'

Jameson shrugged.

The nurse appeared in the shot doing her hourly checks, which included tapping the IV bag.

'Computer, stop the video. Go back five seconds.'

The nurse's left hand was in view. She had candy-pink-coloured nail polish on her fingernails.

'That rules her out,' Jameson said. 'Are you going to inform the site director?'

'Not until we have more evidence.' Joe stood up. 'Thanks.'

'What for?'

'For showing me this. I just assumed... you know.'

'Yeah, I know.' Jameson coughed. 'What are you going to do now?'

'I need to speak to the doc.'

'What about the lieutenant?'

'I'll think about what to do after speaking with the doc. Don't worry. I'll look into it. Just let me do things one step at a time.'

Jameson slowly nodded.

'And Sarge, leave her to me, will you? Promise me.'

'Yes, sir.'

***

'What? You're telling me that the professor was murdered, and Nathan was too?'

'We have footage of a person injecting something into the IV drip bag the night before the professor died.'

'What was it?'

'You tell me?'

The doctor rubbed a hand over his face. 'The drip bag and line will have been destroyed. It was six days ago.'

Joe nodded. 'Did you do an autopsy?'

The doctor hung his head. 'No. I assumed he'd died from complications arising from toxaemia.' He looked up at Joe. 'Sickness brought on from sustained inhalation of poisoned air.'

'So, no evidence remains.'

'Unless, of course, you want me to conduct an exhumation?'

Joe paused before replying. 'What do you need to dig up the casket at night?'

'A written order from the site director or the minister for transport and Project Exodus. Once I get that, I would need four floodlights and two fit men to volunteer to do the digging.'

'I'll have to think about it.'

'You're not on speaking terms with her at the moment then?'

'You could say that her focus is on the bigger picture.'

'What is bigger than murder?'

'Oh, only the attention of the world's press and the fulfilment of Project Exodus to save mankind.'

***

'Computer, bring up the personnel file on Lieutenant Fowler.'

Joe scanned the file line by line but couldn't find any indication that she was a saboteur or spy.

'Computer, change the security code of the subterranean laboratory.' He paused. 'To one-nine-one-eight.'

'Security code changed.'

Joe reached for the walkie-talkie but then realised he wouldn't trust any information from Lieutenant Fowler anymore—even if she were only providing details such as future weather patterns.

Where did she get the information from?

'Computer off.'

The screen went blank, and Joe moved into the corridor. *That looks like where she got the news from.* He smiled, seeing the **Meteorological Office** sign hanging just past the site director's office.

He tapped on the frame of the open door.

A young man looked up from what appeared to be a selection of miniature plastic building blocks in various colours.

'Major Wolfe, how can I help you?' The man pushed his spectacles up the bridge of his nose.

His eyes were magnified to such an extent that he appeared wide-eyed and naive as a child did upon recognising colours for the very first time.

'What is your name?' Joe asked.

'Sam Howe.'

'What do your initials stand for?' Joe asked, pointing at Sam's name badge.

Sam looked down as if in doubt that it was there. 'Oh, yeah. Samuel Charity Jonathon Howe.'

'Charity?'

Sam nodded. 'I know. My parents had wanted a girl for so long, and along I came to disappoint them.'

'What are you building?'

'My Lego? Sorry, sir. I didn't expect anyone. Well, maybe only the lieutenant.' Sam pulled out a drawer from his desk, put an arm around the Lego, and was about to shove it all into the drawer.

'Don't.'

Sam looked up.

'There is no need to hide it just because I'm here.'

'I'm building a structure called a death star. It's from a series of films... sorry, movies called *Star Wars*.'

'Never heard of it. Anyway, I would like to know what the weather is expected to be like today and in the near future.'

Sam nodded. 'Computer, bring up the meteorological map of Scotland.' He pointed at lines of various colours and told Joe about cold fronts, warm fronts, cumulonimbus and cirrus clouds, all of which went over the major's head.

Joe couldn't stop himself from yawning. 'Sorry, Sam. I haven't had much sleep recently.'

Sam nodded. 'I'm not surprised, sir. What with everything happening recently and the shuttle being delivered tomorrow? In a nutshell, sir, you will probably need your hazmat suit at least for a couple hours every day for the next fortnight.'

'Any idea when those two hours will be each day?'

Sam shook his head. 'I may be good, but I'm not that good, sir.'

Joe laughed. 'Well, I had to ask.'

Sam smiled.

'What about right now?'

'Right now, you would be best wearing protective gear if you're spending any length of time outside.'

Joe pointed at a black circle on the screen. 'What is that, Sam?'

'Computer, run a one hundred percent screen and colour recalibration.'

The hologram disappeared in an instant. A band of yellow light was replaced by green, then blue, purple, and red. The lights faded.

'Screen and colour calibration complete, Samuel,' the voice said in a soft female Scottish voice.

Joe raised his eyebrows.

'Thank you, computer. Show meteorological map of Scotland.'

The hologram appeared once more, and it again had the black hole of light in the centre of the screen.

'Is that...?'

'Perth?'

'It seems to be over the site of Tower 17,' Sam said in a whisper. 'No weather at the centre of the site.'

'How can that be?'

'I dunno, sir. Maybe the tower is casting a shadow.'

'Well, thanks for the weather info.'

'Will you be passing it on to the lieutenant?'

Joe shook his head. 'I shall see you again, Samuel,' he said in a fair imitation of a Scottish accent.

Sam's cheeks coloured up.

Joe went all the way to the end of the building and peered out of the window.

It's not worth risking just to check on the lab today.

'Sir, do you want to see him?'

Joe turned around and saw the woman with corporal's stripes whom he'd seen out and about on her duties.

He smiled. 'Yes, perfect timing.'

She opened the door behind her and waved him in. 'Just knock on the glass of the door when you're finished, and I'll open it up to let you out.'

'Sir, I'm sorry.' Corporal George Swift sat on a bench seat. His hair was unkempt and greasy, and his eyes were shadowed, with red spider webs visible where they'd once been pure white.

'Why did you do it, George?'

'I thought you were responsible for my father being beaten up. I should have known differently.'

'What do you mean?'

'I've seen how you treat people. How you treat the people in the tents outside, and how you treat everyone in the security team.'

Joe inclined his head. 'So, how are you Benjamin Dawson's son? And does he know about you?'

A frown passed across George's face. 'He met my mother at work. She worked in the R&D department of Coben Engineering when he was there.'

'That would have been over twenty-seven years ago.'

George nodded. 'My mother loved Benjamin Dawson and thought he loved her just as much. I was born, and Benjamin Dawson disappeared. She was so upset she signed up to go to Planet 27 on a flight that took off just after I was born.'

'They allowed her on with a newborn?'

George nodded. 'It meant that we had to live through the journey.'

'And you grew up aboard the ship and then...?'

'When I was old enough, I knew I needed to know more about my father. The only way I could see it being easy to do would be as part of the security department. When I was accepted, I could search through the files and find out what I thought was the truth.'

Joe nodded.

'The court martial I was a witness at wouldn't have been on any files on Planet 27. But did you speak to Benjamin Dawson—your father?'

George's voice faltered. 'It was never the right time. There was always some emergency. I must have arrived just as you disappeared. What happened to you?'

'I was stabbed and left in an ore container that took me to Earth. Luckily, I survived.'

'Who stabbed you?'

'Commander Trent.' Joe stared at George. 'I was told you'd killed him and his side-kick Zimmer.'

George nodded. 'I don't know what came over me. I felt that they had something to do with my father.'

Joe shook his head. 'No, there was an old man in the hospital who was responsible for the team who beat up your father.'

'There is no need to worry about that old man anymore.' George looked into the distance.

'Did you...?'

George shook his head. 'Nah, I didn't get the chance. He had a brain embolism. I think that's what the nurse said.'

'What's your mother's name?'

'Was.'

'What?'

'My mother died on the flight.'

'Oh. I'm so sorry.'

'Why? Why are you sorry?'

'My mother died whilst travelling to Planet 27 too.'

The flash of hurt in George's eyes was replaced with sorrow. 'It's been years, and yet it still hurts, doesn't it.'

Joe nodded.

'You should take a couple of weeks R&R.'

'What? Are you not sending me to jail?'

Joe looked steadily into the younger man's eyes. 'Are you going to try to hurt me again or anyone else here?'

George shook his head.

'So, a couple of weeks R&R it is then.'

'Please, I don't want to be on R&R. I don't know what I would do with myself. Plus, with the site getting busier and busier, I could be of use here, couldn't I?'

Joe paused and looked at Corporal George Swift. 'What about dropping to private and being on gate guarding duties for six months?'

As soon as he said it, Joe was shocked to see George actually smile and nod repeatedly. 'Of course, you'll have to report to Sergeant Jameson every week.'

'Yes, sir. Of course, sir.'

'Wait here until someone comes for you. I have to speak to people.'

***

'You what?'

'I've forgiven him.'

'Why?'

'He thought I had something to do with his father being beaten to a pulp.'

'And you didn't?'

'No, I stopped his father being killed.' Joe smiled. 'So Private George Swift will report to you every week and is on gate guard duty for six months.'

'Ouch. And this is you forgiving him?' Jameson grinned. 'Remind me not to get on your wrong side.'

'Can you see to it that he gets a chance to sleep and freshen up for his 0600 duty tomorrow?'

'Yes, sir. You do remember what is happening tomorrow, don't you? The shuttle?'

'He won't be on the gate by himself. So, yeah, it will be okay.' Joe remembered the professor. 'I have something else to do now.'

Chapter Twenty-One

Joe typed in 1-9-1-8, and the catch unlocked with a click. He glanced at the camera above his head and felt the emptiness of the building he was about to enter.

With a contained oxygen and carbon dioxide filtration system running automatically and powered by the solar panel array, the air was always clean, even in the deepest parts of the underground laboratories. The corridor light came on as soon as his first foot touched the floor. Despite the professor being his greatest fan for obtaining the additional ore for the tower, he'd never given Joe a guided tour. Joe took his mask off and pulled down his hazmat suit bottoms. He breathed in the bland fresh air, thankful he didn't have to worry about the weather. The top half of the safety suit was placed on top of the mask and bottoms, and Joe automatically put it safely out of the way in the corner next to the central doorway.

Every time I've been down here before, it was to see the professor and nothing else. Time for a looky around. Joe smiled.

The first few doors opened up to offices devoid of personal effects and ready to be occupied. There was a room set aside as a small canteen, followed by a janitorial closet, and finally, the stockroom, where the spare safety suits and face masks were stored. Joe turned at the end of the corridor and was faced with a matching corridor but with fewer doors on each side.

This place must have taken some time and effort to build.

Joe tapped in the code to the security console and felt the air being sucked in past him as he entered the room. There were four glass-encompassed pods filled with an array of foliage, and all were lit with imitation natural lighting. Each of the glass pods had a computer console connected to it. The plants within had nothing unusual about them, and Joe checked the consoles, which appeared to be the humidity and lighting controls for each glass pod.

He made his way back to the entrance, only to find that just as he had to enter a code to enter the lab, he also had to enter the numbers to exit. Joe entered the code for the next lab along. Each of the glass pods in the lab was empty, and Joe did a sweep of the room just to be thorough. The glass pods were lit, and on closer inspection, he saw dead and decaying remains of plants. Desiccated fronds and stems drooped into piles of dust.

Looking back at the glass pods, Joe frowned, tapped the code into the security console, and the door opened to let him out. He knew the next lab was different before he tapped the keypad. The nearest glass pod to the entrance was visible from where he stood. A vibrant green filled the pod, and the plant was crushing itself in its attempt for freedom.

As he pressed the last key, a shadow moved within the lab. The door opened, and the air hissed as it was sucked inwards.

'Hey, is anyone in here?'

No answer.

Joe took a moment before placing a foot in the lab. 'It's Major Wolfe. Joe Wolfe,' Joe corrected himself. 'Nothing to be alarmed about. I'm coming in.'

The door began to close, and Joe placed a foot in its path, still hesitant to enter the lab. It retracted and didn't move again.

Who could it be? His mind flew through the candidates, and only one came out on top.

'Charlie? Are you in here?'

Still no answer.

Joe crept into the lab, constantly scanning the room as he placed each foot down.

'Charlie? Is that you? We need to talk. We have to go over plans for tomorrow, and we have to review the security of the site after Nathan's death.'

'I didn't kill him.'

'Who was it? Do you know?' Joe was slowly edging anti-clockwise around the outside of the room. He stood for a second too close to a glass pod, and the light reflected off his face.

Damn. She could have seen me.

He moved back into the semi-darkness. 'Charlie? Do you know who it was?'

'It wasn't me.'

'What were you asking the professor in the medical ward?'

'I was trying to find out what his tests involved.'

'They were about the ore.'

'But why is it so much of a secret?'

'Why did you kill him? Was it because he didn't tell you?'

Silence again.

Joe took another step. A hand holding a pistol smacked him across the bridge of his nose. Pain erupted and stars blossomed, filling his vision.

'Charlie, stop!'

He heard her run out of the lab and up the corridor. He staggered after her towards the main door. It was just closing as he reached the inner decontamination door.

'Charlie, no! Don't, it's bad weather outside,' Joe said, his voice fading, knowing she hadn't heard him.

He finished putting his hazmat suit back on and tightened his face mask before blowing hard to force the old air out of the mask. As he opened the outer security door, the last of the sunlight was creeping below the horizon, leaving him alone and vulnerable in the dark.

Will she be waiting for me? Where would she go?'

Joe lifted his wrist to his eyeline and saw the red warning light of the air quality sensor. It blinked incessantly, highlighting that the poisonous air was at its worst level possible. He moved out towards the nearest light source. A figure dashed between two buildings ahead of him.

'Charlie, no! It's not safe,' Joe whispered as he continued walking towards the main gate.

He saw her dash past the gate guard, who was fully suited and not expecting any traffic in the terrible conditions.

I hope you find safety, Charlie; I really do.

***

Standing in front of the console of an overly filled glass pod, Joe saw that the branches of a plant had grown in circles around the inside of the container. Some leaves had been crushed against the glass and smeared, causing the clear glass to change to semi-opaque in a bizarre self-mutilation. The top of the container was strengthened by a band of stainless steel securing it to the ceiling.

Why was Charlie in here, of all places?

Joe looked back at the door and the security keypad, shaking his head with a wry smile on his face.

If she were in here when I changed the code, I would have locked her in.

He tapped the console, and a ghostly shape of a hand appeared. He placed his own onto the outline.

'Hello, Major. What can I do for you?' a crisp, English-accented voice asked.

'Bring up results of all recent tests conducted in this laboratory.'

A flurry of holographic files opened up in a continuous stream.

'Computer, stop.'

Joe eyed all of the reading material.

'Computer, open up all test files completed in this laboratory that involved ore from Planet 27...' He paused briefly. 'In the last seven days.'

A handful of files appeared.

'That's more like it.' Joe stared at the title and blinked. 'What does Electrical Resistivity and Conductivity mean?' Reading the following line, his question was answered.

This test is designed to measure the electrical resistivity and conductivity of P27-ferrum.

Joe's eyes quickly passed over at the data before settling on the bottom of the screen.

Results: Minimal effect occurs when mild electrical charge is passed through P27-ferrum. A significant response occurs as the electrical charge is increased. Reanimation occurs and lasts longer the greater the number of amperes that pass through the ore.

Joe flicked open another file.

The title read: *What occurs when reanimated P27-ferrum is added to plant-growing media?*

This test aims to determine the benefits that growing media offers to plants when reanimated P27-ferrum is added to loamy soil.

Again, Joe ignored all of the technical data and went straight to the bottom.

Results: Benefits in plant growth occur in direct proportion to the level of reanimation of P27-ferrum.

Joe stared at the glass container, which held a plant struggling to escape its confinement. *You probably had some highly reanimated ore added to your plant feed, you lucky thing.*

He flicked on to the last test file.

The title read: *What occurs when reanimated P27-ferrum is left in generalised polluted air?*

Joe's walkie-talkie squawked. 'Major, come in. Major, over.'

'Wolfe here.'

'Major, Sergeant Jameson instructed me to remind you to review security measures for tomorrow over.'

'Noted.'

'Sergeant Jameson also told me to inform you that Lieutenant Fowler was reported to have run out of the front gate without a hazmat suit or mask during the period of the highest level of poisoned air.'

Joe frowned. 'On my way, over.' He glanced at the holographic screen in front of him. 'Computer, close these files and make sure they are for my eyes only.'

'Security classification restricted to Major Wolfe eyes only confirmed.'

***

'I'm here as requested, Sergeant,' Joe said with a wry smile.

'The gate guard, Private Swift, reported to having witnessed Lieutenant Fowler running out of the front gates less than an hour ago, sir.'

'Yes. I know.'

Jameson frowned.

'She was running from me,' Joe said before gently massaging the bridge of his nose.

'You've got the start of a bruise there, sir. I hope it doesn't hurt.' Jameson smiled. 'Did you get hit by Lieutenant Fowler?'

'Technically, I was hit in the face by her pistol.'

'Shall we go after her?'

'She wasn't wearing any protective gear. She'll probably feel worse in the morning than I will. That is, if she survives.'

'Okay. What about security measures for the arrival of the shuttle tomorrow?'

'This week's increase will suffice, Sergeant.'

'But what about the lieutenant?'

Joe shook his head. 'She will not affect tomorrow.'

'What about Nathan's murder?'

Joe frowned.

'And the professor's death?'

'Our only suspect has run out the gate, likely to have suffered enough poisoned air to incapacitate her if not sufficient to kill her. We need to focus on getting through tomorrow successfully before returning to carry out any investigations. Wouldn't you agree?'

'Yes, sir. But I have one question.'

'Go on.'

'What do you consider a successful day tomorrow?'

'Getting through the day with no deaths and limited bloodshed.'

***

'It has been a while,' said Dr Wardle, holding up a half-filled tumbler.

'It has indeed,' Joe replied, copying the salute with his glass of whisky.

'So, how was your day?' The doctor pointed at Joe's facial injury. 'Do you want me to take a look at that?'

'I've had better days, and I've had worse.' Joe smiled. 'This is all in a day's work for being Head of Security for Tower 17.'

'I can give you a poultice of ore from Planet 27.'

Joe shook his head, then remembered the scientific test files from the laboratory.

'A penny for your thoughts.'

'What? Oh, yeah, I remembered looking at some scientific test results of the professor's.'

'Do tell.'

'He seemed to be testing the ore to see what would happen when he passed an electric current through it.'

'And?'

Joe got up and closed the door to the doctor's office before continuing. 'The term "reanimation" kept on coming up.'

The doctor didn't say a word but sat staring at Joe.

'It may even affect the air.'

'Really?'

'Oh, I'm guessing. I didn't get a chance to go through all the test files before I got called away.'

'What? What is more important than that?'

'Security procedures for tomorrow.'

'What is happening tomorrow? Oh, yeah. I forgot. The delivery of the shuttle.' The doctor smiled. 'I hear it's getting transported in three sections.'

'Only three? How is it you know more about it than I do?'

The doctor laughed. 'It must be my bedside manner and great listening skills.'

'Humph.'

'Was there any reference to DNA?'

'What?'

'Did the professor mention in any of his notes about DNA repair?'

Joe looked into the distance, recalling all that he'd looked at. 'No, Doc. There wasn't a mention of DNA. Why do you ask?'

'Just a theory I have. Just a theory.'

Chapter Twenty-Two

'You couldn't sleep either, sir?' Samuel Howe asked.

Joe rubbed his face and nodded at the screen. 'What is the forecast for the day?'

'No change from what I told you five minutes ago.'

Joe looked at the cup in Samuel's hand. 'Coffee?'

'A cup of tea. White and two sugars, if you're asking,' Samuel said, grinning.

'You're asking me to make a cup of tea?'

'It's okay, sir. I shall make it. Another coffee for you? Sugar? Milk?'

Joe shook his head. 'Just black, thanks.' He continued to stare at the incomprehensible, slowly moving lines that were allegedly showing clouds moving from the west coast across Scotland.

'Why didn't you use the creationary?' Joe asked about Samuel's late return.

'Sir, I don't know about you, but I never get a good cup of tea from that device. A classic old-style electric kettle and a tea bag never fails.'

Joe sipped the instant coffee, closed his eyes, and felt his synapses awaken. When he opened his eyes, he was alert once more.

'So, Samuel, run me through your hourly forecast for today.' He huddled down next to Samuel Howe as the young man pointed at the lines.

***

The screen showed a news reporter pointing at the first of three parts of the new Helius class of space shuttles.

'As you can see, this has a hybrid engine. There is the flammable liquid methane ring of ten propulsion rockets around the latest zero-point energy propulsion rocket.'

The female co-anchor chipped in. 'Gus, why the two types of propulsion?'

'Thank you for asking Jackie, that is a great question. The liquid methane rockets propel the shuttle through the remains of the Earth's atmosphere, where the zero-point rocket takes over. This has been the biggest improvement made to the shuttles, as there is no longer a need to jettison any booster rockets. The methane tanks can be refilled at a refilling station.'

'Like a gas station in the heavens,' Jackie said with a laugh.

'Exactly. This middle section, which will be the second delivery to arrive on site, houses storage, accommodation for the sleeping passengers, the green module, and water filtration.'

'And Gus, please tell our viewers how many sleeping pods this new Helius space shuttle can transport.'

'Jackie'—Gus turned and faced the camera with a smile—'viewers. This Helius class shuttle can hold fifteen thousand souls.'

Jackie paused for a rehearsed, awkward, jaw-dropping silence.

'And remind us, Gus. What is the green module?'

'The green module contains specimens of all plant species from Earth and DNA for all species of animals.'

'So, you could call this ship the Scottish Ark.'

'Indeed, Jackie. The last part of the shuttle is navigation and wormhole technology.'

'So, the first shuttle launching from Tower 17...'

'The tallest tower ever built...'

'Tower 17... the tallest tower ever built,' Jackie concluded for her colleague.

Joe left the rest of the security team to watch the end of the report and put on his hazmat suit. He passed by the site director's office to see that she was finishing her attire, putting on a pair of gloves. He frowned momentarily before moving on.

A weak breeze was pushing the evil, pale orange-and-brown clouds across the site, and despite the weather, Joe felt the bubble of excitement in his gut when he heard the first of three deliveries. Four massive helicopters could be seen in the distance, and beneath them was the tethered bottom portion of the space shuttle.

The shuttle had been built at the English spaceport and was now concluding its first and only journey before being joined together to form one gigantic working space shuttle.

Joe smiled at the thought.

'Sir, are you okay?'

'Jameson, it's an awesome ship, isn't it?'

'Yes, sir. She is. *Helius 7* will be a beauty when she's put together.' Jameson looked from the horizon back at Joe. 'Did you get much sleep?'

Joe grinned. 'Of course not.'

'And you will be staying up until all three pieces arrive?'

'Of course, Sergeant. Aren't you?'

Jameson nodded.

'How's the team for today?'

'We have four on the main gate. Four on roving patrols along the inside of the perimeter fence line and four protecting the *Helius* engineers.'

Joe opened his mouth to ask another question.

'And there is a four-hour rota shift system in place with the whole team being replaced by a fresh team on the fourth shift change.'

Joe nodded, well satisfied.

Any further conversation was impossible as the roar of the twin sets of blades of four helicopters shredded the air, getting ever closer to their site. Joe and Jameson stared upwards through their face masks as the massive part of the shuttle flew over their heads on the way to the landing site. Everyone had been warned not to attend the landing of the shuttle parts as the downdraft from all those massive rotors could flatten the strongest of people.

Joe remembered the engineers' drawings. The shuttle component would be lowered onto a platform, which would then be moved cautiously into the largest hangar he'd ever known, awaiting its siblings. Last night's security team had voluntarily walked the landing zone, removing any detritus well after their night shift had ended.

He glanced at the base of the tower nearest him and shook his head in wonder. Although he couldn't understand how *Helius 7* would end up at the top of the tower, he bravely accepted that the engineers, who were far more intelligent than he, had each step of the journey meticulously planned out to the nth degree.

As his hearing returned to normal, he turned and smiled at Jameson.

'You go and check on the guys looking after the shuttle, Sarge. I'll check on the main gate.'

Jameson nodded, and Joe headed to the site's entrance. The hairs on the back of his head stood on end, and he paused mid-stride to look around. Helen stood at the doorway, staring at him. She was recognisable with fluorescent orange tabs on her shoulders and her face mask being of the larger and newer variety.

Model 72X face mask, if I remember correctly.

Joe raised a hand in acknowledgement, and she gave a slight nod in response. He felt her stare as he turned back towards the entrance to the site. He was aware of the guards trying to ignore him and focus on their duties. He was there more to see if any members of the encampment had decided to make their presence known.

Some figures had moved towards the front gate but stood staring at the sky, hoping to see more of the shuttle as each part was delivered.

Is that Charlie Fowler? Joe leaned forward, staring at a figure set apart from the group, but he couldn't make out any distinguishing features at such a distance. The person wore a safety suit, which could have been military issue, and a readily available standard face mask.

The sound waves of the next delivery swept over the site, and Joe stared into the distance. He didn't see a crowd forming to the side of the front gate. Three helicopters on each side were stretched out at various heights, bearing the weight of the biggest and most unwieldy section of the shuttle.

'How did they manage to arrange that?' Joe mouthed as the mammoth lump of technology came bearing towards him. Even though it would have been over 150 metres in the air, he still ducked as it went overhead.

'Oi!' one of the gate guards yelled.

The klaxon sounded out and wasn't distinguishable under the downdraft of six helicopters and their labouring engines.

Joe saw smoke trailing from the lead helicopter and couldn't decide which way to look.

In the end, he didn't have to decide, as people in full safety suits and masks poured in through the gate, with the four gate guards powerless to help them. One guard raised his weapon and fired a warning shot, but just as the klaxon was silenced by the roaring helicopters, so too was the sound of the single shot.

Joe was buffeted by rioters passing him, and he stared with his mouth hanging open behind his face mask.

'Where are the roving patrols?' he shouted into his walkie-talkie, unsure whether anyone could hear him.

The second section of the ship was placed on the platform, and the noise of overwhelmed rotors diminished before stopping completely as the helicopters landed nearby. The klaxon continued unabated.

Joe raised a hand at the four gate guards and pointed for them to stay where they were just as four more guards appeared all at once, having run from different directions. He was just about to shout at them before recognising their laboured breathing and sweat pouring down the sides of their temples. Despite every roving team member having been kitted out with the best line of face masks, some of them were still steaming up from the insides.

'Come on. We've got intruders to find and remove.'

'How many of them, sir?' a winded team member managed to get out.

'Too many to count. Come on.' Joe turned and ran towards the space shuttle landing platform.

***

They arrived out of breath only to realise that their numbers, adding to the overwhelmed guards facing off the horde of intruders, would create minimal improvement.

'We have to try!' Joe tackled the nearest intruder, who turned out to be one of the visitors from the first group. 'What are you doing here?' he yelled at the man.

The man whipped his head back and forth, wild-eyed and incoherent. Joe looked at the melee about him, then dragged the man to his feet and pulled him to stand next to the fence. He tied the man's hands to the fencepost with one set of his ten automatic restrainers and jumped back into the throng.

Joe grabbed another intruder who was only a youth but again was beyond reasoning. He dragged the struggling teenager to the fence line and tied the hands to the nearest post. He turned and saw Jameson fighting off two intruders.

Jameson boxed the temples of one of them, who crumpled to the ground. Joe grabbed the arms of the second one and dragged him away to attach to the fence line.

'Did you see her?' Jameson shouted on Joe's return.

'Who?'

'Fowler! That bitch has returned. She didn't die.' Jameson punched a passing intruder, who staggered in a circle before sitting on his haunches in a daze.

'Use the restrainers!' Joe yelled before grabbing a passing person by the arm and hauling the woman off her feet.

Once Joe returned to stand beside Jameson, he watched as the sergeant struggled one-handed to get a restraining device out of his pocket. Joe held out an active restrainer.

'Sorry, sir, it's been a while since I did the training.'

Joe nodded at the fence, and Jameson dragged the unfortunate individual along the ground before attaching them to the fence. Looking around, Joe was pleased to see that his team had followed suit and that over a dozen people were attached along the fence.

He recognised her through the face mask and was even more surprised when he saw who she was with. The site director turned her face to hide her identity, but she was too late. Fowler stared at Joe with cold, clinical contempt for a moment before turning and sprinting back towards the main gate.

Joe looked around and saw that, with the roving patrol guards, the four guards assigned to look after the yet-to-arrive engineers and Sergeant Jameson, they were making some headway in breaking up the mass of intruders.

'Use the automatic restrainers!' Joe yelled at them.

'Restrainers!' Jameson bellowed.

A few of the guards raised their heads, recognising one if not both of the commands, and Joe was pleased to see that the guards were in a position to snap the restrainers onto the intruders and secure them to the nearest post or structure.

'Come on,' Jameson said before rejoining the throng.

Joe followed him and grabbed the arm of one person. Someone's elbow clashed with Joe's head, and he collapsed. Bright lights clouded his vision before darkness crept in from the edges. He breathed in deeply, and his vision cleared. His head ached, and although he didn't feel like standing, he forced himself up off the ground.

'Sergeant, have you noticed what I have?'

Jameson looked around and took a step back to take in the bigger picture. He shook his head.

'I haven't seen any Russians, Koreans, Chinese, or Americans.'

Jameson looked at him quizzically.

'Every one of them I've stopped seems to be wild and...'

'Drugged?'

'Yeah.'

'Which means they could be a—'

'Diversion. Frick.' Joe saw that the guards were doing okay without them. 'Let's check out the rest of the site.'

Jameson nodded and ran after Joe towards the underground labs.

***

The two men stopped and stared at the dripping paint of the logo sprayed onto the security door of the underground bunker.

'Do you recognise that symbol, sir?'

Joe nodded slowly. 'That, Sarge, is a very old logo of what used to be known as Greenpeace.'

'I thought so too. The last time I saw something like that was on the voyage to Planet 27.'

'I know. Seems a big coincidence, don't you think?'

Jameson pulled the door open wide, and Joe frowned.

'How the hell?'

'Someone must have guessed the code,' Jameson surmised.

'Or they overheard me instruct the computer to change it,' Joe said, thinking about why the site director had been out and about during the site being overrun by intruders. 'Hey, is anyone in here?' he yelled into the corridor.

'Let me go in first,' Jameson told Joe, already holding his handgun in the ready position.

They went into the building and checked each room and lab individually. Not a soul was seen. Nothing was out of place from what Joe could remember, and Jameson was soon itching to get back to ground level.

'Come on. Let's go and check the building's topside.'

Joe nodded before taking one long look at the lab they were in. He had to run to catch up with the sergeant, who was waiting at the security door, ready to lock it behind him.

The door was slammed shut with the satisfying click of the automatic lock kicking in.

Joe stopped to take a deep breath. *I'm exhausted.*

'Come on, sir.'

The office block had been ransacked.

'Frick.'

The control office was locked from the inside. Joe took off one glove and rapped on the door. 'It's Major Wolfe. Are you okay in there?'

'Yes, sir. I locked the door as soon as I heard what was happening,' Emma said.

'Great. Well done. Stay safe until we secure the rest of the building.'

Every office had been ransacked. Furniture was upended and drawers had been emptied, spilling out whatever personal possessions had been stored there. Joe made a mental note that Lieutenant Fowler's office and the office of the site director were in a similar dishevelled state.

'Samuel!' Joe pushed open the met office door.

'Major Wolfe? Is that you?'

The door to the cupboard squeaked as it opened about a centimetre.

'Samuel?'

Samuel Howe's fingers appeared out of the cupboard and the door opened, revealing a ghostly white-faced young man.

'Awww, no!' Samuel picked up the pieces of his old-style computer. 'This was an antique.' He held up the remains of a monitor screen to show Joe.

'At least you're safe, Samuel.'

Samuel looked at Joe, his expression bleak.

'Sir, let's go and speak with the ones we captured and get some answers,' Jameson suggested.

Joe nodded and turned to the young man, who was stooped over the remains of his prized possession. 'You gonna be okay, Samuel?'

Samuel pulled a face but nodded anyway.

'What about the doctor?' Joe said, turning back down the corridor.

The doctor's door was locked, and Joe had to pound at it to get a response.

'Doc, it's Joe here.'

'Joe who?'

'Doc, you can recognise my voice. Major Wolfe, Head of Security.'

The door was unlocked with a click and opened a fraction so Joe could see the doctor must have been at the single malt.

'Jameson, check the remainder of the offices, then tell the girl in Communications it's safe to come out.'

'Yes, sir.'

'Joe, come in. Come in before they return. I need to tell you something.'

'It's okay. We have everything under control now.'

'Do you?'

The look Dr Wardle gave him burned through the cloud of alcohol and pierced Joe's soul so much so that he flinched.

'We think so.'

'This has given me a wake-up call. I need to tell you before something could happen to me.'

'You really are safe now.'

'Shut up and listen.'

Joe stared at the frightened man.

'It's about the ore.'

Joe was about to say something, but the doctor held a hand up. 'Just listen. Something could happen to me, so I need to pass on my secrets just in case.' He breathed in deeply. 'You may not have known, but I've been doing my tests with ore from Planet 27.'

Joe nodded.

'Firstly, it was with mice. The results were far beyond what I could imagine,' the doctor said, his eyes shining with excitement. 'Then I tested its use on hamsters.' He held his hands up again, stifling any attempts at questions or protests. 'I know they aren't much bigger, but they were all I had until you arrived.'

Joe's eyebrows raised.

'Your wounds,' he said, pointing first at Joe's shoulder and then the top of his leg. 'The poultice. I remember reading your case file when you awoke on the ship returning from the planet. You'd survived a stomach wound, according to the crew of the ship, but on closer inspection, there was no evidence that you'd been wounded at all.'

Joe nodded. 'The ore,' he whispered.

'The same thing happened with your shoulder. There was no evidence of a wound. So, I gave you the poultice, and that proved everything beyond a shadow of a doubt. The ore has healing capabilities. It appears to work at that deep a level that it repairs the very DNA of a person.'

Joe glanced at the door to make sure it was closed.

'I remember vaguely when we had a few nips of the old nectar.' The doctor eyed the half-empty bottle of whisky on the table in front of him. 'You mentioned seeing gleaming parts of a ship on the planet when they should have been worn and rusted. It got me thinking. How do I replicate the event? The ore has worked wonders once, before I have to use new ore. Time and time again, I couldn't repeat the events. Then the professor wanted to remove the lightning spike, and that got me wondering. Why?'

Joe nodded.

'What if the ore can be shocked into repeating itself? An electric charge may renew its healing capabilities.'

'What?'

The doctor lifted a mobile defibrillator unit and placed it in between them. He raised the pair of shock paddles with a gleam in his eyes.

'Whoa. I'm not up for you trying that theory out on me.' Joe backed away from the table.

Just as he stood up, there was a knock at the door.

'Sir,' Jameson interrupted them. 'That's this building safe. We need to check on the intruders. Maybe the doctor can give his professional judgement on whether they were drugged or something.'

Joe opened the door. 'Good idea.' He turned and looked at the doctor. 'What say you, Doc? You up for looking at a few intruders?'

The doctor shrugged. 'Are any of them injured?'

'Maybe.'

The doctor grinned, and Joe smiled.

'You're not going to give medical assistance to them, are you?' Jameson was mildly outraged.

'I have to. I'm a doctor.'

Chapter Twenty-Three

When Joe, Jameson, and the doctor arrived at the shuttle platform area, the four guards, whose primary task was to keep the engineers safe, were standing, pointing at one or two of the intruders who were bound to the fence. All face masks were off, and everyone was breathing freely. The intruders, though, were mainly slumped down on the ground with their heads hanging in shame.

'Hey, sir.' One of the guards pointed at the clear sky. 'We have a gap of safe air.'

Joe removed his mask and let it hang against his chest. Jameson and the doctor followed suit. He raised his face to the sky and closed his eyes, momentarily absorbing the glorious sunlight.

'What are we gonna do with the prisoners, sir?'

The moment of bliss was shattered.

Joe looked at the prisoners and then turned to the doctor. 'All of these people were acting strangely when we were trying to take control of the situation.'

The doctor walked over to the nearest intruder and cupped the man's chin. He turned the guy's head one way and the other. He pulled out a small torch and flashed it into the man's eyes. He then lifted the face mask and inspected it thoroughly. He unclipped something and took it over to Joe and the sergeant.

'What is that?'

'It appears to be a vial. Don't get too close. It may contain a neurotoxin.'

'What would that do to him?' Jameson asked.

'This one probably increased cerebral blood flow in the occipital regions and activated the anterior cingulate cortex, but bilateral deactivation...'

'In layman's terms, Doc?'

'It could increase impulsive and aggressive behaviours exponentially. With group mania and a neurotoxin, it could account for rioting.'

Joe didn't say anything straight away. He'd immediately gone back in time to the riots at the Russian tower. He couldn't remember if anyone had investigated why the riot had occurred or what had sparked it off. He came back to the present moment to watch Jameson picking off a vial from every one of the prisoners' face masks.

'Who would have the know-how, Doc? And who would have the capabilities to set this up?' Joe whispered to the doctor.

The doctor tapped a finger on his chin. 'It would have to be somebody intelligent enough and with significant resources.'

'Such as international clandestine operations?'

The doctor raised his eyebrows. 'Spies?'

Joe nodded.

'I guess so. A country or an international conglomerate that has a bio-engineering arm.' He looked at the people along the fence line. 'They probably didn't have full control over their actions. One thing would have led to another, and Bob's your uncle, a riot.'

'Did they have a choice?' Jameson asked.

The doctor shook his head. 'All it would have taken is one word or sentence, and that would have sparked the whole event.'

Joe looked along the line until he found one of the men he vaguely recognised as having asked a question on one of the site visits. 'Do you know who I am?'

The man barely nodded and continued to stare at the ground.

'I understand that you may not have had control over your actions today.'

The man looked up.

'All I need to know is what you can remember before you came on site.'

The man looked into the distance. He coughed. 'I, umm... I recall being in my tent and hearing a lot of shouting. When I went out, other guys were complaining that we'd been given faulty face masks from your inventory.'

'Who told them?'

'I don't know. But that girl... Charlene? She was doing a check of all of our face masks.'

Joe stared at the man.

'She kept apologising. She'd handed out the free masks and some suits,' the man said, looking up at Joe. 'She said that someone wanted rid of us. She said she wanted to make sure the masks were safe.'

'Did she check all of your masks?'

'I think so. Then the anger came. It was in all of us. Everything after that is a bit of a blur.'

Joe nodded. He turned to the guards. 'Undo the restrainers.'

'What, sir?'

'Undo all of the restrainers and take them back to their tents. They were all drugged. It wasn't their fault.'

A guard with a black eye stepped forward. 'Are you serious, sir?'

Joe stared at the guy. 'Deadly.'

'Come on. You heard the Major. Restrainers off.' Jameson waved them over to the intruders.

***

Joe, Jameson, and the doctor walked at the tail end of the group that was being escorted off the site.

'So, who do you think it was?' the doctor asked quietly.

Jameson stared at Joe, hanging on every word.

'I'm guessing it was Charlie Fowler.'

'Your deputy?'

'She *was* my deputy—until she ran away off site during my investigation into the death of the professor.'

'Oh.'

Joe nodded. 'It seems that I picked the wrong person to be my deputy.'

'That reminds me. The connector of the drip hadn't been destroyed.'

Joe looked up in hope.

'Yes. It seems that we're trying to recycle the fitments and destroy the drip lines and accessories. Anyway, I have news.'

'Go on. Tell us.'

'There was a hole in the rubber seal. A completely round hole.'

'So, it wasn't a rip or a tear.'

'It wasn't. It could only have been pierced by a needle.'

'So, the professor was most likely to have been murdered.'

'It looks that way.'

They'd reached the main gate, and the guards had stepped aside, allowing all of the intruders to walk through the gap. As they turned right towards their encampment, there was a shouting and yelling of questions. To Joe's dismay, all of those shouts were directed at him.

'Major Wolfe, what has happened?'

'Major Wolfe, the site director told us that you're in charge of security. Can you tell us what happened?'

'Why were these civilians allowed on site?'

Jameson whispered in Joe's ear, who nodded. Joe walked calmly through the gap.

'I am Major Wolfe, Head of Security here at Tower 17. We've just concluded a test of our riot contingency plans.'

The questions paused.

'I'm sure you're aware of what happened at the Russian tower when there was a riot.'

The reporters were holding out their mobile phones, digital recorders, and web cameras to capture every word he said.

'Thank you, guys!' Joe shouted at the back of the intruders. 'Stay safe.'

'Are you still in contact with the Russian ex-president's daughter?'

Joe smiled. 'I haven't seen her since the riot.'

'What happened to that guy?' One of the reporters pointed at the guard, who had a black eye.

'We asked for realism on the test today. I think someone got carried away.'

'Major Wolfe...'

Joe held his hands up and quietened the reporters down. 'Thanks for all your interest and goodwill, guys. We've got a job to do.' He pointed at the distant horizon. A blob could be seen, which slowly transformed. The blob split apart to show six helicopters pulling the third and final piece of the ship.

All of the reporters turned to face the imminent delivery. Jameson waved to the guards and indicated that they should close the gates. Joe and the doctor turned away from the entrance and headed to the offices.

'So, how are you going to deal with the site director?' asked the doctor.

'What do you mean?'

'You think it was her, don't you?'

Joe pursed his lips but didn't reply.

The one-sided conversation didn't last long, as the helicopters brought the shuttle's top right over their heads to the landing platform. Joe and the doctor looked up, and again, the size of the piece was staggering. The surface was smooth yet lined with regularly placed windows. As it passed overhead, Joe was surprised to see that the joints between the surface and the dark windows were seamless. No joins were apparent, and only the change in colour and shade gave any indication that the surface had changed.

As the piece of shuttle reached halfway over their heads, Joe saw a black structure attached to the shuttle stretching down its length. The structure was rectangular, with two thick pipes continuing down to the end of the section, finishing just before the joint,

The doctor held open the door to the building. 'After you, Major.'

Joe frowned, realising he had to speak with the site director and wasn't looking forward to it. He passed the communications specialist, who looked up at him as he went by, and then Samuel Howe smiled as he went by. Too soon, he was standing outside the closed door of **Dr Helen Ogilvy – Site Director**. He rapped his knuckles hard on the door.

'Come in.'

Joe pushed the door wide and took a pace into the office.

'Ah, Major Wolfe. You're just the person I wanted to see.'

Joe raised his eyebrows involuntarily. 'Oh?'

'Yes. I wanted to congratulate you on your handling of the press this afternoon.'

Joe was taken off guard.

'Yes. See...' She carried on talking and pointed at an antique computer monitor playing the real-time news. 'Brilliant idea, saying the rioters were testing our reactions. Brilliant idea! Then, being open about the Russian tower and bringing in your heroic past to diffuse any hostility.'

'Hostility?'

'Yes. The press has flip-flopped on which side they support. Sometimes, it's the establishment and the necessity of our tower, and the next moment, they're just as easily siding with the... what did you call them? Oh, yes—the visitors.'

'The idea for the training was Jameson's.'

'What? Oh well, you were the one who carried it off so well,' she said, smiling. 'Here.' She held out a filled champagne flute.

'What is this for?' Joe asked as the glass was forced into his hand. *Is she wearing make-up? It looks like she's wearing lipstick and eyeshadow.*

'A celebration, of course. First one of many, I hope.' She moved around to the front of the desk, perched herself on the edge, and crossed her legs. 'Tell me, Joe, what was Russia like? What was it really like?'

'Director...'

'Call me Helen. Joe, loosen up a little, will you? Today was a win.'

'Director, I have come to speak to you about Lieutenant Fowler.'

'What is it now?' Her smile quickly turned into a serious frown. 'Have you got another paranoid delusional tale to tell?'

Joe stayed silent until she settled down. 'I went to speak to her, and she ran off.'

'She ran off? Where did she run off to?'

'Charlie Fowler ran out through the main gate and off site.'

'Well, she couldn't have gone far. I spoke with her when you were trying to deal with intruders.'

Joe didn't know what to say.

'Why were you chasing her?'

'What? No. I wasn't chasing her. I was wanting to ask her about the professor. I wanted to know why she shook the professor on the night he died.'

'Why?'

Joe looked at the site director. 'Are you not curious as to why Fowler physically shook a patient having medical treatment on the night that he died?'

'Not really, no. I have more important things to think about.'

'Would it alarm you to learn that the professor was probably murdered?'

'Here you go again. Murder, plotting, machinations. You've been reading too many murder mystery stories, Major Wolfe.'

'But she ran away from me.'

'So?'

'She ran away during the worst weather conditions and without wearing a safety suit or mask. Is that not a sign that she feels guilty about something?'

'Does it? You tell me.' The director dropped down, landing lightly on her toes, stood upright, and then stepped to the back of the room to stand behind the desk, creating a barrier between the pair of them.

'You always seem to be assuming the worst in people and that there is some big, murky scheme going on.'

'But...'

'No buts, Major Wolfe. This is the last time you come to me with accusations about my team with fantasies about murders and plots to sabotage."

'I didn't say anything about sabotage.'

'Get out.'

Joe stood in the corridor as the door was shut in his face. He shook his head and walked slowly towards his own office. He thought about obtaining some alcoholic sympathy from the doctor and instantly dismissed the idea, at least for the time being.

He quietly closed the door and pressed it firmly until he heard the confirmatory click.

'Computer, open up all files and records referring to Sergeant or Lieutenant Fowler.'

There were hundreds of meteorological reports, weekly and daily. She'd even requested hourly updates.

'Humph.'

I could tie these times and dates to events, but I already knew that she was up to something. I don't know if she was up to no good on her own or if she was instructed to do it. Think Joe, think.

He closed all of the weather forecast requests and focused on her personnel file.

What am I missing? What didn't I see before?

Joe scanned the information again. He looked at every field of data for the umpteenth time, but nothing was different. He didn't see anything new.

'What about the sponsor? Who sponsored you, Charlie? There must have been someone.'

Joe moved his finger down the screen, making sure he didn't touch the light waves.

'Feck.'

The sponsor field was still empty.

Joe swiped closed the files one by one and paused at the very last one. It was a draft message addressed to Major Joe 'Howling' Wolfe.

Dear Sir,

I am writing to submit my resignation from the position of Sergeant of Site Security. Although I have enjoyed working at the site of Tower 17, I have found that my position has become increasingly untenable.

Having romantic feelings for you that are unreciprocated is something I can handle, but these feelings also bring back many memories of my time in Russia. Although I don't show my heart on my sleeve, my feelings run deep.

I suggest you choose Sergeant Jameson as your deputy, as he is steady as a rock and has plenty of experience under his belt.

Sorry to send this as a message, as I would feel too embarrassed saying this to your face.

Yours,

Charlie Fowler

Joe looked at the date the document had been created and saw that it was the day before he'd promoted her to lieutenant.

'Humph.' He sighed. 'Computer, archive this draft message and restrict access to Head of Security only.'

'Access to file draft DfSgt.C.Fowler.57476. Restricted.'

'Computer, open the personnel file of Doctor Helen Ogilvy.'

'Unable to comply.'

'Computer, this is Head of Security Major Wolfe. Open Doctor Helen Ogilvy's personnel file.'

'Unable to comply.'

Joe frowned. 'Computer, who has sufficient access to open Doctor Helen Ogilvy's personnel file?'

'Security access of Tower 17 Site Director is restricted to the Head of Global Project Exodus, the Minister for Transport, and the Prime Minister of the United Kingdom.'

Joe pursed his lips. *Dare I go above her head?*

It took him half an hour to draft his first-ever message to the Minister for Transport, and he had to change and redraft it several times. Even then, he found himself uncertain about the most significant decision he would ever make.

Do I include the Head of Global Project Exodus and the Prime Minister?

Joe typed the holographic keyboard and hit Send.

'Computer off.'

Chapter Twenty-Four

Joe watched a team of engineers crawling over the three components of the space shuttle, just like the colony of ants he used to watch as a child. There was a common goal, and each worker carried out their tasks with complete autonomy while still being part of the team.

'Major, Jameson here,' the walkie-talkie squawked.

'Go ahead, Jameson.'

'Lap of the inside of the perimeter fence complete. Fence line is secure. I've found something. Wait one.'

'What is it?'

No response.

'Jameson? What's happening?'

''I'm back, sir. I found a note, and I'm bringing it in.'

'What is it?'

'It's best for you to see it in person, sir. We don't know who may be listening in, over.'

'See you shortly.'

***

'And you said this was stuffed into the crack between the rear gate and the post?'

'Yes, sir.'

Joe looked at his name written on the envelope in blue ink in sloping handwriting.

'Are you gonna get it checked out in the lab? That would be the safe thing to do.'

'You know that the new head of science and his assistant aren't due in for another three weeks. Anyway, what is the worst that could happen?' Joe looked at Jameson and grinned.

Jameson smiled, shaking his head.

'Some role model, sir,' he said under his breath.

'What was that, Lieutenant? You're still under probation.'

Joe looked at each seal of the envelope before ripping it open. No gas or powder spewed out, and both Joe and Jameson exhaled loudly.

Jameson shifted closer to Joe and peered over his shoulder. 'Come on, sir.'

'Patience, Lieutenant.' Joe shook the envelope upside down. A folded letter peeked out, but that was it.

He removed the letter and unfolded it on top of his desk.

Dear Major Howling Wolfe,

It is known that you are aware of our existence outside of the fence line of Tower 17, so it will come as no surprise that we are aware of the recent incursion on-site by rioters. It gladdens our hearts that you and your team suffered no fatalities and that you managed to expel them without getting accused of brutality by the press.

We recommend that you investigate Officer Fowler's background before she joins the security team in our country. We did not fall for her trick with the face masks, and if she returns to our campsite, we will terminate her.

If you find what she was looking for, your anonymous friend in Russia would appreciate it if you could share the information.

Your comrade,

Captain Tyurin

Shotlandiya gruppa

Joe frowned.

'I thought we'd seen the last of Fowler,' Jameson said. 'And who is your anonymous friend? A Russian?'

'It seems that Fowler is still haunting us. My anonymous friend shall remain nameless.'

'I'm guessing that it's the father of the woman you saved. Wasn't he the president of Russia?'

Joe's eyes narrowed, but he didn't say a word.

'Remind me not to play poker with you, sir. I noticed that Captain *Tyurin* didn't mention the site director.'

Joe nodded. 'I don't know if she's guilty of anything.' He paused, glancing at the door to remind himself that he'd closed it. 'She could have spoken to Fowler and was innocent of anything else.'

'Other than being someone who is destined for politics,' Jameson grumbled.

Joe couldn't help but smile. 'Computer, open Sergeant Fowler's application for employment and reference checks.'

Several documents appeared on the holographic screen. The first one they looked at was the medical form, which they gave only a cursory glance. Joe was about to swipe it closed when Jameson grabbed his hand.

'Wait, sir. Look at that.' He pointed at the field titled *Distinguishing Features or Marks.*

Tattoo: five-pointed star surrounded by four small blemishes. Marks consistent with incomplete tattoo(s) removal.

The individual may have had cosmetic surgery that affects her facial appearance.

'She was Chinese?' Jameson asked incredulously.

'So, it seems.'

***

Joe stared at the back of her head as the site director was driven off site in an open-topped Land Rover.

'Her monthly Project Exodus meeting. Where did she say it was this time?' Jameson asked.

'She didn't, but the communications desk told me that Paris was the destination on her flight booking.'

'Did they tell you when her return flight was?'

'She'll be away a week.'

'And how long for the engineers to finish putting together the big toy?'

Joe couldn't stop himself from laughing. 'When is your next perimeter check, Lieutenant?'

'Now,' Jameson grumbled. 'I still can't believe that you haven't allowed me to delegate this task.'

'Remember, we're still down two sergeants.'

'Don't you mean one?'

'Two. Fowler was never replaced, and now there is you. Your position as a sergeant is now vacant.'

'Good luck recruiting.' Jameson smiled. 'Who will want to come to a site that has had two murders anyhow?'

'Get walking before I bust you back down, Jameson.'

Lieutenant Jameson rolled his eyes for comic effect and started walking. Joe returned to his office and sat back to relax for a moment.

'Computer,' he said with a sigh.

'Major Wolfe?'

'Computer, open up the messaging panel.'

Joe typed in the address that he'd memorised the day he was given the details on a card.

Dear Anonymous friend,

Thank you to your acquaintance, Captain Tyurin, for the pointer on who to look into; it was much appreciated.

Joe rubbed his chin thoughtfully.

Unfortunately, the tip was not sufficiently valuable to offer much information in return. Other than confirming that the ore from Planet 27 has, as you suspected, one-time-only healing properties, that is all I can say at the moment.

Your friend,

Joe

***

Joe was quite surprised to receive a message in response almost immediately.

Dear Joe,

Thank you for confirming our suspicions, but it is, as you say, not sufficiently valuable information to us. Holding back your best information is a good tactic, and I compliment you on your tradecraft.

Although I will always be indebted to you for saving moya printsessa, do not think that my favours are endless.

Until next time,

your anonymous friend

Joe read it several times before sitting back and smiling.

The weather was clear and ideal for his run. He stood up, bent down, and touched his toes. He straightened and bent again to put his hands flat on the floor.

'Humph.'

He exited the building and jogged straight to the main gate. He nodded to the guards and swung right, towards the encampment. Since the incident with the intruders, the number of people camping outside the site had been diminishing daily. Some of them could barely look him in the eyes, such was their embarrassment, but others had a fire in their eyes that he hadn't seen before.

Joe jogged across the front of a few tents, and the occupants ducked deeper into the tents, avoiding having to interact with him as he passed. His route went up and down the slight inclines and the ditches, which had been exacerbated by the recent footfall, and he was amongst the military-style tents before he knew it.

'*Dobryy den*,' Joe said as he slowed to negotiate a way around some muddy patches.

The man with Slavic cheekbones inclined his head but remained stonily silent, and Joe increased his pace when he was back on generally flat ground. He saw no Asian campers on his journey, and operatives from other nations stayed undercover if they were there at all.

Even though Jameson had confirmed the secure status of the fence line, Joe couldn't help but routinely glance along the geometrically shaped wire fence. When he reached the back gate, he was mildly disappointed not to find a note for himself, so he spent little time entering the site again and began his warm-down phase of the run. He finished with leg stretches outside his accommodation block. He was so keen to compose a new message that he didn't even have a shower before starting up the computer.

He typed out a message after a brief pause.

Dear anonymous friend,

Although I am doing my best here, if your acquaintances don't see me on my daily run, that's when you should start worrying. The site director has ignored murders here despite my reports, and there is no interest in the facts. She may or may not have been working with Fowler, as they had been seen together during the intruder event the other day.

I need to verify the facts before I send you the information you require. It could be a game-changer.

Your friend,

Joe

Not waiting for a response, Joe instructed the computer to switch off and went to the external door. He peered outside but couldn't see much through the small square of glass. On instinct, he turned the corner and went back to his desk.

'Computer, on.' Joe saw the holographic screen light up the room. 'Computer, messages.' He saw that his Russian friend had already responded.

Dear Joe,

We are curious about the information you plan to share with us. Regarding the other matter, we find that it is very useful to message your friends from new message locations. But that could be me, just getting old and careful.

your anonymous friend

***

Joe left his accommodation block and walked quickly between buildings to see Samuel.

'It has been suggested to me to change my message location. Is that something you can help with?'

Samuel nodded and began typing furiously at the old mechanical keyboard. He grabbed a tissue paper and wrote down a new address and password.

'Untraceable and non-recordable. Ideal for the head of security,' Samuel said with a grin.

'Thanks,' Joe said and turned to leave Samuel's office. A moment later, he popped his head back in, but before he could say anything, he was interrupted.

'You'll be fine the rest of today, but take your safety suit and mask to your sleeping quarters as you'll probably need it first thing in the morning.'

Joe opened his mouth to speak again.

'You're welcome,' Samuel said, smiling.

Joe nodded. 'Thanks, Samuel.'

'Call me Sam. All my friends do.'

'Thanks, Sam. Call me Joe. It's what my friends call me.'

'My mother told me it's good to make new friends,' Sam said, blushing, probably realising Joe would think that he still lived with his mother, which he did.

'Wise women, mothers.'

Sam raised his eyebrows and then nodded slowly.

Joe grabbed his hazmat suit and face mask before leaving the building for the day. He saw the incredible spectacle of the sunset and felt the comforting glow of the late-in-the-day sunshine on his face. Sounds of the space shuttle engineers floated over the buildings, strangely soothing to Joe's ears.

He remembered the tissue paper and walked quickly back to his accommodation.

'Computer, on. Message login screen.' Joe typed in his new details and sent a quick message to his anonymous friend.

A response arrived within moments.

Dear Joe,

Click this link.

Your anonymous friend

Joe clicked on the link, and a panel opened titled *'Secure Video Call.'*

'Hello friend.' The ex-president, Kafelnikov, appeared on his screen.

'Hi, sir.'

'I have asked about your site director and was given quite a file on her.'

'What did it say?'

'Your site director lost her parents when she was in her teen years. She managed to complete her schooling to scrape an acceptance to a university. She left university with a doctorate. The doctor was assigned to a job in Project Exodus, where she met her future husband. They got married, had a baby, and then she applied for the role of Tower 17 Site Director, leaving her husband in China. There is a note on the file that it is believed she seduced the professor's assistant—'

'Nathan?' hissed Joe.

'Yes. She had an affair. When her husband found out, he applied to go to Planet 27.'

Joe nodded but said nothing.

'We recommend that you have as little interaction with your site director as possible. She is listed as volatile and remorseless.'

Joe thought about the message he'd sent to the Minister for Transport and shuddered.

'You have done something that you may regret?'

Joe nodded.

'Do not worry at the moment as she will be in France at the meeting. When she gets back, make sure you are not alone with her or by yourself for any length of time.'

'Thank you.'

Ex-president Kafelnikov nodded and waited.

'I have no proof, sir. But I think the professor was researching re-animating Planet 27 ore by passing an electric current through it.'

'What voltage? How many times... in a vacuum or in open air? Any delay between test and re-animation?'

'I'm sorry, that's all I know.'

Ex-president Kafelnikov stared at him and finally nodded.

'I will instruct the captain and his men to keep an eye on you when the director returns. Until then, keep running the fence line.'

There was a knock at Joe's door.

'Gotta go, sir.'

'Until next time, Joe.' The face of the former president of Russia vanished.

'Major?'

Joe opened the door. 'Doctor, how are you?'

Dr Wardle held out a bottle of whisky. 'We have to discuss security arrangements.'

'Good to see that you've come prepared,' Joe said with a grin. 'What plans do we need to go over?' He opened the door wide and offered him the nearest chair.

The doctor closed the door behind him and took a seat. 'Have you seen the plans for the medical induction unit for onboarding?'

'I know of it, as we're getting another bump in security staff numbers, but I haven't looked at any plans yet.'

'A whole new hangar is going to be built with waiting areas, medical induction, suspended hibernation pods, and then pod storage so that they can be ready for transporting onto the ship.'

'And do you see a problem with those plans?'

The doctor sat back. 'There will be a complete medical team arriving just before the passengers arrive.'

'Won't that take any pressure off you and your team? You won't need to think about dealing with all of the passengers.'

'Humph.'

'I thought the ship was travelling to Planet 27 anyway. Doesn't it have wormhole travel technology?'

'So I heard. Why do you ask?'

'If they use wormhole travelling, that cuts the journey down to a matter of months. I wonder why they're using the suspended animation pods.'

'Remember how many are going on the one ship. If they're travelling in suspended animation, there will be less staff needed to look after them for the whole journey.'

Joe nodded before taking the first whisky of the evening that the doctor was offering.

Chapter Twenty-Five

The spaceship appeared to be complete, as far as Joe could tell. The transporter the ship was lying on had multiple sets of wheels that dwarfed Joe, making him feel insignificant in comparison. The inflated tyres towered above him, and he saw the inner circle of each tyre was over a metre above his head. Struts from each set of wheels supported the base of the transporter. The transporter itself had a cabin where the driver could monitor the journey whilst the ship lay on top, dwarfing anything and anyone nearby.

'Can I help you?'

A bespectacled engineering team member walked over to Joe. The engineer wore a brilliant white hazmat suit and his mask hung down his chest, tethered by rubber straps. With a completely bald head and being clean-shaven, only the white, wispy eyebrows gave any indication that he was older than the rest of the team.

'I'm sorry. You are Major Wolfe, aren't you?'

'That's me. You are?'

'Head of Engineering Popple. Doctor Keith Popple,' Dr Popple said with a smile.

'Nice to meet you, Doctor Popple. Call me Joe.'

'Joe, would you like a personal tour of the ship?

'If you have time?'

'For you, Joe, I can make time. It has been a while since I spoke to anyone who has travelled in suspended animation and been through a wormhole.'

Joe raised his eyebrows. 'I didn't realise it was common knowledge.'

'I try to keep up with all of the fleet's comings and goings.'

Joe nodded. 'And how does this ship compare?'

Keith smiled. 'This beauty is the next generation of star ships. With the most up-to-date propulsion unit, storage for twenty thousand suspension pods, flora units, water generation and recycling, communication... I could go on and on. It is the most advanced ship in the fleet so far.' He gestured for them to walk towards the rear of the ship.

Joe's mouth dropped open as he looked up at the enormous propulsion jets surrounding a circular, shiny silver surface.

'Methane jets surrounding the zero-point energy propulsion unit.'

Joe nodded, attempting to appear as if he knew exactly what Keith was describing. 'How does that work?'

Keith smiled, clearly enjoying talking about his work. 'The methane jets work as all the propulsion units worked up until now. Jets of ignited gas provide enough thrust to propel the ship through the Earth's atmosphere. Then, when into space, the ZPEP is started up and takes over.'

'Who decides when the... ZPEP kicks in?'

'The autopilot.'

'So, it's not manual then?'

'It's all programmed. But there will be a manual override.' Keith frowned. 'We've never experienced a need to manually override the programming in all of the hundreds of tests completed. The electrical charge has occurred exactly when required.' He pointed at the silver metal surrounded by the methane propulsion rockets. 'Behind that cover is the best technology so far.' His eyes were gleaming. 'The ZPEP,' he whispered in awe.

Joe waited for him to continue.

Keith looked sombre. 'If only the ZPEP had been created back in the twenty-first century, then we wouldn't have been in this situation.' He looked up at the tower, which was so tall the printing platforms were no longer visible to the naked eye.

Joe nodded.

Keith sighed and looked at the ship. 'The use of such freely available energy would have cancelled the need to burn coal, oil, and gas.' He lifted his mask. 'And we wouldn't have to use these things.'

Joe stayed silent.

'So that's the methane propulsion rockets and the ZPEP.'

'Why the two? I know you've mentioned methane as a means to escape the atmosphere and ZPEP in space. Why can't the ZPEP do both?'

'The methane rockets create the boost of energy for the ZPEP to activate. We haven't found out how to dissipate the heat that naturally occurs when ZPEP starts up. The ZPEP could create a wave of heat that incinerates whatever it comes into contact with, except for the methane propulsion rockets. The movement of heat out of the rockets essentially sucks the heat generated by the ZPEP, causing it to flow out in the same direction. And once it starts going in the one direction, it continues to do so.'

Joe nodded, not quite sure if he understood, but he suspected that no matter what the doctor said, he wouldn't understand it any better.

After a pause, Keith remembered Joe and smiled. 'Would you like to see inside the ship?'

'Yes.'

'Back to the front we go, then,' Keith Popple said with a laugh before leading the way.

Joe couldn't help but stare at the ship above him as he walked along every section of the transport platform carriages, which were linked just like trains of old.

'She's a beauty, isn't she?'

Joe nodded.

***

At the front of the transport platform, Keith slid back a nondescript panel and typed 1-9-6-9 into a small computer screen. Joe heard a hiss as a hatch above their heads dropped open. A shiny, stainless-steel ladder immediately extended down in front of Joe, missing him by millimetres.

'After you, Joe.'

Joe glanced at Keith, who was grinning. Major Joe Howling Wolfe scrambled up the ladders and into the cab of the transport platform as if he were a five-year-old. Keith's excitement was contagious.

'I never saw much of the ship before travelling to Planet 27. Well, not that I can remember.' Joe looked at the roof of the cabin they were in and realised it was the underbelly of the ship. 'How do we get in?' He eyed steps to the surface of the ship.

Keith turned to the front of the cab and put his hand on a screen.

'Doctor Keith Popple recognised,' intoned the computer.

'Open hatch 1-A.'

'Hatch 1-A opened, confirmed.'

Above the steps, the ship hissed angrily, then sucked in the warmth from around Joe, leaving him shivering and instantly nervous. 'Do all the passengers board this way?'

'No, they'll be brought onboard in their suspended animation pods. That is, after all the components are installed, checked over, and given the green light.'

'Who gives it the green light?'

'That would be me,' Keith said, smiling.

Joe clambered up into the spaceship and once more felt small. The passageway he found himself in went in three directions. Straight ahead, the corridor led into the centre of the ship's diameter. Turning left, he guessed, would take him in the direction of the tip of the ship, while turning right would take him all the way down to the propulsion section.

'Go left,' Keith advised.

'What are these black panels?' Joe pointed along the side of the corridor that was closest to the outside world.

'These are electrostatic photovoltaic windows.'

'Photovoltaic... is that some sort of solar panel?'

'Yes. The panels can transmit the energy from light through the cell structure onto the electrical circuit of the ship as well as the glass being looked through as one would a window.'

'A dual-purpose window.'

'Exactly. Even with a ship this size, we've always tried to maximise every item, every component, and every nut or bolt to be as efficient as possible and used in multiple ways. Condensation is collected and added to the water supply. Used water is harvested, recycled, and processed so that it retains the same taste, if not better than it originally had. Biowaste is used to fertilise the flora. The vegetation grown using manure from biowaste expels oxygen, which humans then breathe in. Everything is cyclical.'

'What about animals?'

Keith nodded. 'We thought about that, but with the cost of transport, each suspension pod is more valuable to transport a human than it would be to transport an animal. If we had animals on board for short period flights, there would have to be more staff to look after them during the journey.'

'Plus suspension sickness.'

'Exactly. How do you think an animal would react if it couldn't remember anything when it awoke?'

'What is down there?' Joe pointed down a corridor that went towards the centre of the ship.

'That is one of the many access points for the green works. Either recycling gas, fluids, and electricity, or fields of grass generating oxygen.'

'You've got a grass lawn creating oxygen?'

Keith nodded. 'Multiple layers of lawns.'

Joe looked dazed.

'Turf with a natural light source above it as it's constantly fed and watered nutrients and with a robotic lawn mower trimming it. Then, a metre or so above the light source is another lawn, and above that, a natural light source, and so on. The mowers deposit the trimmings into a compost area, which is then converted into compost and fed back to plants.'

Keith motioned for them to move forwards towards the front of the ship.

'So, how will this ship get up the tower?'

'The transporter platform will take it to the base of the tower. Then it's over to you lot.'

'Me? I don't know a thing about its transportation.'

Keith laughed. 'Don't worry. Everything has been planned out down to the last detail. I understand that this ship will be hoisted up the tower until it's vertical and then slowly pulled or winched up. You lot have also got some anti-gravity device to reduce the weight of the ship until it reaches the top of the tower.'

Joe stopped asking any more questions, and they continued walking in companionable silence.

'Here is where the magic happens,' Keith said, opening up the door to the control room.

At the front of the room was a wall of solar panel windows that went from floor to ceiling. There was a long bank of computer access points and three chairs. Behind that were two chairs, and three metres behind that was one chair. In front of each chair, Joe saw the floor had a multitude of lights inset just below the surface.

'Holographic computers?'

Keith nodded. 'Only the best.'

'A crew of six to pilot this ship?'

''Technically, one person could pilot this ship alone without the help of autopilot. Ideally, there is an engineering officer, a wormhole specialist, a medical doctor, a communications expert, a deputy, and a captain.' Keith pointed to each of the chairs as he said the titles of each role.

Keith saw Joe pursing his lips. 'I know. At the moment, it's probably somewhat of an anti-climax. But think about it. You're in the control room of the most advanced ship in the fleet. I even let them put on guns.'

Joe's eyebrows shot up.

'I know, I know. The armaments are primarily for defence, designed to destroy any meteors that come too close. Although we haven't seen or heard of any space pirates, it's only a matter of time before they will be out there causing trouble.'

'Really?'

'Based on the history of Planet Earth, it's only logical to assume that some rogue nation will attempt to take over one of the ships.'

'There can't be any nation with the technology to attack one of our ships, can there?'

'Does it have to be a nation? A multinational conglomerate has to be big enough to siphon off a few billion dollars for R&D to build something capable of taking us on.'

'Or to impregnate one of the launch teams with a few spies,' Joe said under his breath.

Keith's eyebrows rose as he overheard Joe's comments.

A knock on the door sounded out.

'Ah, it's you, Keith. Showing off my ship to anyone interested enough to stay awake, I see.'

'David, you're a pilot, not commander of the ship,' Keith told him with a frown.

'And you're just an engineer.' David slammed the door closed.

Keith turned back to face Joe with a flushed face. 'Sorry about that. David has had a bit of a rough patch recently trying to get over the death of his girlfriend.'

Joe nodded.

'She was working with me on the propulsion rockets and didn't get her mask on quick enough.'

'She died from poisoned air?'

Keith nodded.

'Didn't she get medical attention?'

'Medical attention? That doesn't stop it. They can't prevent the poisoned air from killing.'

'But up here, medical attention can treat it. I survived a dose. Others have survived too.'

'The air must be worse down south then, as it's lethal. Anyway, don't be bothered by Commander David Cooper just because he blames me.'

Joe nodded, keeping quiet, seeing Keith frown again.

'If I had only insisted that she wear her mask whilst working on the fuel cells, then maybe...' Keith's softly spoken words tailed off.

The two men retraced their steps back to hatch 1A in silence, and Joe realised his tour was over for the day.

***

'Major Wolfe, there you are.'

'What is it, Jameson? You look worried.'

Jameson grabbed Joe's arm and steered him clear of Keith and out of earshot of the head of engineering.

'It's the site director. She's back from the Paris conference, and she looks as though she's in a foul mood. She has been asking after you.'

Joe turned and waved at Keith. 'Great to meet you, and thanks for the tour.'

Keith waved back and headed towards the engineering hangar.

'Feck. I've already been on my run today.'

'What has that got to do with anything?'

'Just ignore me, Jameson. I'm a rambling, doomed man.'

'What the hell is going on, sir?'

'The less you know about it, the better.' Joe continued walking towards the office block.

'Do I get a choice in the matter, being your deputy and all that?'

'This is way beyond our roles at Tower 17. For your sake, continue with your duties and feel comforted that you informed me that the site director wanted to see me.'

'As you wish, sir,' Jameson said, frowning and continuing walking but angling away to do his daily check of the inside of the perimeter fence.

Joe breathed deeply and opened the door to the building. The amber air safety warning light was flashing, alerting everyone inside that they would need their safety suits when leaving the building. Joe felt the woman's stare as he passed her, manning the communications, and he carried on. The doctor saw him and ducked back inside his office. Joe was approaching the site director's office when Samuel saw him pass and jumped out into the corridor to catch him.

'Major Wolfe.'

'Samuel?'

'I'm posting an updated warning.'

'Yeah, I saw the amber warning light.'

'That's what I'm trying to say. I'm about to post the update. It's now a red warning. No movement...'

'Outside unless in full protective suits and grade 1 face masks,' Joe finished the sentence for him.

They both looked at Joe's C-5 face mask.

'Thanks for the warning. Best you go and post it site-wide.' Joe's smile wasn't convincing.

'Yes, sir.' Samuel ducked back into his office.

Joe stood outside the site director's office and heard Samuel hammering the manual keyboard in his haste to alert the site. Facing the door, he paused before knocking firmly on the frame.

'Come in.'

He pushed open the door and saw Helen Ogilvy with a furious scowl on her face. Standing at her side was the Minister for Transport, wearing a full hazmat suit with a brand-new face mask hanging down against his chest.

'I was told that you wanted to see me, Doctor.'

'What the hell did you—'

The Minister for Transport raised a hand and cut the site director off. 'Major Wolfe, I have just been telling Doctor Ogilvy about the message you sent me.'

Dr Ogilvy was about to burst, but the minister put a calming hand on her shoulder.

'Your boss, it seems, has given you so much latitude in running your department that she hasn't pulled you up on the repeated failings that you yourself have identified.'

The warning light above them started flashing red. The minister continued talking, and Joe watched as Dr Ogilvy began putting on her hazmat suit. A face mask, labelled A-1, lay on the desk in front of her.

'So you see, Major Wolfe, despite your historical impeccable record, your recent activities, systematic failings, and attempt to blame all the wrongs on your boss, the site director, you are now in a predicament.'

Joe glanced down and watched as Dr Ogilvy removed her wedding ring and put one hand into safety gloves before doing the same with her right hand.

'Are you listening to me, Major?'

Joe was staring at the wedding ring on the desk.

'Major!'

Joe slowly looked up at Dr Ogilvy. 'You...'

'Major, have I got your attention?' The minister tried again to catch Joe's attention.

'You... you killed the professor.'

Dr Ogilvy's face drained of all colour.

The minister stepped between Joe and the doctor, breaking the shock-inducing spell that had Joe under its influence.

'That is enough, Major.'

The site director pulled the rubber glove up over her wrist and let it go. The elasticity of the rubber snapped down against her wrist with a loud sound.

'Minister, I think we may have a solution,' she said, nodding towards the red flashing light.

'I don't understand.'

'I believe that Major Wolfe here has an old face mask that is not up to the task of the current air rating.'

'Does he?'

'Yes. But with his level of incompetence being evident with all the failings you've discovered, he obviously doesn't know the ramifications of being outside wearing his old mask.'

'I still don't know what you're saying.'

'I think that the major here should wave you off as you leave the site now. After all, we wouldn't want you wasting any more of your valuable time looking into what seems to be just a matter of internal politics.'

Joe felt a sting on his forearm and, still in shock, stared incomprehensibly at the hypodermic needle in Dr Ogilvy's hand.

'Just a gentle relaxant, Joe. We wouldn't want you getting distressed on our walk out to the main gate, would we?'

The minister nodded. 'I'm pleased that you have this situation under control, Helen. After all, we wouldn't want the prime minister getting wind of this. I know I'm not one of his favoured few, so the least said, the better.'

'Come on, Joe, let's go outside now.' Dr Ogilvy held Joe's arm in a vice-like grip and walked him towards the door.

'One moment, Helen.' The Minister for Transport lifted Joe's face mask and placed it gently over Joe's face before snapping the rubber straps into place. 'That's better, don't you think?'

The minister left the building first, with Dr Helen Ogilvy marching Joe behind with their arms intertwined.

Joe was running on autopilot, his thoughts sporadic and fleeting in his mind. On the walk towards the main gate, he saw the Minister for Transport get into his chauffeur-driven vehicle as the site director continued marching him to the front gate. He didn't register the fact that a large crowd was outside the gate, shouting and expressing their sentiments through their masks.

The gate opened, and the minister drove off down the track. The site director gave Joe a gentle push, which sent Joe tottering towards the group of visitors. The crowd parted as Joe staggered into them, and they surrounded him, shielding him from view as they closed their ranks around him.

Joe collapsed onto the ground, unaware that his mask hadn't been up to preventing the toxic air from getting into his lungs. He was only aware of the pain in his chest.

Chapter Twenty-Six

Joe's eyes flickered open, and he saw a face that he thought he recognised behind a mask.

He croaked, and more masked faces peered down at him.

'Quick, switch the mask.'

'Where are the spares?'

'Are we to trust them? After all, that Fowler woman gave them out.'

'Shhh. She'll hear you.'

'What? We should forgive her just because she gave us better masks? She did poison us.'

'She explained what she did. She asked for forgiveness. Were you not there?'

'Why should we believe her?'

'Ach. There is no pleasing you. You dimwit.'

The mask was pulled off Joe's face, and a new one was put on him. He was aware of the smell of rubber with a faint hint of bleach.

'On the count of three. One... two... three.'

Joe closed his eyes as he was lifted off the ground. The toxins from the air he inhaled when the masks were swapped over had an immediate effect. Dysentery turned his guts to water.

'Oh god. He has shat himself.'

The six people carrying Joe above their heads staggered.

'Don't drop him.'

'You're okay. You're at the back.'

'Don't drop him,' a voice rang out.

The six men quietened.

By now, the pain in his lungs had decreased, and Joe was aware enough to be ashamed of defecating on himself.

'For god's sake, this guy stinks.'

'Just as well that we're wearing face masks,' someone else laughed.

'Where are we taking him?'

'The Chinese quarter. She said the Chinese had a spare double tent.'

'Who's gonna look after him?'

'What do you care? You were complaining about him stinking a moment ago.'

'Just wondering. That's all.'

'She said she was going to.'

'Humph.'

Joe felt the darkness coming on and succumbed to sleep.

***

'Charlie?'

The masked head turned, and the face behind the glass flushed.

'I read your resignation message.'

'But I didn't send it.'

'I was trying to figure out why you ran away.'

'I'm not who you think I am.'

Joe nodded. *'Ni hao ma*?'

Charlie bowed her head. 'I'm well, thank you. Your pronunciation isn't bad.'

'I'm sure it is.'

She looked into his eyes. 'I ran because I couldn't do what I was ordered to do anymore.'

Joe stayed silent.

'I was to seduce you and get all the information I could out of you.'

'But you didn't.'

She shook her head. 'My controllers will not be pleased with what I've done. They will want to know the secrets that the professor was finding.'

'You got them to carry me here?'

Charlie nodded.

'You saved me.' Joe tried to raise himself off the makeshift mattress.

'Don't get up. Any energy you feel you have will soon go.'

'I was making sure we were alone.'

Charlie moved over to the tent flap, peeked out, and then returned. She smiled. 'We're alone.'

'The secret'—Joe paused to formulate his words—'is that the ore from Planet 27 has healing properties. Limited healing properties only good for one time.'

Charlie's eyes were open wide.

'Now it's your turn. What's with you and Doctor Ogilvy?'

'She wanted to know what secrets the professor was keeping.'

'I thought she killed him because he knew about her and Nathan.'

'Her and Nathan? The professor's assistant, Nathan?'

Joe nodded.

'She thinks she's a spy. She thinks she's good at espionage.'

Joe raised his eyebrows.

'Nathan rebuffed her. He was in love with the professor.'

'What?'

'She probably killed Nathan to stop him from telling the professor. I think that was pointless. He told me about her advances and felt proud of himself that a woman of her class was attracted to him.'

'She killed the professor.'

'I guessed that was her. Again, pointless, as a dead man tells no secrets.'

'What were you two speaking about when all the intruders piled on site?'

'She demanded that I give her access to the labs.'

'But how? You wouldn't have been able to get in. I changed the security code.'

'I'm sorry. I had your computer bugged.'

'How? The computer is holographic.'

'The base unit isn't. I just had to add a connector between the computer and the network,' she said and saw that Joe was wilting. She took out a hypodermic needle and raised it to the light. She forced any air bubbles out and was only satisfied with the needle when a bead of fluid popped up at the point.

Joe's eyes went wide when he saw the needle. 'No, don't.'

'It's okay. It will help you recover from the toxins.' She plunged the needle through the material, into the side of his thigh and then stuck a band-aid on the minute hole she'd created in the fabric. 'That is to stop any more poisoned air into your system.'

'There's one thing I don't understand.'

'What's that?'

'Why was there a Greenpeace symbol painted on the outside of the underground labs?'

'That made me wonder too. The site director told me to paint that. Don't ask me why. I don't know.'

Joe's brows were furrowed.

'Don't worry about it now. It's time for you to relax and recover. I've got some fences to mend with my controller. Thanks for the information, Joe. You didn't have to tell me, but I'm glad you did.'

Joe nodded and closed his eyes as Charlie darted out of the tent.

***

He opened his eyes, alerted by someone outside the tent.

'What about here, Trev?'

'What's the ground like?'

'It seems soft there. Chuck me the shovel, will you?'

'Be quiet about it. You never know what type of sensors they have at this site.'

'You worry too much.'

'Aye, but that is what has saved my skin more often than nought.'

Joe raised his wrist and saw the air sensor was showing green. Taking his mask off, he got a whiff of his faeces.

I stink.

'What are you two doing?' Joe recognised Charlie's voice.

'Piss off.'

'Who are you, anyway?'

'My name is Charlie. What are your names?'

'Charlie? The poisoner Charlie?'

'You could call me that, although I did apologise to everyone here.'

'Sorry, Charlie. We don't mean to piss you off... I mean annoy you.'

'Yeah, we only want to see what is going on in there.'

'Do you happen to know if they have motion sensors on the fence?'

'No sensors, but the inside of the fence line is walked once a day, every day. So, you'll have to cover your tracks.'

'Thanks, Charlie.'

Charlie lifted the flap and entered the tent carrying a large bucket of water. 'I thought you could do with a wash.' She pulled a face.

'Yeah, sorry about that.'

'No need to apologise. I understand. You didn't have any control of what happened.' Charlie put an arm under his back and helped him sit up. 'Let's get you cleaned up.'

'I can do it myself, thanks.'

Charlie smiled. 'Go on then. Let's see how long you last.'

Joe untied the fastenings of the top half of his safety suit. He breathed heavily.

'Here, let me help you.'

'I've got this.' Joe grimaced and pulled the safety suit over his head. He let it drop to one side, and he wobbled.

'Lightheaded, are we?'

'Humph.' He shimmied out of his safety suit trousers and Y-fronts in one go, and that's when the stench hit him. 'Oh, for the love of...' His stomach rolled over in protest.

'Here, let me take those from you. There is a fire going in the centre of the camp. Best place for them.' Charlie stood up.

'Will they burn?'

'Of course. They're lined with charcoal, after all.' She pushed aside the tent flap and held the soiled clothing out in front of her.

Joe managed to get to his feet. He cupped his hands and threw water over himself. Grabbing a nearby towel, he alternately drenched himself and wiped himself dry until he was satisfied that he was as clean as he could get given the circumstances.

Charlie wolf-whistled at the entrance to the tent.

Joe wobbled on his feet. 'I think I've tired myself out.' He fell onto the ground, still naked.

Charlie lifted him back onto his bed.

'Don't get any ideas, Lieutenant,' Joe whispered before his eyes closed and he passed out.

Charlie gave a small laugh before covering him with a thin blanket.

***

When Joe awoke, he was once again alone in the tent, but he felt more human.

How long have I been out of it?

Shovels hitting the ground sounded out just outside his tent.

'Shhh. Someone is coming.'

'Don't "shhh" me.'

'Someone is coming. Quick, cover this up.'

It went quiet again, and then he heard footsteps. Jameson was still undertaking his duties seriously. Even with Major Wolfe, his superior, no doubt reported as missing, Jameson was walking the fence line. Joe thought seriously about calling out to attract Jameson's attention, but the fact was that he had no idea whether he was safer outside the fence than on the inside.

'He's gone. Come on, you lazy turd.'

'Who are you calling lazy?

Both men sniggered and resumed digging.

Some of the soil hit the outside of his tent and slid down the side panel.

'Hey, watch out,' Joe shouted, more reacting to the surprise than being annoyed.

'Sorry, buddy.'

'Yeah, sorry, mate.'

Joe felt his stomach before it growled in annoyance at being so empty for so long. He looked around and saw a tin of food, and nearby was the tin opener.

'Don't mind if I do.'

His luck was in as the tin contained peaches in thick, sweet syrup.

Charlie entered the tent frowning.

'What's up, Lieutenant?'

'No need to call me that anymore. I think my cover is blown after all these years. Plus, I'm on the move.'

'What?'

'Yeah, my controllers were pleased with that information you gave me, and they've decided that there is no point in me staying here any longer. With me being either discovered as a mole or a deserter, I'm not in a good position for any further secret-gathering. Plus, they think that there are no more secrets for me to obtain.'

'When are you going?'

'Now is as good a time as any.'

'What about me?'

Charlie's eyebrows furrowed. 'What about you? You don't expect me to take you with me, do you?'

'No, but... Who is going to look after me?'

'It's been three days since you got air poisoned. You're recovering well. I shall leave you the tent, some rations, and water. I only need to take my rucksack.' Charlie nodded to a bulbous rucksack in the corner.

'Please stay. I'm sure we can sort it all out.'

Charlie shook her head. 'You've got a battle on your hands with Doctor Ogilvy if you're thinking of going back in there. Anyway, there are too many questions I don't want to answer and too many crimes that she can pin on me for me to stick around for.'

'And me. She has already blamed me for all sorts of crap.'

'Well, goodbye it is then, Joe.' Charlie bent over and kissed him fully on the lips.

When Joe opened his eyes after the kiss, he realised she'd gone—no tears or prolonged farewell. Lieutenant Charlie Fowler had left for good.

'You okay in there, buddy?'

'What are you getting involved in now, Trev?'

'She left with tears streaming down her face. Something has happened. I wanna make sure he's okay.'

'You're just a nosy bastard.'

'Hey, less of the nosy.' Trev chuckled and pushed up the tent flap. 'You okay, buddy?'

Joe sat up. 'I'm a lot better, thanks.'

'Cool. What's your name? I'm Tommy.'

'I'm Joe. I thought your name was Trev.'

'That's just in case one of the guards hears us. We want to make it difficult for them every step of the way.'

Joe nodded, grinning.

'This is Mally,' Tommy said as his pal popped his head under the tent flap, peering in.

'What did you do to Charlie to upset her?' Tommy asked.

'Me? Nothing. She had to leave.'

'You better go after her and make it up to her. She's a looker.'

'Yeah, probably an eight or a nine.'

'I'd say a nine and a half.'

'Your standards are too low. She's at most an eight and a half.'

Both Tommy and Mally carried on bickering playfully as if they were an old married couple. Joe relaxed and felt at ease more than he had for a very long time. He only half-listened to their random conversation and was caught off guard when they stopped and stared at him.

'Well?' Tommy demanded

'What?' Joe stared back at him.

'What did you do before all this went down?'

Joe looked wistfully into the distance. 'I used to be a tracker in the army.'

'Cool,' Mally said, nodding.

'That is awesome. But you don't look that old. You couldn't have been in long. What are you, twenty-five, twenty-six?'

'I think I must be about thirty or maybe thirty-one.'

Tommy and Mally looked at each other and burst out laughing. 'You don't know how old you are? What are you, senile?'

'Guys, it's been a helluva journey recently.'

'That's for sure,' Tommy agreed.

'Yeah,' Mally said, nodding.

Joe looked around the inside of the tent and frowned.

'What's up, Joe the tracker?' Tommy asked, spotting that Joe looked anxious.

'Umm. It isn't very comfortable. I have no clothes, and she burnt my safety suit.'

'She's a bitch,' Tommy said, shaking his head.

'Yeah, I never liked her. Why would she be so heartless, nicking all your clothes?'

'And burning your suit! That's pure evil.'

Joe laughed. Tommy and Mally looked bemused.

'So, what's the joke?'

'We like a good laugh. Go on, tell us.'

Joe smiled. 'She didn't steal my clothes. She saved my life. I only came wearing my safety suit, and it was better off on the fire after I'd used it.'

'You're a right pillock then.'

'What's a pillock?'

'An idiot. You're just plain daft. Why come to stay with a bird like Charlie only in a safety suit?'

Joe shook his head, struggling to keep up with their banter. 'Can either of you guys help me out?'

Tommy and Mally looked at each other.

'I could give you a T-shirt,' offered Tommy.

'Not your Bob Dylan shirt? That's your favourite. It's a classic.'

Tommy nodded. 'I see it as helping a man out after the love of his life left him without any clothes.'

'In that case, I have a pair of denim shorts that I will donate to the cause.'

Joe was overcome. 'Thank you, guys. It means so much.'

'Hey, don't get all gooey on us, pal,' said Mally. 'It's not like I'm giving you a pair of my favourite grundies.'

'Grundies?'

'Grundies. Undies. Underwear. Boxers. Y-fronts.'

'Yeah, you'll have to go commando.'

Joe stifled a laugh and was thankful that although Tommy and Mally weren't the same height as he was, they were both thickset and broader than him.

Fingers crossed, their spare clothes will fit me.

'So where have you come from to serenade Charlie?' Mally asked Joe.

'I didn't...' Joe decided it wasn't worth the energy of trying to correct Tommy and Mally from their concocted storyline of the reason for his current situation. 'I was thrown off site.'

'Woah. Seriously?' Tommy's eyes went wide.

'You can tell us how to break in without getting caught, then.' Mally's eyes flashed, and he grinned.

Joe considered the situation. *Do I owe them any loyalty?* He remembered Jameson, the doctor, and the head of engineering. *Would they understand? Do they care that I'm missing?*

'So, what did you do on the site? Were you a guard or an engineer?'

'I was in the security team.'

Tommy and Mally nodded.

'So, you know how to get in?'

Joe thought about the site and remembered the back gate. *Will Jameson know how to change the security codes? Will they have thought about that? For all I know, Doctor Ogilvy may have told them I was dead... out walking in the worst poisoned air levels with an inferior face mask.*

'I may know a way. But why do you want to be on the site anyway? What are you gonna do on there if I help you in?'

Tommy grinned and nudged Mally. 'Go on, tell him.'

'We want to be the first-ever space stowaways,' Mally said, staring at Joe.

Joe thought about telling them that he'd been a stowaway but looking at them, he didn't want to shatter their dreams. He nodded thoughtfully.

'That is truly a worthy goal.'

'See, I told you. This guy knows his stuff,' Mally said, boxing Tommy on the shoulder. 'He gets us.'

Tommy stared at him and waited for any joke or laughter to erupt from Joe. Joe stared back equally as seriously looking. Tommy nodded and beamed. 'You are a pal.'

'Good enough for your favourite Bob Dylan T-shirt?' Joe quipped.

'Ha. Yes. The Bob Dylan T-shirt is my second favourite. The Queen T-shirt is my best.'

'Why do you like vintage designs like those? They're ancient.'

'Did you ever listen to their music?'

'Now you're gonna tell me about David Bowie,' Mally said, rolling his eyes.

Joe relaxed back down again and relaxed once more. The banter reminded him of the good times he'd had while in the army. Although he was a loner at the time, he'd always listened in to the other soldiers' bantering. They'd left him alone, knowing that he was a tracker. He knew how to hunt anything and anyone. To them, it was magic, and he was the sorcerer.

'I'll get my spare shorts,' Mally said, breaking Joe's dream.

'And I'll get my T-shirt.'

No sooner had they darted out of the tent than they were back with clothes. To Joe, it was a veritable treasure.

'I brought my flip-flops. I never wear them, so you can have them.'

'And I brought a spare pair of socks. They aren't made of polyester, so they'll absorb water if you get them wet. Wool. Some people swear by it, but I'm not one of them. Give me bamboo or polyester any day.'

'Say, how about we ask everybody around for clothes for Joe?' Mally turned to Tommy.

'Yeah, and if anyone has a spare suit?' Tommy said nodding.

Joe held up his hands.

'I thank you both for your generosity. But it's best that the less said about me, the better. My boss either thinks I'm dead or AWOL.'

'But...'

Joe shook his head. 'If word gets back to the guards, then they'll come for me. And if they do, I don't know what will happen to me.'

'But Joe'—Tommy smiled—'they all know about you being here. They haven't said a word about you.'

'Yeah, Charlie made them promise,' Mally added. 'She was a keeper. You shouldn't have kicked her out for burning your suit.'

'We loved her. Truly thought she was mad to shack up with you.'

Joe laughed.

'So, it's settled then. We'll get some spare clothes.'

'We'll put the word out.'

'On the QT, though. As you requested.'

Joe grinned. *These guys are a tonic.* 'I'll get you on site without getting shot at.'

Tommy was already out of the tent, and Mally turned around at the flap. 'We'll hold you to that.'

***

A heap of assorted clothes was piled on top of his legs. Joe was wearing a T-shirt with a barely recognisable print of Bob Dylan on the front, a pair of Mally's old denim shorts, a pair of socks of indistinguishable colour, and bright yellow flip-flops.

Joe held up a promising pair of black trousers although, on closer inspection, he realised that they were several sizes too large around the waist.

'That's a shame.'

Tommy held out a leather belt. 'They'll work. Here.'

Mally held out a pair of mud-stained running shoes. 'UK size eleven, I'm guessing, would fit you.'

'I'm ever so thankful.'

'It was their way of saying thanks. You showed them around, and then they ran about the site.'

'Yeah, they're still so ashamed.'

Joe looked at them. 'Did you two run about with them?'

They shook their heads. 'No, that was the day before we arrived here,' Mally said.

'Unfortunately, nobody had a spare suit, and they said you got the only spare face mask.'

'That's okay, guys,' Joe said, looking up. 'I think I've got an idea about that anyway.'

He stood up and put on his new clothes. A thick woollen top finished his attire. He was bent over, tying up his shoelaces, as he heard Tommy and Mally whispering.

'Come on, guys. What is it?'

'You've recovered, haven't you, Joe?' Mally was the first to speak.

'And you promised to get us on site?'

'Without getting shot at,' Tommy quickly added.

'Yes.'

'What about tonight?'

Joe stood up and pursed his lips. *Is there any reason why not?* He shook his head.

Tommy and Mally saw Joe's head movement, and their shoulder slumped in resignation.

'Tonight is as good as any night,' Joe said, smiling.

Tommy and Mally pumped their fists in the air.

***

Joe followed them out and saw the sun setting in a glorious showing of colour. There wasn't a cloud in the sky. His face mask was hanging down his chest on a women's narrow pink belt that would have been too small for him anyway. He breathed in deeply and savoured the fresh air.

'Scotland is beautiful, isn't it?' Tommy whispered.

Mally and Joe nodded.

Floodlights clicked on and shocked the three men out of their reverie. The light stretched to the base of the fence and no further.

'Come on then,' Joe encouraged them. He set off walking westwards along the fence line.

Tommy and Mally had mercifully quietened down, and Joe no longer had to worry about their constant banter attracting unwanted attention from guards on any roving patrols.

After a few minutes, Joe had to pause their walk as a stitch caused a piercing pain through his guts.

'You shouldn't have eaten that whole tin of haggis,' Mally offered his opinion in a quiet voice.

'That is sacrilege, if you ask me,' Tommy added.

'It was tasty. Spicier than I expected. And I never would have thought haggis would be in a tin.'

'Welcome to apocalyptic Scotland,' Tommy said.

The three men fell silent again, all thinking about why they were there, as Joe set off once more, Tommy and Mally on his heels.

***

'Okay, you two stay back there out of the light, and I'll open the gate.' Joe stepped forwards on the lit ground until he stood at the security access pad.

He punched in the number he remembered and saw the light remained red. 'Damn,' he whispered under his breath. He punched in the code again.

'Damn.'

'What's happening?' asked Tommy. 'I thought you said you would get us inside.'

Joe shrugged. He looked up at the camera in frustration, then turned, ready to admit defeat.

The latch clicked, and the panel's light was green.

'Come on, guys,' he said, gesturing them over, relieved.

'Ya beauty,' Tommy said, already sprinting through the gap, closely followed by Mally.

'Thanks, Joe.'

'See ya laters.'

Joe smiled and closed the gate after himself as he stood once more on the site of Tower 17. He stood still for a moment, breathing in the air.

'No different smelling air here compared to the other side of the fence line,' he muttered to himself before moving off.

Before he reached the first building, Jameson and George Swift came running towards him.

'You're alive!' George said in a hushed tone.

'The site director told us some cock and bull story about you wandering out through the front gate and collapsing in the poisoned air pollution that was the worst ever. She told everyone that you'd died on the spot.'

'Obviously, I didn't.'

'Obviously.'

'What are we going to do with him, sir?' George asked Jameson.

'She made me Acting Head of Security,' Jameson said sheepishly.

'Don't worry. I'm not jealous,' Joe said, grinning before getting serious again. 'But I think you realise she is not to be trusted.'

George and Jameson nodded.

'So, what do you want to do about it?' Jameson asked.

'Did you change the code for the underground labs?' Joe looked at Jameson.

'No. I couldn't. For some reason, the computer kept refusing me access to that code.'

'I can hide out down there to start with while I think about what to do.'

'Tell him about tomorrow. He probably doesn't know who's coming.'

Joe turned from George to look at Jameson.

'We have a big VIP coming.'

'What, the Minister for Transport?' Joe asked.

'Bigger. The prime minister... And the head of Project Exodus.'

'The head of Global Project Exodus?' Joe asked.

George and Jameson nodded.

Joe rubbed his chin. 'Any idea what the weather is gonna be tomorrow?'

'I can ask the met office guy,' Jameson said, already turning to leave.

'I'll be in the labs,' Joe said.

'What can I do?' George asked.

'Whatever you're supposed to be doing. But thank you. It's good to see a friendly face here.'

'You do remember he tried to kill you,' Jameson said with a grin.

'That was a mistake. And the major knows it was.'

Joe nodded.

Chapter Twenty-Seven

Joe stood at the device with his belly rumbling. Its ping announced to the empty room that his meal was ready.

He looked at the imitation cheeseburger and fries, knowing it wasn't his healthiest of choices, but it was what he desired. He ate his first solid meal. He'd enjoyed the haggis in a tin but knew that it wasn't a complete meal by itself.

He wondered what Tommy and Mally were up to and whether he should have let them on site. Joe shook his head, banishing any potential self-recriminations. He finished his meal and took the cardboard plate over to the garbage bin.

What do they call it here? Oh, yeah. It's a rubbish bin.

He tapped the monitor, allowing the gallery to scroll through the different cameras. As the image of the front door appeared on screen, he saw someone enter the building and held his breath.

Jameson looked up at the screen and pushed his hood back before giving him a wink.

Joe exhaled loudly. He pressed a button. 'Jameson, I'm in the third lab on your left.' The Tannoy sent his words echoing through the corridors.

Jameson knocked and pushed the door to the lab open. He poked his head in and looked around before pushing the door wide.

'Come on in.'

Jameson sat on a stool next to Joe.

'So?'

'Samuel gave a depressing picture of the weather tomorrow.'

'Okay, any specifics?'

'Clouds are expected to roll in from the southwest, bringing in poisonous air from Glasgow. He said it was going to be just as bad if not worse than last week.'

'The week I was severely poisoned,' Joe muttered.

Jameson nodded.

'Has everyone got the newer face masks?'

'Yes. That was the only good thing about your disappearance. The site director made sure that everyone checked their face masks. If anyone had the old version, they had them replaced immediately.'

Joe nodded.

'What are you planning, sir?'

'Best you not know for your own sake,' Joe said with a smile. 'Just run me through the timeline tomorrow, would you?'

***

Joe opened the door and looked at all of the new and unused hazmat suits. The empty racking on his right, he guessed, had supplied the new guards, engineers, and technicians who were now working at Tower 17. He ran his hands down the suits, looking at the sizes marked at the top of each hanger. He stopped at Large, pursed his lips, and then continued before finally pulling out an Extra Large. He also grabbed the rope to attach to his face mask, as the last one had been removed due to being vomit-stained and had been burnt along with his previous suit.

Joe got back to the table and he looked at the half-eaten breakfast knowing that nerves would prevent him from enjoying a meal. The remains went straight into the rubbish bin, and Joe realised that he would have to get over his technology phobia to learn how to use the composting device before the remains of previous meals started to make their presence known again.

On went the trousers, and he pulled the drawstring at the waist tight. Then on went the oversized jacket. Joe pulled a glove onto his left hand and secured it over the end of the sleeve. He did the same with the right hand. He tightened the hood around his face before securing his face mask in place. Standing in front of the glass pod, he saw himself in the reflection and realised that he couldn't recognise his face. If Joe couldn't identify himself, he doubted if anyone else would recognise him.

Standing at the exit door, he breathed in deeply and pushed open the security door, allowing himself to be revealed to the morning light. Thankfully, nobody was in the vicinity to witness him leaving the underground building. Knowing that there being a roving patrol today was his ticket to going about the site unchecked and unrecognisable, he headed off in the right direction.

Jameson was walking between buildings and was cutting across his intended path.

This will be the first test.

The acting head of security spotted Joe and paused mid-stride.

Joe flung his arm up and saluted Jameson, aping the British way of saluting an officer.

Jameson responded in kind and continued on his way.

Joe breathed out in relief. *Test passed.* He looped around the site buildings to the perimeter fence and walked within touching distance of the wire.

My plan relies on timing and a bit of luck.

He thought about Dr Ogilvy and tried to be the devil's advocate, but with each angle he tried and each perspective he considered, Joe found no logical reason for why she'd acted the way she had.

Joe tapped his wrist and the sensor lit up, showing two orange bars lit out of ten. The panel also confirmed that he was on time. He breathed out, and some misting occurred on the inside of his mask.

Some things don't always improve when they're upgraded.

He heard the helicopter before seeing it. The aircraft was flying just in front of the poison clouds, and he realised that it was ahead of schedule. Joe increased his stride and headed directly to the designated helipad area. When the helicopter appeared over the tops of the trees, he recognised as one of the newest American Sikorsky models.

'Damn, I'm not going to make it.'

His stomach dropped as he saw the site director move forwards to welcome three figures who had exited the aircraft onto Scottish soil.

'Damn. I assumed she would wait in her office for them. Damn, I should have guessed.' Joe turned on the spot and headed to the office block which housed his office.

He tapped his arm, and the sensor showed six orange bars out of ten. On entering the office block, he thought twice about hiding out in his old office and realised it was probably being used by Jameson nowadays. So, he went along to see if Samuel was in his office and up for seeing a friendly ghost.

Joe stepped into the met office and closed the door softly behind him as Samuel looked up.

'Can I help you? Who are you?'

Joe pulled his hood back and removed his face mask.

'Major Wolfe!' Samuel gasped, wide-eyed. 'We were told you'd died.'

Joe held a finger up to his mouth, and Samuel's voice lowered instantly.

'Where have you been? How are you?'

Joe stepped alongside Samuel and whispered in his ear. 'The site director lied about me. She wanted me out of the picture as things are going on here that aren't great, Samuel.'

Samuel's eyes widened further.

'Do you trust me, Samuel?'

Samuel nodded slowly. 'I've always felt there was something dodgy about Doctor Ogilvy. What is she up to?'

'I don't know exactly. But my guess is something very dodgy indeed. Can I stay in here and think of what to do next?'

Samuel nodded furiously, his face reddening with excitement.

Joe stepped next to the door and pressed his ear to the gap.

'Prime Minister, it's so nice to see you again. It must be several years since we met at the UK Exodus planning meeting. And sir, I don't think we've met before. I know you by reputation. I'm honoured that you're here visiting Tower 17.'

The two men didn't reply, not that Joe could hear anyway.

'Please come into my office.'

'We've come for answers, Doctor Ogilvy,' said the head of the Global Exodus project in a rich, deep baritone.

'Oh?'

'Yes. We've received word that not all aspects of your site, Ogilvy, are running smoothly. Some concerning news that, if brought to the public's attention and that of reporters, would bring Project Exodus into disrepute. Just as public opinion on the validity of the project is hanging in the balance, we have to come here and deal with you.' The prime minister sounded distinctly cold and formal.

'What news? What information?' Dr Ogilvy's voice was pitched higher than Joe had ever heard before.

'Where is your head of research?'

'Who has been talking to you?'

'Where is your head of research?'

'What?'

'Do you not understand English?' the prime minister asked icily.

'Sir? Prime Minister. There must be a big mistake.'

'Is your head of research alive?'

Doctor Ogilvy didn't respond.

'Where is the assistant to your head of research, Doctor?'

'But... You don't need to see him.' Doctor Ogilvy was on the back foot.

'Come to mention it... where is your head of security?'

'Yes, where is Major Wolfe?'

'Major Wolfe died last week,' she said, managing to get some composure back.

'That is very convenient, isn't it?'

'What do you mean?' Her voice was high-pitched again.

'The one person we trust to give a fair and true report on what has been going on at the site of Tower 17, which would probably show you in a bad way, is himself dead?'

'Yes, that is three too many deaths at this site, Doctor Ogilvy. Care to explain yourself?'

'It was that Major Wolfe. It was all his fault,' she hissed.

'So very convenient blaming someone dead who cannot defend himself.'

Joe opened the main office door and took a few steps to stand at the open entrance to the site director's office.

'Prime Minister and your Highness, I am Major Wolfe,' Joe said in a calm voice, looking at the Prime Minister for the United Kingdom and Prince Al Atarique of Oman—the current head of the Global Exodus Project.

'You are alive, Major Wolfe,' intoned the prince.

'I'm alive,' Joe confirmed.

'I didn't kill them,' the site director blurted.

Joe, the prince, and the prime minister turned to face Dr Ogilvy.

'Kill who?' The Prime Minister asked.

'Nathan. You know he laughed at me, don't you? I offered to sleep with him,' Helen Ogilvy said, snivelling. 'I only wanted the research. He laughed at me.' Her eyes flashed with the anger of a woman scorned. 'He was nothing. Just a youngster in the way of the truth. He had to go. He would have told the professor.'

'You stabbed him, didn't you, Helen?' Joe asked quietly.

Tears were running down her face. She sniffled and nodded slowly. 'I had to, you understand. He laughed at me. At *me*!'

The prime minister whispered in Joe's ear. 'Have you got an armed guard?'

'Wait, sir. I think there may be more to listen to.' Joe nodded at the woman in front of them, who was crying.

'He was going to expose me. I saw him looking at Lieutenant Fowler. He was gonna tell that bitch.'

'What did the professor do? He was suffering in the medical ward. Why him?'

'He wouldn't share his research. It could have changed the world. My daughter. She shouldn't have to live in a world like this. And he...

he wouldn't tell anyone what he'd found out. He was keeping it to himself.'

The prime minister was about to call for a guard, but Joe held his arm to hold on a moment more.

'The Minister for Transport agreed. We should have access to all the research. But that professor looked at me like I was scum. The minister told me I was in charge. I was responsible for everything at Tower 17. I was responsible for who lived and who died.' Helen Ogilvie looked around the room and the three men. Heartache, pain, and bitterness battled across her face, rising from the depths of her soul. Hate flourished amongst the pain. 'So, I chose to end his suffering.' She looked up again at Joe. 'I killed him because he was selfish.'

'That is sufficient for your court of law, I believe,' the Omani prince said.

'Major?'

Joe stood, shocked to silence.

'Major!' The prime minister said loudly.

'Yes, sir.' Joe stepped out into the corridor and saw a group of people, white-faced with mouths agape. Despite the end of the corridor being filled, you could hear a pin drop. Standing at the head of the group was Jameson.

'An armed guard, please, Jameson.'

Two armed guards in full hazmat suits waited to enter the site director's office as the prime minister and the head of the Global Exodus Project stepped into the corridor and out of the way of what was going to happen next.

'Sir?' the tallest armed guard asked the prime minister, who nodded towards Joe. 'Sir?' he asked again, this time of Joe.

'Take Doctor Ogilvie to the police station in Perth. I shall phone them and let them know you're on your way.'

Joe watched Helen Ogilvie remove her wedding ring and place it on the desk before putting on rubber gloves. She looked up at Joe. 'Make sure my girl is looked after, Joe, will you?'

Joe saw how calm she was after all the emotions and torment had spewed out of her. 'I will.'

'Please don't let her be affected by me or anything I've done.'

Joe nodded, watching a murderer calmly and matter-of-factly check that her gloves, hazmat suit, and face mask were all fitting correctly.

The guard attached a pair of restrainers to the doctor's wrists and guided her out into the corridor and down to the exit. The group of onlookers parted to make way and then disappeared back to where they'd come from.

Prince Al Atarique grabbed Joe's hands. 'We owe you a debt of gratitude, Major Wolfe.'

The prime minister nodded. 'Thank you for alerting us to this... situation. We heard that you almost died.'

Joe nodded. 'If it weren't for Lieutenant Fowler, I would have.'

'Where is she?' the prince asked.

'I understand her handlers in Beijing have recalled her.'

The prime minister and prince nodded, apparently neither being surprised by the information.

'What can we do for you? As a sign of our gratitude?' the prince asked.

'Well'—Joe rubbed his chin—'we could do with a new site director.'

'Of course, of course,' the prime minister agreed.

'But this time, someone who is a bit more stable.'

The prime minister smiled. 'That we can do.'

***

Prince Al Atarique's bodyguard appeared in the doorway. 'Sir, that is the helicopter warming up.'

The prince nodded and turned to Joe. 'Thank you again, Major.' He placed a thin golden card on the desk. 'Should you ever need to call in a favour.'

The prime minister shook Joe's hand, gloved surface to gloved surface. 'I believe you know how to keep this secret. Or as my teenage daughter would say—on the down low.'

Joe laughed, nodding, then cocked his head sideways.

'There is one thing though, sir.'

'What is that?'

'Neither of you asked me what the professor's research involved.'

The two men nodded but didn't answer his question.

The prime minister allowed the prince back out into the corridor first before turning to face Joe with a smile. 'So, you're going to ensure Ogilvie's daughter is taken care of?'

'Yeah. I promised.'

'Let's get our flight, Your Highness, shall we?'

Joe followed them down the corridor and saw Dr Wardle's head pop out of his office doorway.

'Doctor,' the prime minister said, nodding once.

Joe stared at the doctor, who flushed with embarrassment at being acknowledged by the prime minister.

Everyone in the corridor put on their face masks as the door to the outside world was opened and poisoned air seeped into the building. Joe raised his arm and saw the sensor instantly turn red. He tightened the straps to his face mask and followed the prince's bodyguard towards the helipad.

The prince, the prime minister, and the prince's bodyguard ducked as they walked under the speeding rotors and stepped up into the helicopter.

Joe breathed deeply and relaxed as the helicopter took off, growing smaller and smaller on the horizon until it was a mere dot.

Outside the office building, Jameson was waiting for Joe's return. 'Sir, the police have been on the phone. They have bad news.'

'Oh?'

'I think it's best if you speak to them directly.'

Joe closed his office door behind him.

'Computer, on.' He put his face mask on the desk and pushed back his hood before rifling his hand through his hair. 'Computer, return call to Perth police station.'

Joe's heart sank as soon as he saw the senior officer appear on his screen. He checked the rank on the man's shoulders and counted the three pips.

'Chief Inspector, I was speaking to your desk sergeant earlier today. What do I owe the pleasure?'

'Major Wolfe...'

'Please call me Joe.'

'Unfortunately, Major, this call is not informal. It's about Helen Ogilvie.'

Joe's mouth tightened into a thin line.

'I have the unfortunate task of informing you of her death.'

Joe's eyebrows raised, but he remained silent.

'She arrived at Perth unconscious and suffering from extreme air poisoning.' The chief inspector paused to gather his thoughts. 'Although we have yet to begin a full review of the case and interview all staff at every step of her journey, it's thought that she intentionally made a hole in her safety suit.'

'She committed suicide,' Joe whispered.

The chief inspector nodded. 'Was Helen Ogilvie under significant stress or mental strain before her journey to Perth police station?'

Joe sighed and looked down. 'You could say that. She'd admitted to murdering two members of staff up at the site of Tower 17.'

The chief inspector pursed his lips.

'She made the admissions in front of me, the prime minister, and the head of the Global Exodus Project. She was upset.'

'I see.'

'And she asked me to ensure her daughter was looked after.' His sentence tailed off.

'I'm considering cancelling the full review following what you've just told me—that is, of course, if you have no objection. If there is nothing to be gained by the review, it would save us valuable manpower when it's in high demand.'

Joe nodded. 'Robbing and looting still an issue, Chief Inspector?'

'You can call me Freddy, Joe,' the chief inspector said, nodding.

'I'm sorry to hear that.' Joe ran a hand through his hair. 'Yeah, no need to conduct a review. We both know what it will find... Are your guys okay? The ones who booked her in and looked after her?'

'Thanks for asking. Yes, they're seasoned veterans to the deaths by air poisoning.'

'Are there many? For them to be seasoned by.'

The chief inspector nodded. 'Unfortunately so. Many in this region alone. It seems to be a favoured suicide method.'

'You have many suicides?'

'Yes. In the towns and cities, many people are unable to cope with... their future.'

Joe nodded. 'I can understand if they haven't got the option to join Project Exodus.'

'Shall I advise the medical officer on duty that neither you nor your team have an objection to a finding of suicide.'

'Yeah. Thanks again, Freddy.'

'Joe,' the chief inspector said with a final nod.

He sat in his chair in the silence after such a busy day. *So, what do I do now?*

'Computer, message dashboard.'

It took two minutes to type out a message to the prime minister and the head of the Global Exodus Project. He typed 'Minister for Transport,' then deleted it after shaking his head.

Joe left his office and knocked on his deputy's door.

'Sir?' Jameson asked on opening the door.

'Did the chief inspector tell you about Doctor Ogilvie?'

'Yes, sir.'

'Please make sure you don't tell anyone before I address all staff.'

'You, sir?'

'Yeah, it will be my second action as Acting Site Director and Head of Security for Tower 17.'

Jameson's mouth dropped open, and it took a while before it closed.

Joe nodded and pursed his lips.

'If you don't mind me asking, sir, what was your first act as acting site director?'

'I notified the prime minister and the head of Global Exodus Project that my predecessor, Doctor Ogilvie, had passed away, and it was my recommendation that any investigation and/or any charges against her be dropped.'

'Why the hell should they do that?'

'For the safety and emotional well-being of her daughter.'

'Humph.'

Chapter Twenty-Eight

'Friends and colleagues,' Joe said, opening his arms. 'You are all here for me to give you some unfortunate news. Site Director Doctor Helen Ogilvie has died.' He paused, allowing everyone to absorb the news before carrying on. 'Following long conversations with both the Prime Minister and the head of Global Exodus Project, I have accepted the role of Acting Site Director until the new site director is appointed.'

Jameson nudged Joe.

'Unfortunately, Doctor Ogilvie received a lethal dose of poison air yesterday afternoon. Her safety suit had a hole in it, enabling toxins to be absorbed and inhaled.'

The large crowd of staff, who didn't include the guards on duty, began muttering all at once.

Jameson held his hands up. 'Hey, everyone. We understand it's devastating news, and we want everyone to check over their safety suits as soon as possible. You must be extra vigilant over the seals and quality of your safety suits every time you put them on.'

The majority of staff dashed away to check on their safety suits.

'What is your next act as site director, sir?' Jameson smiled.

'Breaking the news to Doctor Ogilvie's daughter.'

'I don't envy you that task. Boss, if you need anything, just let me know.'

Joe nodded. 'Keep on top of the security. I wouldn't want anybody to think that because of her passing, we're easy pickings.'

'Consider it done.'

Joe went back to his office and frowned. 'Computer, open Doctor Ogilvie's personnel record.'

'Insufficient access.'

'Computer, make a note on Doctor Ogilvie's record of her death as per the police record on file.'

'Notation confirmed.'

'Computer, make a record that the prime minister and the head of the Global Exodus Project have promoted me to acting site director.'

'Record confirmed.'

'Computer, open the late Doctor Ogilvie's personnel record.'

'Access granted, Site Director.'

Joe moved his eyes past each field that had no reference to the daughter. He tapped the next page and saw what he was looking for. But what he was looking for wasn't what he was expecting.

Kathryn Ogilvie.

Known as Kittie.

Age seventeen.

Joe scratched his head. *I was expecting her to be much younger. I only heard one side of the phone conversation.*

***

The drive to the private school was the quietest it could have been, considering George Swift had been asked to drive. George had been the only one on the team who wasn't on shift and knew how to drive on the left-hand side of the road.

'Where are we off to, sir?'

'I'm off to tell Doctor Ogilvie's daughter that her mother has died.'

'Sorry, sir. I shall leave you to your thoughts.'

Joe nodded appreciatively and returned to staring out the window.

When the sky was clear of toxic clouds, the Scottish countryside was magnificent. Trees, shrubs, and bushes on either side of the road appeared to thrive despite the weather. The truck was hitting a top speed of a hundred kilometres an hour on the road, and George seemed to be confident driving that fast on an unknown route.

They ascended a slope, and their stomachs lurched as the vehicle dropped quickly on the undulating surface.

'If it weren't for the fact we came from Tower 17, I wouldn't have guessed there was anything wrong with the Earth's atmosphere,' Joe whispered.

Out of the corner of his eye, Joe saw George nodding slowly but staring determinedly at the road ahead.

The first sign warned them to drive carefully, as there was a school nearby, and the one after instructed them that the entrance was on the right.

They drove slowly down the lane towards a magnificent stone building that must have been hundreds of years old. George parked to the left of an archway and killed the engine.

'Stay here, George.' Joe got out of the vehicle and went to the door marked **Reception**.

A grey-haired woman wearing a pair of half-moon glasses scowled at him as he entered her domain.

'I'm Major Wolfe.'

'You're expected, Major.' The woman pointed at a small camera on a tripod on the counter. 'Please stand in front of the camera for a security scan.'

Joe raised his eyebrows but complied.

A thin, horizontal red beam of light scanned his face and confirmed it had finished with a click.

'Please keep this on you at all times when on the campus and return it here when you leave. The head will be with you shortly,' the woman said, handing Joe a visitor's badge, pointing at a chair in the corner.

Joe sat down only to hear the door chime as a large, ebullient man in an academic gown stood before him.

'Major Wolfe, I assume?'

'Yes, sir.' The deferential word came out automatically.

'Follow me.' He left the reception as quickly as he'd arrived, and Joe stepped quickly to catch him up.

'It's an impressive place you have here.'

The head nodded. 'You're here about Kittie Ogilvie?'

'Yes, sir.'

'Bad news, is it?'

'How could you tell?'

'Normally, we expect one of the parents to collect Kittie at the end of term.'

'Oh, I haven't come to collect her. Only to tell her about her mother.'

'Shhh!' A finger to the man's mouth silenced Joe immediately. 'Walls have ears.'

Joe saw a couple of children's heads popping out of doorways as they continued their forced march to goodness knew where.

'Where are we going?'

'The exam centre. It's Kittie's last exam today.' The headmaster checked his watch without slowing his stride. 'Five minutes ago. Let us hope she hasn't disappeared on us again.'

'Again?'

'Some headstrong students like Kittie sometimes go for a walk to clear their heads after sitting their exams. Nothing to worry about. I'm sure we'll find her regardless of where she is.' The headmaster glanced at Joe's shoulder. 'Major, eh? No insignia showing.'

'Ex-army tracker in a past career. Currently Acting Site Director of Tower 17.'

'Acting Site Director.' He nodded slowly. 'She has died then, has she?' he asked quietly.

Joe nodded.

'Air poisoning?'

He nodded again. 'How...'

'Your Samuel provides all meteorological updates for us. We would have been scuppered on numerous occasions without his accurate forecasts.' An imperious finger extended out from under the man's gown. 'There she is.' He raised his voice to call, 'Miss Ogilvie, over here please.'

Kittie Ogilvie was the spitting image of her mother, except for the fact she was in her late teens. Wearing a short skirt that made the headmaster pull a face and let out a tut-tut, she exuded the vibrancy of youth and the twinkle in her eyes that indicated she knew she was stunningly beautiful. She wore a green tweed jacket buttoned over a brilliant white blouse, and her lustrous, dark hair bounced on her shoulders as she walked towards them.

Joe could feel her eyes scanning him as if she were determining that he was from her mother's workplace.

'Mummy has sent one of her staff to collect me.'

Joe's eyebrows arched, and she smiled at his reaction.

'Let's go into the office,' the headmaster said, indicating the nearest building as a crowd of students walked past them, staring and pointing.

Joe saw Kittie blush and scowl at the unwanted attention of her peers.

'Kittie, why don't you sit down? The major here has something he needs to tell you.'

Joe saw the break in her confidence, and her mouth trembled.

'What's happened to her?'

'I'm sorry to say that your mother passed away yesterday.'

The air in the office stilled.

Kittie nodded slowly.

'Kittie, do you want the housemistress to talk to?'

'No, Headmaster, thank you. Oh, and please call me Kathryn from now on. My mother called me Kittie, and I always hated it.'

The headmaster, who had probably gone through similar conversations over the years, merely nodded. 'If you're packed, bring your luggage down to reception, and the major will take you.'

Kathryn promptly left the office without another word.

'I haven't come here to collect her.'

'You aren't abandoning her, sir.'

'Abandoning her?'

'You are the nearest thing... Kathryn has to be a next of kin. I hope you're taking your duties seriously, Major.'

***

Joe sat in the front passenger seat, stunned.

'Shall we go, sir?'

Joe shook his head.

'What are we waiting for, sir?' George asked just as the back door was opened and a large suitcase was flung in.

'Her.'

George glimpsed a young woman climb into the vehicle and sit directly behind him.

'Now we can go. Oh, and eyes on the road, George.'

Joe saw the glimmer of a smile on Kathryn's face and wondered at the type of relationship she'd had with her mother. His thoughts meandered in and around the situation he found himself in on the journey back to the site, and he only half appreciated the countryside on the return leg.

'So, Major, sir,' Kathryn said calmly as George held open the door for her. 'When can I start?'

'Start what?'

'My job here.'

'I don't understand. You have a job here?'

'Yes, didn't my mother tell you? As soon as I finished my exams, I was to start employment here at Tower 17.'

'Umm, what job did she promise you?'

'Assistant to the assistant to the head of research.'

'Ah, about that. I'll need to talk to you about recent goings on.'

***

The guards on duty lowered their weapons and stepped aside to let their vehicle through. Joe had initially been against armed sentries but ever since the event, with the overwhelming numbers of intruders getting on site, he'd relented. Jameson, on the other hand, had cajoled, persuaded, and made jokes about him being a pacifist until he agreed to arm his team. The armoury had been well stocked when it was opened. Those who designed the layout of the site had anticipated the need for an armed force to ensure the security of Tower 17.

Jameson was waiting for him outside of the office building as Joe walked over from the car parking area. Behind him followed Kathryn, who was looking at everything, intent on missing none of it. George carried the suitcase and a rucksack for Miss Ogilvie, and Joe guessed that he was already becoming smitten by the teenager.

'Sir, I need to speak to you,' Jameson said, looking over Joe's shoulder and seeing Kathryn. 'Who is she?'

'This is Kathryn Ogilvie and Kathryn, this is Lieutenant Jameson. My deputy.'

'A deputy. Are you like the sheriff around here, Major?'

Jameson grinned and looked at Joe, who rolled his eyes.

'Lieutenant, Kathryn has been promised employment as the assistant to the assistant to the head of research.'

'But that means...'

'Yes. I have yet to brief Miss Ogilvie on that department being closed for the foreseeable future.'

Jameson closed his mouth and nodded, instantly recognising another topic of conversation not to be discussed with the daughter of the deceased.

'I shall take Miss Ogilvie to the doctor to have an arrival medical, and I'll be right back.'

'But I'm fine,' Kathryn objected. 'I don't need a medical.'

'Tell that to the doctor, Miss Ogilvie. Every new member of staff is required to undergo a thorough medical before starting their job.'

'Okay, as you put it that way, sir,' she said, overemphasising the word 'sir.'

***

'Doctor, I have a new patient for you. She's a new member of the team. She goes by the name of Kathryn Ogilvie. A new starter medical, if you will.'

Dr Wardle raised his eyebrows but didn't say a word. He caught Joe's eyes and nodded once.

Joe reached the door to Jameson's office and knew what his deputy wanted to speak to him about. He could see Tommy and Mally lounging about in the background.

'So, Jameson, what is on your mind?'

'I found this pair of idiots hiding behind the base of the tower. They said they knew you. When I was investigating why they were there, they informed me that you'd hired them. For what, God only knows.'

Tommy and Mally grinned at Joe, and Mally gave a conspiratorial wink.

Joe pursed his lips. 'It's true they're on site because of me. I thought they were the right young men for the task.'

'Which task is this, sir?'

'I've tasked them with seeing if they can get onto the top level of the tower. In addition to accessing the tower, once the shuttle takes off tomorrow, their objective is to attempt to stow away on board.'

Jameson suddenly smiled. 'That is good thinking, sir. They can identify any weaknesses in our security plans. Right guys, come with me. Let's get you into new hazmat suits, and I think we can improve upon the face masks that you currently have.'

'Thanks, sir,' Tommy said, emphasising the word 'sir,' indicating that they hadn't realised he was in charge of the security department.

Joe gave Mally a wink when he walked past. Joe was walking past the communications room and glanced in to see a young woman working the comms.

'It's Emma, isn't it?'

'Yes, sir,' she answered, starting to colour with embarrassment.

'When does your shift finish? I may need your assistance.'

'George is taking over from me in five, sir. What can I help you with?'

'George? George Swift is taking over from you?'

'Yes, sir. He volunteered for a communications duty tasking. He has picked everything up quickly.'

Joe nodded. 'Erm. We have a new starter, Kathryn Ogilvie. Yes, the daughter of Doctor Helen Ogilvie. She'll be starting her job at Tower 17 tomorrow. Will you be able to show her around when she finishes with the doctor? She's having her arrival medical.'

'Of course, sir. It would be my pleasure.' Emma smiled. 'Does she know?' she asked quietly.

'Yeah, she knows that her mother died due to air poisoning yesterday. But nothing else.'

'Thank you, sir.'

Chapter Twenty-Nine

It was the day of the shuttle climbing the tower, and Joe lay in bed wide awake, waiting for the alarm to tell him it was time to get out of bed. He'd considered going into his office early, but that would have been a change of location, not a change of state.

Finally, the longest hours he'd ever experienced in his life passed, and the alarm rang out not a moment too soon. He forced himself to take his time getting ready, and he drew out his morning shave in an attempt to battle with his impatience. He made himself do an extra five push-ups, still trying to win his mind over impatience. However, when he entered the office block, he was relieved that he wasn't the first to arrive. A small group stood at the entrance to Samuel's office.

'Well, Samuel?'

'As I was saying to everyone here, sir, I'm waiting for my system to reboot.'

'Did something go wrong?'

Samuel shook his head, smiling. 'No, I always reboot the machine at the beginning of a significant day.'

His face lit up, reflecting light from the monitor. Samuel casually tapped the keyboard and paused for a moment. 'Mmm, mmm.'

'Well?' Jameson couldn't hold it in any longer. 'What is the day going to be like?'

Samuel looked at the group. 'You'll be pleased to know that the forecast is dry, calm, and clear for the next twelve to twenty-four hours. Now be gone, all of you. I have to let everyone know.'

Joe clapped him on the shoulder. 'Well done, Samuel.'

'Sir?'

Joe turned and saw Emma with Kathryn Ogilvie in tow.

'Yes, how can I help you, Emma?'

'I was wondering if Kathryn and I could watch the start of the shuttle climb. And as the research department is closed for the foreseeable, Kathryn could shadow me on comms today?'

Joe looked at Kathryn and then back at Emma. 'Of course. But keep a walkie-talkie on at all times. Just in case.'

Emma and Kathryn held up their walkie-talkies. 'Thanks, sir.'

***

Joe walked over and stood beside Jameson. Everyone held their breath as the end wall of the engineering hangar opened up. The bottom of the massive panel inched outwards, teasing all watchers with its lack of speed. The nose of the space shuttle couldn't wait for the giant door to finish its journey and edged out of the darkness on the transporter platform.

Again, Joe was overawed by the size of the ship that crept out of the hangar on the horizontal section of its journey.

'What are those?' Jameson pointed at a mountain of silver-coloured tubes.

'Those, I believe, are the suspension pods.' Joe watched as a tented frame expanded out over the pods, hiding them from view.

The roar of engines snapped them out of their reverie as the Project Exodus medical team arrived in a fleet of buses. The team was well-practised, and as soon as they disembarked, the group of white safety-suited professionals entered the newly tented area, ready for their shift.

No sooner had the buses parked away from the tent than a squadron of large passenger helicopters circled the site. One by one, the helicopters dropped down. They gently landed on the helipad of Tower 17, only to rise back up again after their cargo of passengers ran out from under the rotating blades towards the entrance to the Project Exodus medical tent.

The queue of well-dressed passengers was already being processed as they entered the tent, each helicopter rising back into the air to join the other circling aircraft.

'That can't be all of them, can it?' Jameson whispered.

Joe cocked his head to one side. 'Wait for it.' He saw the first of many luxury buses drive on site and swing around to deposit its passengers at the door to the tent, only to leave and be instantly replaced by another luxury bus and another group of passengers.

'This will take some time, won't it?' Jameson stared at Joe, looking bored already.

'Come on. Let's go for a walk around the site.'

Joe and Jameson stopped at one side of the main gate to watch the organised chaos. Each luxury bus would stop, and a guard would jump aboard to verify that the occupants were as expected, ticking them off the digital list as having arrived. Then the guard would go through the same process less than a minute later. Each new busload would have to wait until an empty vehicle passed, and as the empty vehicle reached the widening of the road it, too, would be passed by a new full bus. All buses moved in a disjointed yet precise military formation, impressive to witness.

'Come on, ' Jameson said, coaxing Joe away from being mesmerised.

They walked along the inside of the perimeter fence, and Joe remembered meeting Tommy and Mally for the first time.

'What are you grinning about, sir?' Jameson eyed the acting site director with suspicion.

'I remember meeting you for the first time. It seems like a lifetime ago.'

Jameson nodded. 'Another planet, and you've filled that time with adventures.'

'Humph.'

'Not all of them would have been fun, mind you,' Jameson added with a grin. 'But remember what they say. What doesn't kill you makes you stronger.'

Joe laughed. 'What does fighting off a wolf, almost dying from dehydration, getting beaten to a pulp, stabbed, shot, poisoned twice, and ending up as acting site director do to me then?'

'That should make you one of the world's strongest men,' Jameson said, joining in with Joe, laughing.

Joe's laughter dried up as he saw some people on the other side of the fence look at them quizzically.

'Have you considered offering them a site visit today?' Jameson asked.

'That would be opening us up from organised chaos to potential carnage.'

Jameson pointed towards the farm of solar panels. 'What's that?'

'That is the solar farm.'

'Not those, but that?'

Joe followed the direction of Jameson's finger and saw freshly turned earth.

'Bastards,' Jameson breathed.

Joe looked around and made some mental calculations. 'Are you up for a jog?'

'What? The nearest gate must be—'

'The back gate,' Joe finished his sentence. 'If we cut straight across from here, it will be half the distance.'

'If you say so, sir.' Jameson burst into a run. 'Last one there buys a round of drinks.'

Joe grinned and chased after him.

It didn't take long for Joe to catch up to Jameson, as Joe's daily runs proved his fitness level was superior to that of his subordinate.

'Come on, youngster,' Joe hissed at Jameson even though Jameson looked twenty years older than him.

Jameson gritted his teeth and matched Joe pace for pace to the edge of the solar farm. Joe waved him to stop, realising that whoever had dug the ground might still be in the vicinity. He instructed Jameson to circle anticlockwise while he went around the left-hand side.

After a few minutes, Joe saw where someone had cut through the fencing. The ground was too dry to see any footprints, yet not dusty enough to reveal any other evidence of someone passing by. He continued to follow the fence line, looking down the row of solar panels at every gap. Joe turned as he reached the far corner and stopped when he arrived at a metal shed. Although a padlock secured the door, he saw bright marks on it, indicating that someone had attempted to gain entry.

Jameson walked over. 'Didn't see anyone. Not a thing.'

Joe pointed at the padlock. 'At least we know nobody got in here.'

'Humph.'

'Come on, let's see what they got up to digging.'

***

When they reached the pile of freshly dug earth, Joe shook his head. The pipe housing the electric cable had been uncovered and, just like the padlock, there were scratches, evidence that the perpetrator had once again been unable to get through.

'Just as well,' Jameson remarked, eyeing the pipe.

Joe looked at him.

'The person would have probably electrocuted themselves, and we would be looking at charred remains if they had.'

'You got your walkie-talkie? Get an engineer out to patch the fence up, will you?'

'Comms, this is Jameson, over.'

'Jameson, this is comms. Send message, over.'

'Comms, we need an engineer to patch a hole in the solar farm fence ASAP.'

'Jameson, standby.'

'Didn't sound like Emma,' Jameson remarked.

'Probably Kathryn,' Joe said, nodding.

'Jameson, this is comms, over.'

'Comms, go ahead.'

'Engineering too busy today, over.'

Jameson looked at Joe, then turned back to the walkie-talkie. 'Comms, get one of the team to get tools from engineering and bring them out here. We'll sort it ourselves.'

'Will do, comms out.'

Joe led Jameson over to the hole in the fence.

'No real evidence,' Jameson murmured.

'Just evidence that someone tried something and couldn't follow it through.'

'What do you think, a failed attempt to get power for personal use?'

'That would be my guess, but they would need some equipment not only to prevent killing themselves but to make use of any access to the supply. It's not like they can plug a device in.'

It wasn't long before George came jogging over, pink-faced and panting with the exertion.

Jameson took the tools off the youngster, and Joe took the roll of fencing wire that had been tied to the young man's back. It took fifteen minutes for Jameson to make a repair, which impressed Joe, by which time George had recovered and was looking a more natural colour.

'Come on, George, you grab the tools, and I'll take the fencing,' Jameson said, grinning.

'That's only because there is hardly any fence left, sir,' George grumbled.

***

They followed the fence on the way back and arrived near the main gate, which was inactive.

Joe walked over to the nearest guard. 'Hey, how are you all doing?'

The guard snapped off a salute. 'Hello, sir. We've survived today's arrivals and are psyching ourselves up for the next four weeks.'

Something that Doctor Ogilvie didn't get a chance to tell me about.

'Well done, guys. I appreciate all of you. Amazing job.' Joe turned to Jameson and George Swift. 'You guys go back to the office. I wanna pop my head into the Exodus medical tent.'

'See you later, sir,' George said with a smile.

'Don't let it overwhelm you, sir,' Jameson said softly, close to a whisper.

Joe raised his eyebrows briefly but let the comment go. He didn't realise what Jameson was referring to until he opened the flap of the Exodus medical tent and looked inside. Although the tent would have covered three football fields side by side, he could only see a room with a snake-shaped line of people waiting to be medically processed.

A nurse stepped beside him. 'Name?'

'Major Wolfe.' Joe looked at the nurse's head until it rose back up and her eyes locked onto his. 'I'm Tower 17's site director.'

An embarrassed cough. 'Sorry, sir. I didn't recognise you. What can I help you with?'

'I'm interested in seeing the medical tent operating.'

The nurse tapped her computer tablet. 'I see you have several medical processing entries on your file, sir. I would have thought that by now, this would be a routine event for you?'

'You could call me a frequent flyer.'

The nurse didn't respond and continued watching him, waiting for an answer.

'I haven't seen it from an organisational and logistical viewpoint before.' Joe could only imagine what was beyond the first wall. 'How are you all doing?'

'We're on target to process all arrivals today for their embarkation processing.'

'And in layman's terms, as if I didn't understand a word of what you just said?'

'We're doing well, sir.'

'Pass on my best wishes and appreciation to your colleagues.'

The nurse glanced at the corner of the room. 'Here is the lead processing doctor.' She waved over the doctor, who, to Jameson's eyes, didn't look old enough to have finished high school.

'Doctor.' Joe nodded. 'I'm Major Wolfe, Site Director. Just going around the site and being impressed by everyone's professionalism and great work.'

'Thank you, Major.' The young-looking doctor pushed his spectacles up to the top of his nose and ran a hand through his hair. 'I'm Doctor Barclay, head of processing here.'

'How many are you expecting through here?'

The doctor already appeared bored by the conversation. 'Forgive me, Major, but I haven't got any time to spare. I'm a team member down, and I need to fill the breach.'

'No, please don't stop here on my account. Please go. Thank you for your work here. I appreciate all that you're doing.'

The doctor waited, and then when he realised Joe had finished, an embarrassed red spread up his neck and onto his cheeks. He nodded, ran another hand through his hair, and left.

The nurse had already moved on to carry out her duties, leaving Joe alone in the middle of the medical processing room. He looked all around him before leaving them all to it.

Something didn't feel right in there. I'm not sure how to put it.

He took a deep lungful of natural air and walked towards the office building.

I've got it. It was silent. Absolutely silent. Joe cocked his head to one side. *No, I was wrong; it wasn't completely silent. There was the sound of the air purifiers and air conditioning units. But it was the lack of conversation that was more remarkable. Nobody was talking to anyone.*

He shuddered. *They have to process thousands of people and put them into a state of suspended animation. Now I understand what Jameson was telling me.*

He was almost at the door to the offices when he swung away at the last moment and decided to have another look at the space shuttle.

I can't believe it. It appears to be in the same place.

Joe saw that the space shuttle had moved less than a metre, and he frowned. Dr Popple was gesticulating at the ship, and clearly, he wasn't happy with whom he was talking to. As Joe wandered closer, he realised that the two men were having a heated argument. They saw the site director, and one of the men stormed off.

Dr Popple turned to face Joe. 'Good day, Major.' His flushed face was quickly returning to its pallid, untouched-by-the-sun skin tone.

'Doctor Popple, is everything okay?' Joe nodded towards the back of the person who had just left.

'Please call me Keith. Everything is fine. Everything is on track,' Keith said with a deep breath and a sigh.

'Are you sure? Your conversation with—'

'Oh, that was just a difference of opinion with Commander Cooper.'

'Your difference of opinion sounded like a heated argument. Care to tell me what you were discussing?'

Keith frowned. 'Commander Cooper wants the shuttle to move quicker than I have planned.'

'I was gonna ask what the timescale is for the shuttle to go from there,' Joe said, pointing at the nose of the ship. 'To there.' He nodded at the base of the tower.

'Two weeks.'

'What? Why?'

'Although the shuttle looks robust, we aren't taking any unnecessary risks that something isn't secured. By the time the ship reaches the base of the tower, the suspension pods will be ready for placement into the pod bays, and everything inside and outside of the ship will be in its place and secure, ready for lift off.'

Joe nodded slowly. 'And Commander Cooper didn't accept that?'

'No.'

'What does he want to happen?'

'He wants the shuttle to be on the tower as soon as possible to allow him to do checks and train his team through launch procedures.'

'How does he think the pods can be placed in the hold on the tower if it's up there?' Both men looked skywards.

Joe was first to lower his gaze. He rubbed his eyes, trying to dislodge the coloured orbs of the afterlights of the sun in his optic cells.

'The thinks that the pods should go up in the elevators.'

'Is that a viable option?'

'Humph. Not you, as well? Questioning my plans.'

'Doctor Popple... Keith,' Joe said softly. 'I'm only asking for all opinions to understand why your excellent plans are the ones we should stick with. Unlike you, I'm a layman when it comes to the logistics of coordinating filling a shuttle and getting it up that gigantic construction.'

'The commander is still suffering from grief.'

'What has that got to do with it?'

'He seems to hate all the ticket holders of this flight. The commander says that the passengers will be in suspended animation, so they won't be upset at going up in the elevators to then be placed in the hold.'

'Surely it would take a lot longer to get them on board that way?'

'Exactly. That's what I said. But all he cares about is training his team.'

'I shall go and talk to him,' Joe said, expecting to hear an argument against it.

Keith merely nodded.

***

Joe found Commander David Cooper standing at the base of the tower, staring directly upwards into the sky.

'Watch you don't blind yourself staring at the sun,' Joe advised casually.

David Cooper looked much younger up close. In his early twenties, he had a dark brown beard covering his chin and jaw, with matching bushy eyebrows and piercing, cerulean-blue eyes. He stood at just under six feet tall.

Joe stepped over to stand beside him, and the pilot had to look up to look at the site director's eyes.

'Are you that major? The one who got promoted to site director?'

Joe nodded. 'That's me.'

'Can you tell Popple-head to speed up the transportation of my ship so I can just get on with it?'

'I could. But let me ask you one thing first.'

The commander cocked his head to one side, confused by Joe's agreeable attitude when he'd expected another argument.

'What do you love about the ship?'

Commander David Cooper breathed in deeply and a smile appeared, shredding the aggressive attitude to pieces. 'It's just so... perfect. Up until now, the technology has always been catching up. But now...' He stared back up into the skies. 'Now we can traverse galaxies in the blink of an eye.'

'Through wormholes?'

'Exactly. The most up-to-date technology. This beauty's very skin can stretch and bend to travel through the cosmos.'

Joe nodded.

'There is only one ship better than this.'

'Oh?'

David Cooper's face lit up with the most beautiful smile. 'The *Da Vinci*. Some call it Leo, but it's magnificent. It's the fastest, most agile thing ever built. With wormhole-creating abilities, it can go wherever it wants in the blink of an eye.'

'Where is it?'

'Do you see the speck of silver up there?' He pointed at the sky away from the tower.

'Yeah?'

'That is the International Space Hub. That is where the *Da Vinci* is, getting provisioned and stocked for the voyage of a lifetime.'

'And you're the pilot of this ship.' Joe pointed along the tracks.

'Don't get me wrong. I would love to be the pilot of the *Da Vinci*. But this transporter shuttle is magnificent too.'

Joe nodded, then rubbed his chin. 'I wonder...'

'What?'

'I've got a few youngsters in my team. They could do with some inspiration, some magic to lift their souls from the humdrum of surviving through the poisonous weather. Would you...'

'Would I what?'

'Would you be kind enough to give them a tour of your ship?'

David smiled again. 'It would be my honour, sir.'

Chapter Thirty

Joe was standing at the door to the comms room when Emma signalled him over. George, Kathryn, Tommy, and Mally stood further down the corridor, waiting for Jameson to come out of his office.

'What is it, Emma?' Joe stepped into the office, careful not to touch any equipment.

'I just thought you should know that Kathryn had been left a message from her mother.'

'How did she do that?'

'Her mother knew that Kathryn would get a job here and sent a message to her before she was taken away. I was showing her how to log in to the system, and the message was already there waiting.'

'Any idea what it said?'

Emma shook her head. 'I gave her space to read it.'

'Thanks for letting me know.' Joe nodded and stepped back out into the corridor.

The group turned to look at him as he approached. 'Let's go and see some modern technology then. Lieutenant Jameson, would you lead the way?'

George was at Jameson's shoulder, keen as mustard and raring to go, whilst Tommy and Mally were next equally as excited. Joe had been torn between whether or not to invite the pair as he remembered their ultimate goal of being stowaways.

Will they cause trouble?

Mally glanced at him and grinned as if he'd read Joe's last thought.

Kathryn was behind them and more reserved than the guys. Joe glanced at her frequently, attempting to assess her mood after reading a message from her recently departed mother.

The nurse from the Project Exodus Medical Processing Team ran over to catch Joe as the group left the office building.

'Sir, Major?'

A helicopter lifted off from the site's helipad, buffeting everyone nearby. At the same time, a coachload of passengers disembarked near the front of the medical processing unit.

Joe turned to face her, and she waited until the noise level dropped and the group were far enough away to speak discretely.

'Doctor Barclay asked if he could have a word. We're so busy he couldn't leave the department. I had to come and ask you on his behalf.'

Joe followed the nurse over to the massive tent, lifted the flap, and waited for her to enter first before going through into the calm and quiet area. The VIPs were already through to the next stage as their tickets gave them instant access to avoid the queues. The passengers who had just been bussed in were already forming an S-shaped queue, building it quickly and without fuss.

The nurse immediately returned to her duties. Joe watched the thread of humanity who had, by all accounts, bought their escape from Earth sheepishly follow the person in front. The queue wound around barriers in the form of a snake.

It's incredible how waiting to be put into suspended animation removes any attitudes or ego.

The doctor came striding over with a pensive look on his face. 'As you're the site director, I need to inform you of something.' He looked about, making sure they weren't being overheard. 'I'm now down two nurses. This puts the team under extreme pressure.'

Joe thought for a moment. 'How long would it take to train someone up to replace them?'

'You're surely not volunteering, Major. Are you?'

Joe smiled. 'No. I was considering asking the site's medical team to help out.'

'That would be ideal. If we have someone medically trained, then it would only take a few minutes of instructions, I'm sure.'

'What's up with the two? Do you know?'

The doctor lowered his voice. 'The first nurse was coming in from a local private school, and she's just never shown up. The second nurse is young and inexperienced. I think she has just been overwhelmed by it all. Realising that she hasn't got a ticket to leave Earth and all these people have has brought on stress.'

Joe nodded slowly.

'Please don't tell anybody what I've said. Her condition is confidential.'

'My lips are sealed. I shall go and speak with our resident doctor to see about getting one or two of his team to assist. I'm guessing you'll want them for as long as possible of the two weeks?'

Dr Barclay nodded.

***

'Doctor, could any of your medics supplement the Project Exodus Medical Processing Team? They're short-staffed.'

Dr Wardle looked up from his desk. 'I suppose it's for the rest of the embarkation?'

'Yeah. I would be grateful.'

'Ha, the new site director would owe me a favour,' he said with a grin. 'I shall sort it out for you, Major.'

Joe rolled his eyes. 'Technically, you'll be doing the medical processing team a favour.'

'You asked. Just a bottle of single malt would cover it.'

Joe left the doctor to sort out staffing levels, smiling ruefully.

'Major!'

He heard the shout from further down the corridor and saw Samuel's head poking out of his office doorway.

Now what?

'What is it, Samuel?' Joe asked, his smile vanishing as he saw fear in the meteorological officer's face.

'What I'm reading on the radar is... Well, I've never seen it before. It looks like a big event.'

'What does that mean?'

'Full sky cover of cumulonimbus, with strong winds.'

Joe was silent.

'Basically, a big storm is on its way, and we're in its path.'

'A storm? How bad?'

'Thunder, lightning, heavy rain, and gale force winds.'

'How strong are gale force winds?'

'Could be over eighty kilometres per hour.'

Joe frowned. 'Timescale?' he stared at Samuel. 'Your best guess?'

'Ten to fourteen days.'

'Margin of error?'

'It could fizzle into nothing.'

'When will you know for sure?'

'Between five to nine days.'

'Frick.'

'Sir?'

'Thanks for letting me know. I want you to give me a daily update on that storm.'

'Yes, sir.'

***

'Doctor Popple.'

'Major Wolfe?' Keith Popple smiled until he noticed Joe wasn't returning a smile. 'Thanks for speaking to Commander Cooper. He let me know that he's showing a group of staff the shuttle.' He paused. 'But I'm sure he was expecting you as well.'

'Yeah, a few things came up, one of which is there is the possibility of a storm with ninety kilometre per hour winds very soon.'

'How soon?'

'Between ten and fourteen days. We'll know for definite between five and nine days.'

Keith pulled a face. 'If we do get the strong winds, what will happen?'

'It depends where the shuttle is when it hits.'

'If it hits.'

'What if the shuttle is on the transporter?'

'If the shuttle is on the transporter, then it won't be flight-ready. If it isn't flight-ready, then the winds could cause significant damage. The best scenario is the shuttle being at launch height on the tower when the winds occur.'

'When would the shuttle need to get attached to the tower for it to achieve that height in time?'

'Two days before the winds.'

Joe rubbed his chin. 'So, worst-case scenario, we need to get the shuttle onto the tower in eight days. In the best-case scenario, if it can be called that, we have twelve days.'

Keith nodded and grimaced. 'It seems that although you've placated Commander Cooper, he may get his wish after all.'

'I think I need to speak to Doctor Barclay again.'

'A site director's work is never done.'

'Thanks.' Joe gave him a wry smile. 'I'm getting daily weather updates, so I'll let you know.'

'No need. Samuel is kind enough to be providing daily weather warnings to me as it is. I shall ask for the long-term forecast too.'

'I'll go and speak to Doctor Barclay then.'

'I shall revisit my engineering launch plan and bring it forward eight days.'

Joe left Keith in a worse mood than he'd met him in and headed back to the Project Exodus medical tent.

***

The nurse, now used to the sight of him, just nodded to the front of the line of passengers as a new group appeared at the entrance to the tent.

'Doctor Barclay?'

The young doctor popped his head around the doorway, and a look of distaste flashed across his face as he recognised Joe.

'Major Wolfe?'

'Firstly, has Doctor Wardle managed to sort you out with a couple more staff?'

'Yes. We're now training them up. Neither of the nurses has experience with suspended animation or the technology. What else did you need to say?'

Joe took a step closer to him and whispered in his ear. 'There is the strong possibility of a bad storm. Doctor Popple, Head of Engineering, is making plans to bring forward plans to attach the shuttle to the tower in eight days.'

Doctor Barclay didn't bat an eyelid.

'Are you not concerned?' Joe inquired.

'No.'

'Why not? Don't you have to process the passengers quicker?'

Doctor Barclay shook his head and smiled. 'No. The storm would give us a much-needed break. We would stop processing passengers, batten down the hatches, so to speak, and wait out the storm.'

'And pick up afterwards where you left off?'

'Exactly. The transportation of the passengers to the site of Tower 17 will no doubt pause their movements and wait out the storm too.'

Joe looked around the tent at the parts he could see and then looked up at the ceiling.

'What about the tent?'

Doctor Barclay scratched the back of his neck. 'If the winds were going to be stronger than eighty-eight kilometres per hour, I would only ask a favour of you to help relocate my team and the remaining suspension pods to safety.

'Why eighty-eight?'

'Anything under that, the tent can withstand. Anything over that, we need to take it down.'

'How long...'

'Thirty minutes for staff and tent. The pods would depend on how many were still to be used or loaded onto the ship.'

'What if we move everything and everyone now?'

'It would delay everything. You said that the storm was possible?'

'Yeah.'

'If it doesn't happen, then moving everything now and setting up somewhere new will be a waste of time. All we need is a couple of hours' notice.'

Joe nodded. 'That we can arrange. Thanks, Doctor.'

Dr Barclay had already turned away to return to his duties.

On the way to rejoin the shuttle tour given by Commander Cooper, Joe sighed and rubbed his temples.

I won't be able to decide for another five days. Even then, it may stretch another four days.

Jameson was heading towards him, smiling. 'That was impressive.'

The group of youngsters crowded around him, and Joe was pleased to see Tommy and Mally had returned.

'Is the tour finished with?'

'Yes. The commander has suggested we come back when the shuttle is up on the side of the tower. All the controls and systems will be in place, making it more interesting to look at. '

Everyone looked up at the side of the tower. Joe shuddered.

Chapter Thirty-One

Waiting was the worst, especially on days when Joe was unable to go for a run. No matter how many times he went to see Samuel, the answer was always the same. There was no change to the forecast, and he was still unable to confirm whether the storm would reach them or pass them by.

The storm system was continuing to build out in the Atlantic Ocean as predicted, yet it didn't give a hint as to which direction it would take. Despite Joe wanting to ask the head of Global Project Exodus or the prime minister about the storm, he refrained, as he knew deep down that Samuel had as much information as his counterparts in the met office would have. The met office would be the ones advising the prime minister.

Only Emma asking Joe to re-task Kathryn, as she knew as much as she could about the on-site comms, was a break in the monotony of being in limbo, not knowing. He'd tasked her with shadowing Commander Cooper as the only way of getting her out of his hair. She still hadn't told anyone what her mother's message was about. Just as he was wondering what else could lift the boredom, Jameson appeared at his doorway.

'Sir.'

'What can I help you with, Lieutenant?'

'Can you do something about Tommy and Mally?'

'What would you like me to do about them?'

'Can you give them to someone else to look after? They're driving me bonkers. They're like two small dogs following me wherever I go.'

Joe stifled a smile. 'Have they shown any other interest on site?'

'They enjoyed the brief show round on the shuttle with Commander Cooper.'

Joe pursed his lips. 'Unfortunately, I've just moved Kathryn Ogilvie to shadow the commander.'

'There must be somewhere else. What about the medical processing department?'

Joe laughed. 'If I put them there, I would probably have multiple staff walkouts and the department shutting down within days. What about guard duties?'

'That would be taking them out of the frying pan and putting them into the fire.'

'I tell you what. I shall get them to follow Doctor Popple, the Head of Engineering.'

'I shall follow you,' Jameson said grimly.

'Are they that bad?'

Jameson just grunted.

'Come on then.'

They found Dr Popple checking his computer tablet, which was hooked up just inside one of the external doors of the shuttle.

'Doctor,' Joe said with a smile.

'Major.' Keith returned the smile. 'What can I do for you? You don't want me to have this spaceship at the top of the tower today, do you?'

Joe cocked his head to one side. 'Now that you come to mention it.'

Both men laughed.

'We have two young members of staff who would love to shadow you around. They may even soak up some of your knowledge about this shuttle.'

Keith's eyebrows furrowed. 'What's the catch?'

Jameson laughed. 'I thought you'd be too clever to take it at face value.'

Joe looked at Jameson.

'That is one big reason that we thought of you as the best person on site to show these youngsters the brilliant technology we have here.'

Joe and Keith smiled again.

'Well, as you're putting it like that, yes, bring over the two gentlemen.'

Jameson gave a loud whistle, and Tommy and Mally appeared from the nearest building.

'Why do I already feel I've been had?' Keith muttered.

'You and me both,' Joe added.

***

Joe sat at his desk and rubbed his face, then breathed out loudly. 'Computer, open messages.'

'Site Director messages opened.'

Joe saw a reply message from Hunting Bear in his inbox.

Hey, Howling Wolfe,

Congratulations on another jump up the ladder. We all hope that you don't get dizzy with being at the heights of a Site Director. And that the responsibility of being in charge of everything is not overwhelming. The son of a drinking friend from childhood (his words, not mine), Silver Fish, said that you would be great. It's not a bad memory for someone over 100 years old. If you have got any of the brains that your father had, you will be a great director.

Everyone here thanks you for thinking of us and offering a one-way ticket to the stars, but we are either foolish for not taking you up on your offer, or we have accepted what comes, what may, and have relaxed into the unknown. Anyway, Jimmy's mom has predicted you will save the earth. Yes, she is blind and keeps to herself these days, so don't feel pressured.

Anyway, enough of my ramblings. Again, thank you for thinking of your old tribe.

We decline the wonderful offer with much gratitude.

Wishing you sun on your face and wind in your hair whilst your howling at the sky is always answered.

much love from the tribe,

Hunting Bear

Joe sat back and found tears at the corners of his eyes. Silver Fish had remembered all his life that Joe had taken him home after getting drunk when they were youths and committing underage drinking with friends. It must have made such an impression on him that he'd told his son and passed the stories on to the next generation.

Well, you can take a horse to water, but you can't make it drink, is what my father taught me.

He saw the time on the computer screen. 'Computer, off.'

The holographic screen dissolved before his eyes.

Out in the fresh air, Joe mentally praised Samuel for being accurate with the day's forecast. Heavy, rain-laden clouds could be seen on the horizon, but for the next few hours, the air would be clear and dry.

He leaned against the wall and stretched his legs one at a time. The roaring of an incoming helicopter reminded him that onboarding was continuing despite the forecasted weather. Joe set off on his run, angling towards the front gate before turning up alongside the inside of the fence line. As well as exercising, the jog allowed him to double-check that Jameson had given the forewarning to the tented visitors outside of the site for Tower 17.

Great! Jameson must have warned them as I'd told him to.

Everyone was either in the process of tying down every item and securing everything they owned or had already done so.

Joe increased his pace and sped past the haphazard tented area on the other side of the fence.

He was relaxing into his stride and felt the strength flow through his legs when something of the shapes of the fence up ahead caught his eye. The typically geometric patterns of the wires in the fence were sitting at weird angles. As he approached the patch that was non-geometrically shaped, he swore under his breath.

A rectangular section of the fence had been snipped and bent back, forming a bulge above the human-sized hole. The tread of a boot stood proud out of the dirt on the inside of the fence line, and Joe stopped mid-stride to change direction.

Frick. I should have got the site director to upgrade the fencing to electric when I had the chance.

Joe increased his speed until he was gasping when he reached the office building.

'Jameson!'

Lieutenant Jameson popped his head out of his office and leaned into the corridor. 'Sir?'

'Put the site on alert. An intruder has gained access to the site by cutting the fence just before the back gate. Send a roving team out to search for intruders and get that fence mended, would you?'

'Yes, sir. Will do. Commander Cooper popped by asking if you were going to be amongst the group to see the shuttle command deck today.'

'Feck. That's today.' Joe shook his head and then headed back to his accommodation to shower and change.

He was just at the entrance to the building when Dr Barclay himself caught up with him. 'Major!'

'Doctor Barclay? What seems to be the problem?'

'Come with me,' the doctor said in a tone that made Joe feel he had no choice in the matter.

***

Joe looked at the suspension pod with the painted Greenpeace sign emblazoned over it.

'Is this the only one?'

'Yes.'

'Is the pod damaged in any way?'

'No. It was the first thing I checked. The passenger inside is still maintaining the minimal life indicators that he should.'

'Is there anything special about this passenger?'

The doctor shook his head.

'Who has access to this part of the building?'

Sunlight lit up the room as part of the wall lifted to allow a forklift truck to enter.

'That answers my question. I shall get Lieutenant Jameson to post a guard on this entrance.'

'Are you going to investigate this vandalism?'

'Maybe after.'

The doctor frowned. 'Maybe after what?'

'I shall speak with Lieutenant Jameson when he returns to his office, and I'll instruct him to begin an investigation.'

The doctor nodded, mollified.

'Any news from your absentee staff?'

'One is due to return tomorrow, and the other...' The doctor looked into the distance. 'The other has told a colleague that she won't ever be coming to work here.'

'Did she say why?'

'Something along the lines of never working where that bitch has been.'

'Where did you say she works?'

'A local private school. Our team has a core that goes from site to site to prep for launches. We get a quarter of the team from within the region.'

'Does any other member of your team come from the same place?'

'Two. The same person who told me what the missing nurse said, and the other is the one who is returning tomorrow.'

'The daughter of the previous site director is working here. She came from a local private school.'

The doctor raised his eyebrows.

'Okay.' Joe breathed out heavily. 'Are you managing without her?'

'As long as we have your site medic.'

'Of course. You've got him for as long as you need.'

***

The wind whipped a strand of Joe's hair across one of his eyes, and he brushed it back without thinking. The dark clouds were ominous on the horizon, and he couldn't tell if they'd moved at all. All he could remember about this morning's weather forecast was Samuel saying no poisonous air was coming this way.

Commander Cooper was standing at the doorway with a grin. 'I thought I was the only one to make people wait.'

Joe smiled. 'Well, I'm here now.'

'Get in quick.'

'What? Why?'

Commander Cooper smiled again but said nothing. He pushed Joe back, making him fall into a seat. 'Buckle up.'

Joe looked about in a panic. Kathryn Ogilvie sat opposite him, her eyes closed, making the sign of the cross over her chest. Tommy sat next to her, and his eyes flashed with joy. He was shouting at Mally opposite him, who was shouting back. Joe glanced at Mally on his right and then watched Commander Cooper sit to Kathryn's right. He buckled his harness, pulled the straps tighter, and looked at everyone's buckles.

Joe raised his eyebrows in question, and Commander Cooper nodded.

A grinding of iron on iron sent vibrations through Joe's spine, and then there was silence.

'What's happening?'

'The magnets have taken hold. We're going upwards,' the commander replied.

'But...'

'It's gonna be okay, Major. Just keep breathing.'

The shuttle tipped backwards until it was vertical and aligned on the tracks on Tower 17. Joe felt his heart beating, and he noticed the same pulse in his arms. He clenched and unclenched his hands to invigorate the circulation to his fingers.

Breathe! Just breathe!

He looked up at the commander, who was looking out a porthole, and pursed his lips.

'Commander, I thought the ship wasn't gonna be ready for another three days?'

'So did I. Good old Popplehead must have wanted my ship to be vertical sooner rather than later,' he said, raising a hand to his headphones. He pressed the Speak button. 'Go ahead, control over.'

'Commander, is Major Wolfe with you?'

'Oh, hi, Emma. Yes, he's sitting opposite me. Wait one.' Commander Cooper pointed at the headset hanging next to Joe's shoulder. 'Major, put those on, would you?'

Joe held the headset in his hands and twisted it the right way around before putting them on.

He pressed the speak button. 'Hello? Major Wolfe here.'

'Major, this is Comms Control. I have a Mister Atkins wanting to speak to you.'

'Major Wolfe, this is Simon Adkins. I am the new Site Director for Tower 17.'

'Mister Adkins. I had no idea you were coming.'

'It's Professor Adkins. You would have been sent a message this morning. I only agreed on the posting this morning, and they flew me up straight up from the UK Spaceport. Anyway, enough about that. Do you want to come down, and you can give me a briefing on what's been happening?'

Joe looked at Commander Cooper, who shook his head. 'Professor Adkins, this is Commander Cooper. Unfortunately, now that we're moving vertically, the major won't be able to come back down until we reach the top.'

There was a pause. 'The top?' the professor asked eventually.

'Yes, the top, otherwise known as the launch platform. It's not a platform, but just the point...'

'I get the picture, Commander. Major, I shall see you as soon as I see you.'

'Comms Control, out,' Emma finished on the professor's behalf.

Joe smiled and then followed Commander Cooper's gaze out of the window. He couldn't see anything but darkness with the routine flash of light that they passed on their vertical journey.

'Trouble?' Joe asked.

'I'm not sure. That bank of cumulonimbus seems bigger than it was.'

'Do you think it's getting bigger or closer?'

'I've got a feeling it may be both.'

Kathryn frowned. 'Is that bad?'

'Depends if we can get above it in time.'

Kathryn made the sign of the cross again and closed her eyes. Commander Cooper and Joe continued staring out of the small window into the darkness.

Weariness suddenly washed over Joe, and he remembered he'd had a hectic day. His eyelids drooped, and a flash of light penetrated his eyelids.

'Shit.'

'What is it?' Joe asked.

'Lightning.'

'We have lightning rods at the base. We'll be all right, won't we?'

Commander Cooper stared into Joe's eyes. 'Do you know if Popplehead... if Doctor Popple has replaced the temporary lightning rods with the permanent rods?'

'I don't know. What's the difference?'

'Size. The permanent ones are so much taller.'

Joe closed his eyes.

Commander Cooper turned to Kathryn and tapped her on the shoulder. As she opened her eyes, he calmly asked her to say another prayer. 'We'll need all the help we can get.'

There was another flash of lightning, and the commander started counting. On the next flash of lightning, his count had reached thirty and he started again from one. Another flash of lightning, and his count had reached twenty before he started again from one.

'Does lightning flash at the same interval?' Joe asked.

'I don't think so, but it's the only possible way I can do it, which may indicate it's getting closer.'

Another flash, and the commander winced. Kathryn's praying got louder. The window turned completely white as the lightning hit the shuttle. Joe saw buttons and screens light up in the cockpit behind Commander Cooper.

'Commander, should we be worried?' Joe nodded at the systems starting up in the cockpit.

'Shit.' Commander Cooper unbuckled his harness and clambered upwards.

'Shuttle *Dionysus* ZPEP drive employed,' the computer stated loudly.

'No!' Commander Cooper screamed. 'No!'

Joe unbuckled his harness and climbed up into the cockpit. 'Can I help?'

Commander Cooper pointed at a seat to the right of the one he was sitting in. 'Get yourself in there.'

As soon as Joe secured his harness in his new seat, a console desk popped up from the floor in front of him.

'Ready.'

Commander Cooper looked across. 'See those five green buttons? When I say "now," press them one at a time. Got that?'

'Green buttons, one at a time. Got it.'

Commander Cooper pressed five green buttons on his console. 'Now.'

Joe pressed each one. 'Done.'

The ten propulsion rockets of Shuttle *Dionysus* fired up with a roar. Everyone was thrust downwards against their seats as the ship took off.

Joe turned and stared at Commander Cooper. His eyes were steady, and his mouth was a thin slit. He saw Joe's stare.

'We had to, or we would have killed everyone on site and us at the same time. The ZPEP drive requires the rockets to direct its flow to initiate operation.'

'*Dionysus*, this is Comms Control, over.'

'Go ahead, Comms Control.'

'Our readings indicate that you're launching,' Emma said in a flustered voice. 'Confirm your status, over.'

'Comms Control, we experienced a lightning strike which set off our ZPEP drive over.'

There was a lengthy pause before a different voice was heard. 'Commander Cooper, did you say the ZPEP started up?'

'Affirmative, Doctor Popple. A lightning strike hit us. By the way, if you lose our signal shortly, it will mean we've reached the exosphere.'

'The lightning rods. I forgot to change the lightning rods,' Doctor Popple lamented.

'Commander Cooper, this is Professor Adkins. May I congratulate you on the successful first launch from Tower 17. I shall notify the Global Project Exodus command. Please let Major Wolfe know that we can postpone our debriefing meeting indefinitely,' he said with humour. 'Can you confirm the number of passengers? Over.'

Commander Cooper tapped his console. 'There are 12,500 souls in the forward suspended animation hall,' he said under his breath to himself. He swiped the screen. 'And 5,507 in the rear hall.' He pressed the talk button on his headset again. 'Comms Control, Professor. We have 18,007 souls in suspended animation and...' He turned around and counted Kathryn, Tommy, and Mally. 'And five awake and lively souls in the cockpit, over.'

'Thanks for confirming the numbers, Commander. Can you please confirm the names of the awake crew?'

'Present in the cockpit are Commander Cooper, Major Wolfe, Kathryn Ogilvie, and Tommy and Mally...' He turned to face the guys. 'What are your surnames?' he hissed at them.

Before Tommy and Mally could reply, Professor Adkins spoke. 'That wouldn't be Thomas Butcher and Malcolm Taylor, would it?'

Joe and Commander Cooper turned to look at Tommy and Mally. Their heads hung down as they looked at their feet in embarrassment. They both nodded sullenly.

'Well, that confirms their whereabouts. They were reported missing from work five months ago.'

Joe turned to face Tommy and Mally. He raised eyebrows and mouthed, 'Where did you work?'

'Yeah, the whole of the UK Spaceport has been hunting the pair of tearaways. I shall let their boss, the head of Space Engineering, know they've been found.'

'Good to know, Comms Command, over.'

The response from Comms Command was distorted and incomprehensible.

'We're now passing through the exosphere and won't hear any more from Comms Control of Tower 17. We're on our own.'

'What do we do now?' Joe asked.

'It depends on whether or not...'

The sun blazed through the right-hand window. Commander Cooper tapped his console a couple of times, and the window darkened, reducing the blaze of light to a glimmer. The glow of the sun, even through the shaded window, moved.

'As I thought. Automatic steering has kicked in.'

'I thought you were the pilot.' Joe hissed.

'Calm down, Major.' He tapped his console again. 'As I thought. We're heading towards the International Space Hub.'

'Why?' This time, it was Kathryn who asked.

'To refill with propellant. The ZPEP will carry on regenerating for all eternity, but my ship may need fuel for any launch again.'

Joe was still trying to grasp the predicament they were all in. 'And where was *Dionysus* programmed to go afterwards? Where did the sleeping passengers pay to go?'

Commander Cooper grinned. 'Anyone ever been to Mars?'

Chapter Thirty-Two

Thankfully, the artificial gravity generator kicked in as they left the outer reaches of the Earth's atmosphere.

Joe eyed Commander Cooper for a second only to see him tap away at his console monitoring his ship. His belly rumbled. 'Does anyone know where the nearest creationary is?'

Kathryn grinned. 'Was that your tummy rumbling, Major?'

'Yeah. I'm starving.'

'Come on, we'll all go.' Tommy pointed.

'What's that on your wrist, Tommy?' Joe asked.

'What this?' Tommy held up his wrist, which had been stained by dark green paint. 'Oh, just some paint.'

'You wouldn't know anything about a Greenpeace logo painted in the medical tent, would you?'

'Might do,' Tommy said with a grin.

'Not that it matters now, but why?'

'It was a nod to my grandmother, who went to...'

'Planet 27?'

'Yes. How did you know?'

'Let's just say she left her mark. What was her name?'

'Here is the cockpit crew canteen. Or, as Commander Cooper likes to call it, the Three Cs.' Kathryn said loudly, cutting off Tommy's conversation.

Joe pressed a button. 'American apple pie,' he said into the microphone grille.

'I suggest you choose British food,' Mally piped up.

'Why?' Joe turned back to see a plate of mushed ingredients.

'The programmer didn't upload all the global menu files. He only did his home country first. England.'

Mally stepped close to the microphone grille and pressed the button. 'Fish and chips.' Moments later, he took out a plate of piping hot fish and chips.

Joe's stomach rumbled again. 'Here goes nothing.' He looked at Mally, tucking into his food already. 'Fish and chips.'

He took his plate of food to a table away from Mally to get some peace, only to be joined moments later by Kathryn.

'You don't mind me sitting with you, Joe? Do you?'

Joe looked at her and, for the first time, saw that she was really just a scared little girl trying to use her guile and charm to get something. He breathed deeply, smiled at her, and nodded. He saw her shoulders relax, and she began to toy with her food.

'What did you choose?' He pointed at her plate.

'Cottage pie. It was my dad's favourite,' She wiped a tear from her eyes. 'Major Wolfe, do we have to go to Mars?' she whispered so that Tommy and Mally didn't hear.

'Where would you prefer to go?'

'Planet 27,' she said without hesitation.

Well, that makes two of us.

'I don't think we have much of a choice at the moment.'

'How long will it take to get to Mars?'

'I believe it would take six months without using a wormhole; that is, if indeed one has been created for movement to Mars.'

Joe saw her bottom lip tremble. She sniffed and wiped her eyes again.

'What happened with your father?'

She glanced up from her food. 'My mother did something, and he left. He left home without saying goodbye to me because of her.'

Joe heard the pain and bitterness in every word.

'That school of mine didn't even let me go to his flight.'

'Where did he...'

'He launched from Paris to work as security for Planet 27. He's a cosmologist. Why did he get such a crappy job?'

Joe's eyes narrowed.

'He didn't say goodbye,' she said just before her whole frame shook with silent sobbing.

All four of them felt the trembling of the ship as it reacted to the ten rockets ceasing. A slight buzz remained as the ZPEP system continued, propelling them towards the International Space Hub.

'I've got to ask. What was in the message your mother sent you?'

Kathryn looked up with red-rimmed eyes. 'Not much. It was mainly about you.'

'What?'

'She told me to trust you with my life. She said that she'd never met anyone who was so honest and sincere. She told me to be truthful with you, and you'll see me right.'

Joe's mouth dropped open.

'Was she right, Major Wolfe? Can I trust you? I've been truthful with you.'

Joe smiled softly and nodded. He stood up, stepped over to her, and kissed her on the top of her head. 'We'll be all right, Kathryn. You eat your food now. Finish your meal. I'll go and speak to Commander Cooper.'

She looked up and gave a hesitant smile.

'Go on. Eat up.'

She picked up a fork and began eating. Satisfied, Joe moved away and went back to the cockpit.

***

'Commander Cooper.'

'Major Wolfe. You know you can call me Dave when not in front of the kids.'

Joe laughed. 'Yeah, I suppose we can all use our first names. After all, we're all in the same boat, so to speak. Please call me Joe.'

'So, Joe. Are you looking forward to visiting Mars?'

'Nope. And that's why I've come to talk with you, Dave. Is there any way that Kathryn and I could be dropped off at Planet 27 first?'

Dave pulled a face. 'Fraid not. After we fill up at the petrol station, otherwise known as the International Space Hub, as soon as I press a button to confirm the tanks are full, we'll be off. The automatic pilot is programmed to take us straight to Mars.'

'Please, there must be a way.'

'I could leave you at the Hub. You can hitch a lift to Planet 27.'

Joe's eyebrows furrowed. 'Could I message someone?'

'Right now? If it's to someone on Earth, they won't receive anything but gibberish. That's one thing that good old Popplehead couldn't finish in time. Look.' Dave pointed at a red light on his console.

Joe stepped closer to read what it said.

Communications module. Programming incomplete. Unable to transmit through the ZPEP ion cloud.

'So you see, Joe. Both of us will be stepping off Shuttle *Dionysus* and onto the International Space Hub. I'll be updating the Global Exodus Project, and you'll be messaging whomever you want to.'

Joe walked slowly back to the canteen.

I can stay on the International Space Hub, hoping to catch a ride to Planet 27, or spend six months on board Shuttle Dionysus *en route to Mars. Not a great choice.*

Joe's stomach rumbled, reminding him that he had some fish and chips waiting for him. When he entered the room, Kathryn and Mally had left. Tommy was just about to dig a fork into Joe's fish and chips.

'Ahem.'

Tommy looked up guiltily. 'Almost,' he said, grinning.

Joe sat down facing him and pulled his plate over.

'You'll need these,' Tommy said, holding a knife and fork.

'Thanks, Thomas Butcher.' Joe smiled. 'Tell me your story of how you came to be here.'

'It's about time I told someone.' Tommy looked into the distance. 'Mally and I were spaceport brats.' He looked up and saw Joe was none the wiser. 'Our parents worked at the UK Spaceport.'

Joe nodded understanding at last.

'We grew up amongst programmers, astronomers, cosmologists. Mally and I met in school and were instantly great friends. School interrupted us having fun and terrorising all the other kids.'

'Were you bullies?'

He shook his head. 'Not quite. We just had fun and ran about chasing everything and everyone.'

'Were you any good at school?'

'The funny thing was, the more we had fun, the easier the subjects were. We must have picked up everything we needed to know from the adults around us, as we excelled in every subject. Our parents expected us to follow in their footsteps, so we ended up being apprentices to an idiot at Space Engineering.'

Joe raised his eyebrows but remained quiet.

'He treated us like shit. We did all the work for him, and he took all the credit. To keep us in his department, he would tell everyone how useless we were and that he was only keeping us there as a favour to our parents.' Tommy snarled. 'Mally stood up for us one day, and the guy laughed at us. He laughed in our faces and told us how lucky we were to have him as a boss.' He smiled. 'We never went back. We walked and hiked, and walked and hiked until we arrived in Scotland. When we needed food, we found people who needed cars, fridges, or washing machines repaired. We were never really hungry. There was always someone who needed something fixed. We were in Edinburgh one day when we heard that the UK tower—Tower 17—was being built in Perthshire. We got there just before that bad spell, sitting outside a tent with a half-dead man who turned out to be the site director.' He stared at Joe. 'You never told us that when we were getting clothes for you.'

Joe smiled. 'You didn't tell me about what you used to do, and I didn't tell you what I used to do.'

'Fair enough.' Tommy raised a hand and ran his fingers through his hair.

Joe saw the remains of the green paint again. 'You never answered me. Who was your grandmother?'

Tommy looked straight at Joe. 'Annabel Lewis. She travelled to Planet 27 on board *La Nina*.'

Joe's world dropped away from him, and he felt dizzy. The memory of his romantic encounter with Annabel surfaced. He relaxed as he realised Tommy's mother would have been born before he had met Annabel.

'You okay, Major?'

He breathed deeply and managed to nod, convincing Tommy to go on.

'I found out that she gave birth to my mother and was forced to give her up for adoption.'

'Who forced her?'

Tommy pursed his lips. 'I think it was the Russians. Back then, every country that was trying to gain control over the off-planet colonies put people in place. Anyone and everyone was an agent for one country or another.'

Joe nodded, dumbstruck.

'So, Grandmother Annabel gave up my mum and had to go to Planet 27. I think she got married and had kids. No doubt it's all a ruse to stay undercover. She left this for my mum to keep.' Tommy held out a tattered fabric Greenpeace badge.

'You might want to come to the cockpit, everyone,' Commander Cooper's voice boomed out over the Tannoy.

***

The International Spaceport was directly in front of them—a massive construction of metal with six legs jutting out of its sides.

'It looks like an insect,' Joe muttered.

'Like a gigantic bug,' Commander Cooper agreed, nodding. 'And we're going there,' he added, pointing at the front left leg.

They all watched as the automatic pilot slowed the Shuttle *Dionysus* and aligned it perfectly with the space hub. With no juddering or noise to indicate they'd docked, Joe was amazed when a green light flashed, and the computer announced successful docking had taken place.

'Do we need space suits, Commander?' Kathryn asked, wide-eyed.

'No. There is a pressurised connection between us and the space hub. Come on, follow me.'

Commander Cooper pressed a button, and a hatch opened up to reveal a corridor in the space hub. Joe and the youngsters followed the commander into the metal bug.

'I didn't expect there to be many people aboard,' Joe whispered to Commander Cooper.

The commander nodded.

A uniformed man stood in front of them, stopping them in their path.

'Welcome aboard the International Space Hub. We weren't expecting Shuttle *Dionysus* so soon, but now that you're here, make yourselves comfortable for the time it takes to refuel your ship.'

'Excuse me, can I send a message back to Earth? It's an urgent one. You see, we weren't supposed to be on board when the ship launched.'

'Major Wolfe, I presume.'

Joe nodded.

'There is a priority one message waiting for you.'

'Do you know who from?'

'The head of Global Project Exodus, I believe.'

***

Dear Major Wolfe,

News of your unplanned emergency launch in Shuttle Dionysus *travelled fast, and I was informed of it just after my morning prayers.*

I have spoken to both the UK Prime Minister and the Head of Coben Engineering in an attempt to determine who is now responsible for you and your shipmates. We were all in a quandary about what to do with you, and then a close friend of mine reminded me of our plans.

Plans are underway to establish a task force to develop a wormhole highway. This had been scheduled for some time in the future. However, you may have created an opportunity a lot sooner.

You see, your being aboard the International Space Hub is fortuitous. Not only are you there, but the spacecraft with the technology is already there.

So, would you like to become the first Squadron Commander of the International Space Consortium's wormhole-building flagship?

Your friend,

Prince Al Atarique

Head of Global Project Exodus

Epilogue

Joe breathed in deeply and tapped the send button. He smiled and breathed out slowly.

I'm now the squadron commander of the flagship for the International Space Consortium. Now I need a crew.

'Computer, off.'

The screen went blank, and as Joe opened the door, the same uniformed man was waiting outside.

'Are you finished with the communications room, Major?'

'For now. What is your name?'

'I'm Bob, the concierge.'

Joe looked at Bob and saw the lines around the man's eyes, the grey hairs at the temples, and the immaculate uniform.

'Well, Bob. I am now the Squadron Commander of the *Leo*.'

'Congratulations, sir,' Bob said without missing a beat.

'The challenge I have is, I don't have a crew.'

'What about your associates from the *Dionysus*?'

'Commander Cooper will be going on to Mars, and he may need a couple of crew members as well. I don't know what Tommy and Mally want to do. Our journey here was unplanned, you see.'

'And the girl?'

'Kathryn? I think she'll be coming with me.'

'So, you may need a pilot, a navigator, a comms officer, and a weapons officer as a minimum complement. Then you may want to consider whether you need a medic, a security officer, a guidance counsellor, an astrobiologist, and an astrogeologist. Possibly most important would be an astrophysicist or cosmologist.'

'I need to speak to my fellow travellers first. But do you have enough people here that I can pick my crew from?'

Bob slowly nodded. 'If not, we can recruit from Earth.'

'We?' Joe asked with a smile.

'I must assist with all requirements of visitors to the International Space Hub, Major. Including recruiting for the greatest mission yet.'

Joe nodded. 'If you can show me where my fellow travellers are, then wait while I ask who wants to come with me... I shall need your help recruiting.'

'As you wish, Major. This way.' Bob indicated down the corridor.

***

'Hey, guys. I have some news.' Joe looked around the four of them. 'I am now in charge of the spaceship, *Leo*. Anyone wanting to come with me, say now.'

Kathryn was the first to break the silence. 'Where are you going?'

'You lucky git,' Commander Cooper muttered.

'Firstly, I'm going to Planet 27 to tie up a few loose ends...'

'Can I come?' Kathryn couldn't wait for him to finish his sentence.

'So, guys, you can choose Mars with me or Planet 27 with the major here.' Commander Cooper gazed at Tommy and Mally.

Tommy and Mally stared at each other.

Mally nodded slowly, looking at Tommy, and then they hugged.

Mally turned to Commander Cooper. 'Can I come with you, Commander?'

Tommy turned to Joe. 'Can I come with you, Major?'

'Shit, now I need more crew.' Commander Cooper rubbed his head.

'Ask Bob here. He may be able to help you recruit for any position you need to fill. Isn't that right, Bob?'

Bob nodded. 'It would be my pleasure to help both of you, sirs, to get your crews together.' He looked at Joe and then Commander Cooper. 'Let me go and compile a list. Then I'll post it on the Hub's jobs board before sending it over to Earth. I don't think you'll have trouble finding applicants. You've got the top two ships of the fleet.' He turned to Commander Cooper. 'Commander, if you can, come with me, and we'll go through the crew positions you want to fill.'

Joe glanced at the youngsters.

'Sir, what is our mission?' Tommy asked.

Joe smiled. 'We are going to create wormholes and plot our way around space.'

'Cool.'

Joe looked at Kathryn. 'But of course, that is after stopping off at Planet 27.'

***

Bob was true to his word and had multiple applicants for all of the roles after two weeks.

Joe had kept himself busy by running around the outer corridors, and one continuous loop was a circuit. He wasn't the only one, either. Some went jogging in a clockwise direction, and others went in a counterclockwise direction. He'd just finished his daily jog when Bob called him into the comms room.

'Major, you have a live interview for your security officer. He's on Earth,' Bob said, pushing Joe into a seat in front of the holographic screen.

'Major Wolfe, good day,' said the familiar voice of Lieutenant Jameson. 'You survived the launch then?'

Joe laughed. 'Jameson, it's good to see you again. How is everything on the site of Tower 17?'

'Boring without you, sir.' Jameson grinned. 'The new site director took over following your surprise departure, and, well, nothing happens now. I heard about your recruitment drive and thought, "Why not?" I may be able to help you when you get into your next pickle.'

'Consider the job yours. You have to get up here as quick as you can.'

'There is one thing you may not have heard about.'

'Go on.'

'After the lightning struck the tower, it started growing.'

'Growing?' Joe caught his breath.

'Yes. Not only growing, sir, but it has improved the air around it.'

'What do you mean?'

'The tower has healed the air.'

'Well, I'll be. The professor was right. The ore has regenerated after electricity has passed through it.'

Jameson smiled. 'Whatever happened, the air quality continues to improve, and it's like the poisonous clouds are scared to come near.'

'So when you get here, our first stop is Planet 27.'

Jameson nodded. 'Unfinished business,' he said softly.

'Yeah. We have to take Kathryn Ogilvie. Her father is there, remember?'

'Someone will be pleased to see you.'

'I hope so.'

***

Can the ore heal planet Earth?

Joe sat, staring into space, with the holographic computer screen flickering in anticipation of the following line of his new message.

Dear Anonymous Friend,

You may have heard about my sudden departure. It was a shock to me as well. The lightning struck the shuttle and the tower, so we had to launch the shuttle, or it would have exploded. Thankfully, our pilot knew what to do.

That isn't the only reason for my message.

You wanted to know about the ore. Well, the professor was right. It has one-off healing properties. The fantastic news is that the lightning has made Tower 17 grow. My security officer has also told me that it's healing the very air about it. I don't know much more, but someone needs to know. This could be a significant benefit for the planet.

Please notify everyone who needs to be informed.

Joe

He sent the message and sat back. The realisation that he would be returning to Planet 27 after all brought a beaming smile to his face.

Launching into space to avoid being blown to smithereens may have other benefits.

'Computer off.'

When the concierge returned, Joe was still staring into space.

'Are you ready for the next interview, sir?'

Joe breathed in deeply and slowly exhaled. 'So, who have we next?'

Afterword

Thank you for choosing to invest your time in reading Tower 17. It means more to me than you can imagine. Speaking of time, I am going to ask for more of yours. Many years ago I learnt the value of word of mouth recommendations and this is just as true for authors. The simplest form of recommendation is to tell friends, family and colleagues – but please no spoilers. If you have a moment it would be great if you left a review online. Honest reviews are very much appreciated and are useful to other readers.

***

Previously in the Series...

Planet 27 **– Book One of the Howling Wolfe Chronicles**

What would you do if you woke from suspended animation with no memory of who you were—or why you were sent across the galaxy?

That's exactly the dilemma facing Joe Howling Wolfe. Stranded on the mysterious Planet 27 with only fragments of identity and a growing list of threats, Joe must navigate a strange new world, confront shadowy enemies, and piece together the secrets of his past before it's too late.

The first installment in G. L. Blackie's thrilling sci-fi series, *Planet 27* is a gripping journey of survival, mystery, and self-discovery. Packed with action, unexpected twists, and an unforgettable protagonist, this imaginative debut will leave you questioning everything—and eagerly reaching for the next chapter.

***

Next in the series...

Follow the continuing adventures of Joe Howling Wolfe in **Wormhole No.** 7.

Printed in Great Britain
by Amazon

8505480e-5020-4825-a275-633eabb85b5aR01